CLOSE TO THE EDGE

DAWN RYDER

St. Martin's Paperbacks

This is a work of fiction. All of the characters, organizations, and events portrayed in this novel are either products of the author's imagination or are used fictitiously.

CLOSE TO THE EDGE

Copyright © 2018 by Dawn Ryder.
Excerpt from *Don't Look Back* Copyright © 2018 by Dawn Ryder.

For information address St. Martin's Press, 175 Fifth Avenue, New York, NY 10010.

ISBN: 978-1-250- 13272-7

Our books may be purchased in bulk for promotional, educational, or business use. Please contact your local bookseller or the Macmillan Corporate and Premium Sales Department at 1-800-221-7945, ext. 5442, or by e-mail at MacmillanSpecialMarkets@macmillan.com.

Printed in the United States of America

St. Martin's Paperbacks edition / March 2018
St. Martin's Paperbacks are published by St. Martin's Press, 175 Fifth Avenue, New York, NY 10010.

10 9 8 7 6 5 4 3 2 1

To all the men and women who serve our communities. Thank you for making this world a better place.

CHAPTER ONE

"These two were murdered."

Dare Servant considered the veteran firefighter-paramedic who wasn't backing down. The guy had weathered skin, but his eyes were still bright and sharp. Those winkles in his skin said he had a lot of experience under his belt. The couple of scars on his chin told Dare the guy had earned the right to be heard out.

Because Dare knew one thing for certain, always listen to the man who'd been on the job a long time. He'd notice things others wouldn't. When it came to cracking a case open, men like this one were the key to pointing out the tiny cracks Dare needed to apply a crowbar to.

"They aren't the first bodies I've fished out of the Los Angles River," firefighter Ramos continued. "I called the Feds because no one is taking this seriously."

Dare flashed his badge. The guy nodded with approval. "I knew calling in Feds was the right move, even if my supervisor is pissed over me going outside his jurisdiction."

"Tell me why you think they're murder victims?" Dare Servant asked.

Ramos pulled down the zipper on the body bag to expose the face of a young girl. Dare noted her age, Asian features, and tried like hell not to let the blue tinge to her skin affect him. She was far too young, her hair so dark and full. Her skin unblemished by time and age. Shit. He hated seeing the waste of a life like this one.

She was dead.

The only thing he could do to help her was listen when the rest of the world was ignoring what an experienced man was saying about how she ended up in a body bag decades before her time. Dare was there to stop other girls from joining her.

"Too well groomed," Ramos said. "Look at the brows, manicured hands, feet, waxed legs, and genitals," he was shaking his head. "Someone put her in rags to make it look like just another junkie who loaded up too close to the water. Look at the eyeliner left under her eyes. That's the professional grade stuff or there wouldn't be any left. And then, there's the family."

The guy's tone took on a thick coating of disgust. The kind truly devoted public servants experienced when they were caught between hard evidence and the law that protected every citizen until they were proven guilty. Ramos had a gut feeling and didn't like being told by his superiors to dismiss it. The guy had an eye for detail, something which served him well as a Paramedic. He was the one who rolled up first on a scene and made the call on who was getting transported first. Paramedics burned out fast on the job, Ramos had far outlasted many in his field. It meant he lived for the job and Dare knew he'd be a fool to dismiss what the guy was picking up about the girl.

Dare looked up from the body. "What about the family?"

"The woman who showed up claiming to be next of kin used to own a dozen or more of those massage places that were fronts for prostitution and trafficking." The firefighter looked at the girl and shook his head. "I used to do the fire-code inspections and I know when the girls are living there. They bring them in, these girls, fill their heads with stories of good jobs and then turn them into prostitutes. and then they threaten the girls with exposing their shame to their families." The guy stopped for a moment, pissed off at the harsh side of reality. "The girls won't go back home, won't accept help from anyone because they won't shame their families. That woman isn't this girl's aunt. She was the madam."

"Why is the body still here if the kin tried to claim it?" Greer McRae asked.

Dare nodded agreement at his partner's question as he reached out and pulled the zipper up to cover the girl's face. It was a tiny shred of dignity, but all he could offer her.

"Me," Ramos said with a good amount of satisfaction. "Just watch the footage from the security cameras. They looked around long and hard before coming through the door and trying to claim the body. They didn't see me in the back and I know that woman. She turned and ran the second she saw me. That's why I called you guys. They'll just wait for me to leave and try again. There's no legal way to hold the body on our end. My superiors are telling me to drop it. I'm telling you . . . there is more going on here than a suicide."

"Good call," Dare replied. "I'll sign the order to hold the body."

Dare left the building behind, his fellow agent Greer close on his side.

"We're getting closer," Greer said as they climbed

into their black SUV. He pulled out some printed photos. "She was with Kirkland the day before her death. I wanted to tell that guy sort of bad."

"He's better off not knowing what sort of case we're working," Dare replied. "Let him enjoy knowing his instincts gained the attention he thought the body deserved."

"He's right, she was murdered." Greer spoke in a grim tone.

It was a heavy topic but one they were both used to facing. It went with the Shadow Ops badges they both carried. They worked with a special class of criminal. Kirkland Grog was proving to be the image of his father who was once known as the Raven. A major underworld crime boss who'd died as violently as he'd lived.

Now, Kirkland was fighting for his share of the Raven's empire. It fell to Dare and his team to catch him before he lined up too many bodies while building his reputation as a man to be obeyed.

Dare was up to the challenge.

In fact, he thrived on it.

"What have you got?"

Dare was used to the way his section leader cut right to the reason for his calls. There was no greeting when Dare punched the button to accept the incoming call. Kagan gave him just enough time to get the phone to his ear before he spoke.

"Two bodies, one was with Kirkland less than twenty-four hours ago," Dare filled his boss in.

"Good," Kagan replied. "Kirkland is using human trafficking to fund Carl Davis's presidential campaign. I want them both out of business."

"The world will be a brighter place for it," Dare answered. "We're going to wire Kirkland's Cliffside house tonight. Just waiting on the window of opportunity to open. Word is, he likes to arrive at his own parties, leaves for a few hours before so the catering staff can set up. We've disabled the chef's car to keep him away from the party location and allow for our team to get onto the property."

"Keep me posted," Kagan said before the call ended.

Dare dropped his phone back into his shirt pocket. He had eyes on the Malibu estate where Kirkland spent most of the winter months. It overlooked the ocean and pissed him off a little because it was vastly unfair of the universe to allow a man like Kirkland to live in such opulence with money he was earning by selling innocent girls into prostitution.

There were times Dare truly loved his job. Today was one of them because he could smell an opportunity to gather hard evidence coming his way.

"He's on the move."

Agent Thais Sinclair's voice came through his ear-piece while Dare Servant watched traffic.

"Looks like Kirkland is clearing out so the party can be set up," Thais continued. "Just the catering delivery guy left, and he's making ready to pull out."

"Copy," Dare responded. "Make sure Agent Bowan has the chef delayed."

Dare killed the call, feeling a surge of satisfaction. Kirkland didn't empty out his house very often. It was the opportunity they needed to bug the place.

One golden hour.

Dare planned to make the most of it.

Jenna jumped for the phone when it rang.

Pathetic . . .

Yeah, whatever, beggars couldn't be choosers.

Or in her case, she couldn't afford to miss a call which just might revive her vacation plans with enough income to make the Hawaiian islands do-able.

Awww Hawaii . . . She seriously loved the tropical islands. If that meant she had her price, so be it!

Being a combustion expert was great, except she worked by the project, which meant when one contract finished she was on the bench until another project was secured. Three days at home and she was going stir crazy. She really needed to blow something up but if she wanted to do it legally, she had to wait for a contract. She smiled as she answered the phone.

"Good morning."

"Jennie dear . . ."

Jenna recognized the tone. Her friend Sam was in need and looking for reinforcements. It wasn't a contract offer but it was her buddy.

"What's wrong?" she asked.

"It's Paul," Sam began. "He's stuck with a dead car and I have this major account with a huge party tonight and there is no way the food will be ready if I don't get someone there within the hour."

"Don't you have tons of people trying to get hired on with you?" she asked.

Sam let out a snort. "Yes, but this is one of those Malibu cliff homes. Background check is mandatory. Fingerprinting, you know the drill. They use gold-plated toilet paper and don't want anyone around who might steal a square or squeal to the paparazzi about their private parties."

Sam and his husband ran one of the most exclusive catering business in Malibu. Along with the glory went the stress because one bad review could translate into disaster among the celebrities who owned the high-priced real estate.

"So what's it going to take to get you to work for me tonight?" Sam asked bluntly. "You have a background check from the government."

"Ah . . ." Jenna muttered, grateful for the fact that she could roll her eyes without her buddy seeing it. "You know, I'm not really a chef."

"Please," Sam cut her off. "You are a chef at heart, you just enjoy blowing stuff up more. You'd work for me if you weren't employed by the space program. Which is why I love you.

"For the record, I don't blow stuff up."

Sam made a scoffing sound. "Fine, combustion expert. Whatever you say. What I call it, is—you have a background check and I *really* need you to get up to Malibu and put the soup on before my client gets pissed and slams my name to all his buddies." Sam paused to draw in a deep breath. "Besides, moping around your townhouse isn't good for you."

"I'm not moping," Jenna said, defending herself.

"You picked the phone up mighty fast."

Jenna gave into another urge to roll her eyes. "Because I know a contract offer is coming. I work by project. It's just the way the space program is. I'm not unemployed, just on the bench."

"Okay, fine, you're going to be back to crunching numbers in a jiffy. In the meantime . . . while you're not moping . . . want to come grill tiger shrimp? With that amazing sauce you haven't been able to teach anyone to make, right? Please? I'm a gay man and I'm begging. Do you have any idea how bad this could be for my reputation? Gay men aren't supposed to need women for anything."

Jenna chuckled. "I can't even see you, and I know you're using the puppy-dog eyes."

"Big . . . corgi ones," Sam confirmed.

"Ugh . . . Okay, send me the address and menu." Jenna caved in. "You're right, I'm picking the phone up too fast. Can't seem too desperate."

There was a squeal of delight from her Sam. "You're the best! The rest of the team will show up later. I just dropped the first load of food but have to go get the fresh sea food so we can meet and exchange the key."

Big corgi ones, huh?

Jenna aimed a rueful look at her phone before she headed toward her bedroom. Waiting on the phone wasn't going to bring in a project offer any faster. She'd get dinner out of it, premium eats, too. Just because she would be cooking it herself didn't really factor in. Sam knew her well, she did love to cook. She just loved making rocket engines better.

But appearing desperate? Well that had to go.

"Is it done?"

Dare Servant was used to controlling his tone. He kept it low and even as he listened to his fellow agent Zane Bowan.

"That car isn't going anywhere," Zane confirmed. "You've got a clear window."

"Copy that," Dare answered. He killed the call and let out a whistle.

Kirkland Grog was his father's son all the way.

Two innocent girls were laying in cold storage, and that matched his father's blood trail alright. Marc had killed anyone who got in his way or learned too much. Kirkland seemed to think that was a fine way to run his businesses.

One of which was porn.

It wasn't that Dare was straightlaced. He liked a good sex-filled weekend at the end of cases, but knowing Kirkland was bringing in girls from impoverished families and forcing them into pornography turned his stomach.

Dare took a great deal of personal enjoyment in knowing he'd used Kirkland's own security rules against him. The guy insisted on background checks. Today, that was going to translate into a window of time when Dare and his team could get into the house and bug it. Sure, the caterer was likely having a meltdown but the guy would live to put on another party.

The girls on the other hand needed him to have a means of gathering the evidence he needed to get Kirkland convicted in spite of the millions of dollars the guy could afford for lawyers.

Dare enjoyed the drive along the winding road that lead up to the exclusive mansion home. Kirkland was getting money from somewhere. On the surface, Kirkland made a lot of noise about how clean he was. Claiming he made his money as a pop singer. But his father had been an underworld crime boss.

He didn't have any concrete evidence against Kirkland, but it was a fact that his promotion manager gave out more tickets than they sold. Packing the stadiums when Kirkland was on stage, but, from what Dare's team had discovered, all the concerts did was break even.

Kirkland was getting his money somewhere else. And the dead girl had been with him the night before she died.

Dare needed to know what was going on inside the house, and he needed to bug a good portion of Kirkland's personal possessions so he could track the guy.

He pressed his foot against the accelerator and sent

his car peeling around the next turn in the road as he gripped the wheel and made the turn in spite of the hairpin curve.

The tires squealed, but the sports car hugged the road with every bit of its promised German engineering.

No, he didn't have the evidence yet but there was a reason he was on the case.

He never quit.

"Turkey."

Jenna jumped back as a wave of gravel came her way from the tires of a sports car. She was pulled well off the road, in a turnout that was big enough for Sam and her cars but that didn't seem to be far enough off the road for some of the locals.

"They all drive like dicks up here," Sam remarked. "Watch the curves, I've found myself facing a car coming at me in my lane more than once because the driver is on a cell phone."

Jenna took the remote Sam was holding out. "You know something? If the universe decides to deliver a mega millions jackpot to me, I'm pretty sure I can make it through life without being a PITA to the rest of the human race."

"I hope you get the chance to prove it." Sam winked at her. "I'm hitting the docks to grab the fresh fish Paul ordered and then I'll be right back, but it's a drive down there. I'll call you when I get up here. That remote thing is the only way inside without setting off the security system. The owner has a bug up his crawl about keeping the house secure. So stay in the kitchen." Sam started to leave but held up a finger. "The guy is also a major dick. Got little bare titty girls all over the place like a buffet. Thinks he's God's gift if you know what I mean."

"Thanks for the warning. Don't worry, I've got plenty to keep me busy."

"Just giving you a heads-up so you don't chop off the guy's hand when he thinks you're part of the party service." Sam shook his head. "Everything is in the back pantry. House is empty."

Sam ducked into the cab of his truck and shut the door. Jenna did the same, buckling her seat belt before looking long and hard at the road and pulling off the turn out. The weather was perfect. The sky was blue and the sun sparkled off the expanse of the Pacific Ocean. It was actually a chore to keep her attention on the road as she made her way up to the house because the view was just so magnificent.

And so completely out of her price range in real estate.

She went past the main driveway, following Sam's instructions to look for a second entrance to the property. The little concrete strip took her around the side of the house to the four-car garage that served as the service entrance.

Four-car . . .

She shook her head at the excess, slightly miffed at having to cross her fingers and do a crazy chicken dance as she hoped for a new job offer just so she could afford a vacation someplace with a view this house had every single day.

Yeah, life isn't fair. This isn't your first encounter with that fact.

She smiled at herself and pointed the remote at the garage door. It slid up in response. She left her car in the driveway and walked into the garage. There were two trucks inside it, one for a gardener and another for deliveries.

A quick tap on the remote and the door slid shut again. She had to point the remote at the door leading into the house and click it to unlock the security system. As the door slid down and the sunlight was cut off, she pushed the door open to the walk-in pantry. Sitting on the island were the promised boxes of ingredients for the night's party eats.

There was also a man.

A huge one with a black ski mask pulled down over his face, standing on the island as he was drilling something into the side of the beam that ran across the ceiling.

Jenna blinked, but he was there, turning to face her as she heard the door behind her close and click as it locked.

Fuck.

She'd dropped the stupid remote into her pocket, and the doorknob wasn't turning.

The guy was cussing, jumping down from the island as she tried to get the dammed remote free of her pocket. Her fingers were nothing but a tangled mess as she fought against the fabric of her pants and felt like her dammed heart was going to burst because it was thumping so hard.

"Stay away from me!" she warned.

Her voice came out in a tone that was far less than confident. Mr. Ski Mask man was less than impressed, too. She caught a hint of his eyes narrowing before he was reaching for her.

"Don't touch me, asshole!"

This time, something clicked inside her. Like a button being pushed. It happened as he reached out for her, a need to survive surfacing above her horror. The self-defense training she'd been required to attend at work kicked in. The guy only gained a partial hold on her arm before she clamped his hand down beneath her own and twisted under his arm, taking his hand and arm along with her motion.

There was a grunt from him as she twisted and tried to lock up his arm.

Unfortunately, he'd had self-defense training, too.

He dropped his shoulder and turned, breaking her hold with a snarl.

"I mean it . . . don't touch me!"

That was another lesson from her classes, be vocal. Make sure you told your attacker to stop.

It made it so much easier to convict them that way.

Yeah? Well you have to survive first.

He came at her, and she popped a back fist into his eye. Practicing on a hand-held pad was no preparation for the feeling of her knuckles sinking into the soft flesh of his eye and hitting the bone of his skull.

She let out a gasp as the impact traveled up her arm and into her shoulder. There was a grunt and then a snicker. The unexpected sound drew her attention to the doorway, which opened into the kitchen. There was a second man there, watching them through the slits in his ski mask.

The distraction proved fatal.

One moment she was trying to decide why he was snickering and in the next the man in front of her had her face down on the island, her arms twisted up behind her.

"Need any help?" the man in the doorway asked.

There was a grunt from the man behind her. He had his weight on her, pinning her to the smooth marble. "Get off me!"

"Greer . . ."

"Yeah." The guy in the doorway moved toward her. He pulled something from his vest.

She caught a glint of light shining off the end of a very sharp needle before she was fighting for her life. The guy behind her underestimated her response. It gave her a tiny taste of relief because she managed to push off the island as his feet gave.

But he pushed her back into place a half-second later.

"Sure you have her?" the first man asked.

"Do it, our window is closing."

There was an unyielding note in the first man's tone. It chilled her blood, making her realize that she'd never really been afraid before.

No, she understood true fear now.

Her heart was racing, sweat popping out all over her skin as she strained against the hold on her. All the while, she watched the guy in front of her coming closer. The man behind her grabbed her hair, using the hold to flatten her head on the island. It gave the first man a clear path to her neck.

She thought she caught a hint of remorse in his eyes before he was tapping the needle against her neck. It stung, but what she felt most was the horror.

Was she going to die?

Normally, she would have questioned her level of drama, but the ski masks just made them look ten times scarier than anything she'd ever seen in her life. The hold the guy had on her was painful and so hard, she felt it bone deep.

And then, relief was washing through her, the pain lessening as thinking began to elude her.

"Ease up on her," The first man said. He popped a cap back onto whatever it was he'd used on her and replaced it in his vest pocket. "She'll be out in a moment."

The certainty in his tone sent her into a panic.

Right.

Wrong.

Hopeless or not.

She jerked and strained against the hold on her.

But she was weakening again.

She felt like her muscles were losing strength, becoming limp. She gasped, trying to draw in enough breath to fend off the fog clouding her thoughts.

Helpless . . .

It was by far the worst feeling she'd ever experienced. Like being caught in the doors of an elevator and aware of every second while those unfeeling doors crushed her.

The man behind her eased his hold as she wilted right in front of him. He reached out and caught her arm, controlling her fall to the floor. Their gazes locked.

Devil back eyes.

It was the last bit of information her failing senses could grasp.

"I would have called you something a little more sordid." Greer said.

"Our window is closing," Dare reprimanded Greer.

Greer shrugged and turned to return to the kitchen. "Your eye is swelling shut, too."

It was a parting jab.

Dare was used to them from Greer and the rest of the team. Shadow Ops wasn't for the thin-skinned.

He knelt down beside his captive and felt something unique. She was petite. From her delicate nose all the way to her slim fingers. Perspiration was coating her, telling him how frightened she'd been.

It wasn't the first time he'd scared someone during a case.

Wouldn't be the last either.

Working with scum meant he had to meet them on common ground. Bad guys played rough, so he did, too.

What was unique was, today, it bothered him.

He drew in a stiff breath and stood. The mission goal was what needed his attention.

As in, undivided attention.

Whoever she was, he'd deal with her after the house was wired.

"How much did you give her?"

Greer McRae was standing in the doorway of the bedroom Dare had carried their unexpected guest into.

"Those trigger pens don't allow for choices in the dosage." Agent Thais Sinclair added her opinion from the hallway behind Greer. "As slight as she is, don't expect any answers until morning."

"She's tougher than she looks," Dare said. He left her lying on the bed, reaching out to pull on the frame. It held steady as he tried to shake it.

"I wouldn't secure her." Thais was still feeling the need to offer her opinion. Dare wasn't in the mood for it, but his frustration gained his attention because Thais was his fellow agent.

In short, there was no reason for him to have his jock-strap in a twist.

They worked together, in each other's back pockets.

He looked at Thais. "We finally have Kirkland's house wired. Team resources need to be focused on the mission, not making sure our detainee doesn't slip out the window and go screaming to the local police. We don't need anyone running their mouth about a federal investigation going on in the area. Kirkland might have a few of the local cops in his pay."

The set of shackles in his hands jingled as he dropped one cuff on the bed next to their detainee and unlocked the second one before securing it around a section of the bedframe.

"That drug nauseates a lot of people," Thais continued.

Dare had picked up the second cuff, intending to secure it around Jenna's wrist. He stopped and looked at Thais.

"We're working here." Thais stated the obvious. "If she throws up all over this room, because she can't make it to the bathroom, we'll be the ones enjoying the scent."

"But if it makes you feel better to cuff her," Greer said, choking on his amusement, "we can see why."

Greer winked, while Thais made a soft, delicate sound of approval. Dare felt his jaw aching.

His eye was swollen, and it was going to be a nice shiner come morning. His teammates left him, but he heard them laughing in the hallway before they turned and went back to where their command center was set up in the living room of the house.

The Shadow Ops teams used personal property to avoid being tracked in a world where operating off-grid was becoming more and more of a challenge.

Houses in probate, ones that belonged to recently deceased accident victims, those were the places they liked to set up in. It would take the locals a few weeks to question if they were new residents or not, and by then, they'd move on.

He looked down at Jenna Henson.

She shouldn't have become a factor. It was an odd twist of fate that the owner of the catering company had a friend with a security clearance who also had chef skills.

Dare didn't let his guilt gain any further hold on him than that.

No, it wasn't fair.

Neither was life. And Jenna wasn't dead, unlike the Asian girls who were lying in cold storage.

His team was doing their best to make sure countless others wouldn't have to come face to face with just how harsh reality could be when men like Kirkland were willing to kill to gain what they wanted.

Okay, he still felt a twinge of guilt as he looked at his detainee.

Jenna had a delicate bone structure, just like the two bodies that had been fished out of the Los Angeles riverbed. Kirkland liked pretty girls, lots of them. He also seemed to like doing business with the same sort of criminals his father had. Dare had pictures of Kirkland meeting with crime bosses and underworld thugs. But no evidence linking him with any crimes.

Yet, anyway.

It would come. There was too much money flowing. Kirkland's legitimate businesses didn't account for all of it.

He dropped the shackle on the floor and left Jenna behind. That was the way it had to be. The only comfort he could offer was letting her have the dignity of not being chained if she did wake up nauseated.

Someone would hear her or he would be getting a new team.

Her mouth was dry.

Like she'd slept with her mouth open and a squirrel had decided to sleep on her tongue.

But that wasn't the only thing off. Waking up was taking a serious amount of effort. Half her brain didn't want to respond, but her bladder was screaming for relief. Jenna reached up and rubbed her eyes. They burned, feeling gritty.

But it was the sight of the ceiling above her that really made her break through the fog holding her down.

It wasn't a very interesting ceiling. Just some shade of white, which wasn't too glaring. There was some crown molding running along the edges of it, too. And a nice little arched opening to a bathroom.

Crown molding her bedroom didn't have.

She sat up and cringed as her body protested. Pain raced along her nerve endings, but it sort of got shoved into a back corner of her mind as she looked around the room and didn't recognize anything.

Her memory decided to reengage. Offering up a perfect recollection of those moments in the kitchen.

Fuck.

And double fuck.

In fact, fuck, just wasn't a dirty enough word for her circumstances.

She looked at the door but scooted off the bed and made a dash for the bathroom first. Wetting herself while escaping didn't seem a very wise choice. Halfway through washing her hands, she realized she needed to prioritize. Getting out of wherever she was had to rank higher than clean hands.

Peeking back into the room she took it in as she tried to decide on a course of action. It was still dark outside, the air had the morning chill feeling to it. She was cold from lying on the bed in just her clothing. The comforter was mussed where she'd been placed.

Someone put you in that bed . . .

A someone strong enough to carry her.

Yeah, like a guy wearing a ski mask she'd recently encountered.

She shouldn't have flushed the toilet.

The sound of the water running was like fingernails on a chalkboard. Her heart accelerated as she decided the window was a good bet for getting out of the house.

She made it only halfway across the room before the door opened.

"Welcome back, Ms. Henson."

Jenna jumped back into a fighting stance. She tried to quell the thought going through her brain about how ridiculous she must look.

Still . . . stupid looking or not, she wasn't going down without a fight.

The light was on in one of the rooms in the house. It gave her a strange illumination of the guy, while leaving his face in shadow. What it did grant her was a very clear picture of how he completely filled the doorway.

He was huge and muscled beyond the normal civilian man. The sight sent a strange twist through her belly because she realized his body was by far the most deadly weapon at his disposal. The gun strapped to his chest in a harness was only one option he might utilize.

"I am Special Agent Servant."

As much as she'd been struggling with believing her circumstances, the introduction took a moment to sink in. She wanted to be relived, but it was hard to come out of her flight mode and really think about what he'd said.

Okay, and the needle in the neck thing was still sticking in her brain.

"You were wearing a ski mask," she mumbled, her thoughts just spilling past her lips because of how fast her brain was running.

He tilted his head to one side and shrugged. "You're being detained."

"Excuse me?" she demanded. "I don't see a badge."

He came through the doorway, his stride too full of confidence for her dwindling confidence. "You can show it to me from right there."

At least she managed to sound more together than she felt.

Fuck, she really didn't need to lose it.

He reached down and pulled something off his belt. The meager light had her squinting to get a real look at it. He moved a little closer while she was trying to read the badge.

It was a fatal miscalculation on her part.

He dropped the badge and clamped a hand on her wrist before she realized what he was doing.

"That thing doesn't say police on it," she argued.

He twisted her around and pushed her back toward the bed.

"Special Agent," he clarified.

His strength was flatly amazing. He moved her where he wanted with the hold he had on her arm. A moment later she heard a click as he secured something cold and hard around her wrist.

"We'll talk more in the morning." He was moving back to where his badge was lying on the floor. One easy motion and he'd plucked it up before turning to look at her while he clipped it to his belt. "You're not in any danger."

But she was chained to the bed with a length of chain. "I want to call a lawyer."

He turned and contemplated her. What bothered her the most was the pity in his eyes. It reminded her of the way someone looked at a pigeon with a broken wing. He might not like the situation, but it wasn't going to change the fact that things weren't going to end well for the pigeon.

For her . . .

"There is a reason you've never seen a badge like this one, Ms. Henson. We're a covert team. Settle down. You aren't going anywhere until we decide you aren't part of the case." He went through the door and started to pull it shut. "Trust me, this is more comfortable than most detainees get. I suggest you enjoy it while you can."

The warning was clear as a fog horn.

"You were the one breaking into someone's house," she argued as she jerked on the shackle.

"I know what I was doing," he muttered. "What concerns you is what you were doing there and what you saw."

It wasn't the first part of his sentence that concerned her. She knew she was innocent of any crime.

But she had seen him and his buddy.

That was a cold, hard, jab of something she wished she'd never seen. An ignorance-is-bliss sort of moment. She was left dealing with the very bitter realization that knowing too much had killed the cat.

At the moment, she was cast as the cat in life's little drama.

He shut the door as she sunk onto the edge of the bed and blinked because her night vision had been disrupted by the encounter. She was left in the dark, waiting for her eyes to adjust while time limped by like a lame tortoise, letting her soak in just how helpless she was to do anything but wait.

The shackle on her wrist was like one she'd seen in reality prison shows. It had a two-foot length of silver chain between two cuffs. One was secured to the heavy bedframe and the other around her wrist.

She was scared.

Fuck that!

She growled at herself and turned around, trying to push the bed. It was a heavy iron frame that didn't budge. Hell, the thing didn't even rock.

Fuck.

You're repeating yourself . . .

Yeah? Well that was sort of low on the priorities list at the moment and fuck was working for her.

The chain was solid, and she didn't have enough strength to break the frame.

There was a nightstand, but it was a basic one, no drawers. The room was just as spartan.

She didn't want to quit.

But circumstances left her with nothing but the fact that he'd said he was an agent to keep her from descending into panic again.

Of course, the memory of him wearing a ski mask was making it sort of hard to accept her circumstances.

Special Agent Servant . . .

The special part likely allowed for the ski mask.

It calmed her down, right until she recalled that Sam had been planning to work that same party. Her blood chilled as she contemplated demanding Servant tell her if Sam was okay.

But her head was pounding and her legs quivering. It

seemed whatever they'd shot her full of, its grip wasn't completely broken.

And Special Agent Servant wasn't exactly the sort she wanted to take on without all of her wits.

But she was going to take him on. That thought kept her company as she settled onto the bed and fought to get the comforter over herself.

Yeah, the guy had another thing coming if he thought she was going to roll over for him.

Jenna Henson never gave up!

"The place is wired," Dare reported to his section leader, Kagan.

The man didn't have a last name, and Dare wasn't even sure if Kagan was a first name. It was just the title the man went by. Dare knew enough about Shadow Ops to understand the need for obscurity.

He had a female shackled to a bed in the back room because she'd seen him.

It wasn't fair, or right, but he had to catch the bag guys, and that wouldn't happen if he played by the rules.

"I have a civilian in custody."

There was a soft sound from his section leader.

"She caught us bugging the house," Dare explained. "Can't let her blow our operation."

It took a moment for Kagan to respond. That was another thing about his section leader that Dare was accustomed to. Kagan would think things through.

Every time.

"Agreed." There was another pause. "Tag her before you turn her lose. Keep her if she even smells like an evidence link."

"Yes, sir."

Kagan killed the call. Dare dropped his phone back

into his vest pocket. He stood for a moment, drawing a breath and letting it out.

"What's wrong, Servant? Digging deep?"

Thais Sinclair was a femme fatale.

Her face was perfectly sculpted, and her lean body combined with it to produce a female that turned heads and made his collar feel too tight on occasion. Her dark eyes could tempt a man to venture too close, which was right about the time she'd be close enough to either use her very accomplished skills of seduction or kill him with her equally polished abilities in hand-to-hand martial arts.

"Interesting."

She also purred when she spoke. It was undermining a man's ability to think straight. Today however, he found it irritating.

"Kagan wants our guest tagged before we release her." Dare was giving Thais an order, but his fellow agent only sent him a little smile that made him feel like she was peeling away his layers.

To get at what, he wasn't really certain.

But he was pretty sure he didn't want to think too long about it.

Thais was good at a lot of things. Pushing men's buttons was at the top of the list.

Greer entered the room.

"Kept if there is any reason to think she has evidence against Kirkland," Dare finished.

"Didn't look like it to me," Greer responded. "She's clean as a nun's sheets. Even has a couple of cooking trophies to support her being there to take over. The buddy called her right after the first chef called in to him."

"Let's get this finished." Dare sent Thais a hard look.

The agent's eyes narrowed with distaste, but she stood up and went toward a long table where they had equipment cases laid out. He heard the chirp of the fingerprint scanner as she opened the case that held the air gun.

Dare was turning into the hallway, but he knew what Thais would be doing. She'd take out one of the tracking location chips and check it against their systems before loading it into the gun. It wouldn't hurt any more than an ear piercing.

Physically that was.

Dare was pretty sure their civilian was going to have plenty to say about how much she disliked knowing her privacy was being shredded.

He stopped at the bedroom door and drew in another breath.

That just irritated him again.

He didn't need to be digging deep over her. There were two mothers who would be burying their daughters once he traced the girls back to their homes. His job was to find the connection between Kirkland and those murder victims. And who knew what else. Kirkland was trafficking humans. Ones he considered disposable. Getting the girls into the country wasn't easy. Ship holds, shipping containers, all of the options were less than comfortable to say the least and there was no way to know how many of them died before reaching U.S. ground. It sickened him to know Kirkland's people preyed on the desperation of those girls, hunting them in the poor parts of Asia and Korea where even the poorest of families still raised their daughters with morality. They were promised nanny positions and housekeeping jobs.

And ended up being turned into prostitutes. A shame they could not see past, which accounted for why they didn't come forward once they had the chance.

Kagan didn't assign Shadow Ops teams to simple cases. His section leader was keeping his jaw tight to prevent himself from tainting the evidence. Dare's job was to dig where the local police hadn't ventured. He had the numbers to support Kirkland's lack of income from his pop-music career. Now he needed to prove where the money was really coming from.

That included ensuring Jenna Henson was as innocent as she claimed. His job was to doubt her, and that was exactly what he intended to do.

There was a single rap on the door before it was opened.

The shade was pulled down on the window but there was enough light in the room to give her a solid look at Agent Servant.

She could have done without it though.

The guy was all hunk.

From his muscle-bound frame to the midnight color of his hair. His jaw had that hard cut to it that came from a level of fitness only movie stars and military personal could claim. The way he took in the room before coming inside only added more fuel to her suspicions of him being some sort of Special Ops guy.

He crossed the room and picked up her wrist, fitting a little silver key into it. There was a click, and she was free. She rolled over the opposite side of the bed and landed on her feet. He sent her a harassed look.

"Please . . ." she muttered with more than a hint of sarcasm.

He lifted an eyebrow.

"You." She pointed at him. "Don't get to look insulted by me trying to put distance between us."

"Wasn't insulted."

She was rubbing her wrist. It was red and bruised

from her tugging on the shackle. "Flashing me a badge, in a semi-dark room, doesn't confirm you are a 'good guy.'"

"If I wasn't a 'good guy,'"—he sent her a hard look— "you'd be dead. Living room, five minutes. Don't make me run you down."

You'd be dead . . .

Her mouth went dry as he left her alone with that pearl of truth.

There was no way to talk her way around it. Even the black eye he was sporting didn't help bolster her courage.

No, all that shiner did was confirm that while she might have gotten a good strike in, she'd lost the battle in the end.

And she could be very dead right then if he'd been the sort who murdered people.

She shied away from thinking "killed people" because she got the idea he wasn't a stranger to shedding blood. The fact chilled her blood, but it also set off another feeling. This one was in direct conflict with her desire to loathe him. That was on account of the fact that she agreed with him. She'd been helpless and at his mercy. The fact that she'd woken up was defiantly a point in favor of him being a "good guy."

Great.

Being deprived of her ability to be pissed at him was really a downer, considering she really needed to have a target for all her emotions.

But that would require her discarding logic.

She let out a sigh and went toward the bathroom to make use of her remaining four minutes.

Good guy? Well, at least he was letting her face him without bed head. That wasn't going to qualify him for any position beyond she wouldn't hate his guts, but it was a step up from kidnapper.

Why had she decided against staying home and moping again?

Sure seemed like she'd made a bad call.

As in—epic failure.

The living room was just that—a standard space with a sofa and love seat that might have belonged to any family.

The computer terminals set up in it and the long table with black cases laid out on top was where the normalcy ended.

And the guns.

There were a crap load of them. At least to her civilian eyes anyway. The three men in the room actually wore chest harnesses. There were guns on tables and next to keyboards as well.

"Have a seat, Ms. Henson," Servant addressed her. "We have some questions for you."

They'd already placed a chair in the middle of the room for her. It gave all of them different angles to watch her from.

"What?" she asked as she sat down. "No super bright spotlight in my face?"

"Disappointed?" Servant asked as he sat down and faced her.

"Well, you were wearing ski masks the last time we met." She shrugged.

But now, they all had badges on their belts. Clipped to the right side, those shiny things just looked real. It helped dispel the last of her fear, leaving her facing the unknown reasons for why she was sitting in a room. She was pretty sure she would be a lot better off not knowing what those reasons were.

"What do you want?" she asked softly. "With me?"

"What were you doing last night?"

Such a simple, mundane question. So much so, it gave her a moment of pause because she realized Agent Servant had a slightly bored look in his eyes. Oh, the guy was focused on her, intently so, but he already knew the answer to the question.

"If you don't already know," she muttered, "you aren't any type of special agent."

It wasn't the wisest thing she might have said, but acting stupid had never been her thing. Okay, to be blunt, she'd put her foot in her mouth countless number of times and couldn't seem to break the habit. Her filter between brain and mouth was about the size of a dime.

Servant's lips twitched. He controlled the little impulse quickly, returning to his stoic expression.

But she'd surprised him.

"Indulge me, Ms. Henson," Agent Servant said.

"My friend Sam owns Joyful Occasions, a catering business for high-end parties and exclusive events. His primary chef had unexpected car trouble . . ." She stopped talking as her brain latched onto that bit of information.

"And?" Servant pressed her.

"And Paul has a brand-new Jeep because he can't be rolling up to client sites in a beater." Jenna said what she was thinking.

"The part where you were at the house?" Servant pressed her.

His tone held a tiny hint of frustration.

Well that made sense, the guy liked control. And he was good at it, she'd grant him that one.

Jenna slowly grinned. "You messed with Paul's car. Thinking Sam wouldn't be able to replace him on such short notice because of the bonding issue." She sent him a hard look. "That's messed up. Know that? Sam could lose his business if one of his clients gives him a bad review."

"You're missing the point . . ."

"No, I get it." She sat forward and eyeballed him. "I walked in on you doing something you don't want anyone to know about. Well, spilt milk now. Don't waste my time by asking me questions you already know the answer to. Or don't special agents have better things to do than trying to intimidate me?"

"I suggest you take this seriously."

"Oh, I am," Jenna assured him. "I'm just saying, let's cut the shit, and get on with whatever it is you've decided is going to happen to me. You already know who I am, what I was doing, and what I saw."

There. Maybe she had more balls than wisdom, but at least she wasn't going down as too chicken to look them in the eye and speak her mind.

Servant got it, too.

She watched the way his black eyes glittered with approval. His expression didn't change, but she knew what she'd seen and held onto that bit of knowledge as he cast a look across the room toward the female agent in the room.

They proved their badges right as they moved. Without a spoken word, the female knew exactly what Servant wanted as the other man came at her from the side.

She held onto the arms of the chair out of the sheer need to prove she could control her panic.

There was no escape.

So, running would only prove her incapable of controlling her emotions.

If her dignity was the only thing left to her, she'd hold on for dear life.

Servant watched her through it all. His dark eyes on her as the male agent grasped her neck and held her steady. The female pulled some sort of gun from behind her and pressed the muzzle against Jenna's shoulder.

Her heart stopped as she heard a click.

There was a searing pain, and then she was free as whatever they'd put into her shoulder throbbed.

"This is a classified operation," Servant informed her. "Speak one word about it and we'll know. That chip will make sure we can find you. Do yourself a favor and make sure we don't have any reason to come looking for you."

"Prick."

Jenna grumbled as the door of the car she'd been in slammed shut after she'd been kicked out on a random street. A moment later, the guy in the front passenger seat dropped her purse onto the sidewalk and the car pulled away into traffic.

"Colossal prick."

She sucked in her breath as she reached for her purse. Her shoulder ached.

Why couldn't she meet one of those tall, dark, handsome, great secret agent men that there were books about?

Because that's not reality . . .

That was why. And reality sucked.

At the moment, it sucked great big donkey balls.

She clutched her purse to her chest as she looked around and tried to get her bearings.

Okay, Servant had some redeeming qualities. His men had dropped her three blocks from Sam's tasting room store front. The wave of relief that swept through her nearly buckled her knees.

But it also drove home just how false her bravado had been when she'd faced down Servant.

Yeah, well, she'd done it.

There was a definite sense of satisfaction attached to that thought. It got her moving toward the crosswalk and down the next couple of blocks before she opened the door of Joyful Occasions.

There was a delicate ringing of bells to announce the front door opening. The receptionist desk was empty, but Sam came ducking through the doorway in response to the chimes.

"Welcome to—thank god!"

Sam had her clasped in a hug that threatened to crush her. "We've been out of our minds!"

There was a scamper of steps on the floor before Paul came through the doorway.

"Jenna!"

She soaked up the hugs, listening to the chattering of her friends. They pulled her through the doorway and into the salon. The velvet-covered furniture was normally intended to impress upon prospective clients the level of taste and quality Joyful Occasions delivered in their services.

Today, Jenna sunk down onto one sofa and just felt like she was home.

And that she'd failed to appreciate how wonderful it was to be there.

"What happened?"

She lifted her head and looked at Sam. Her friend was watching her with wide eyes.

"I found the remote on the kitchen floor," Sam said. "So, I know you were there but your car . . ."

"Was back in your garage . . ." Paul exclaimed. "Like you'd been abducted by aliens or something."

"What happened?" Sam repeated.

God, she wanted to tell them.

Jenna had to clamp her mouth shut and fight the urge to challenge agent Servant's warning to keep quiet.

Even if he was a prick, the guy did strike her as pretty serious.

Okay, deadly serious when she factored in the guns and drug dart thing they'd used on her.

"I can't talk about it."

Her shoulder throbbed right on cue, making it a lot easier to deal with the look her friend shot her.

"Sam, believe me, I wish I could. Just know this, I am so glad to be home," Jenna said.

She'd likely never spoken truer words. They seemed to be the last thing she could really manage before her strength deserted her. Sam was the one who noticed the color draining from her face. They bundled her into a car and drove her home.

Humiliating? Sure was.

But it made her feel so cherished, it was worth the shot to her pride.

Yeah, she'd failed to appreciate the value of the life she had. They said everything happened for a reason, maybe that was the reason she'd run into Agent Servant.

Because it sure wasn't for his charming demeanor!

"Satisfied?" Greer asked.

Dare lowered the pair of binoculars he'd been watching Jenna through. "For the moment. A secondary team is going to be keeping tabs on her."

"In the meantime, we need to cut Norton and Cline loose," Greer said as he pulled into traffic. "Missing that security clearance was too much."

"Agreed." Servant pulled his phone out and pressed in a line of code. "I'll get some fresh fish."

"Nothing wrong with spuds." Greer suggested Army instead of Navy. "The Hale brothers have you too used to squid recruits."

"Norton and Cline were CIA," Dare muttered.

Shadow Ops teams pulled from unique ranks, the happy hunting grounds occupied by ex-SEALS and other special forces because the sort of man it took to make it into those elite fighting units never really retired.

"And you're Scottish."

"The lassies like it . . ." Greer slid into his accent.

"Save it for after the case is closed."

Greer offered him a double-finger salute.

Kirkland liked his parties.

He rubbed a hand across his eyes and sat up. His bed was rumpled, with forgotten bits of feminine attire littering it.

But he was alone.

He never closed his eyes with a woman in bed with him. No, that was a good way to have his defenses undermined. Women were fun, but he needed to keep them in the category of toys. Things he could cast aside when it was time to get back to work.

Kirkland grunted on his way to the mega master bathroom attached to his room. He stretched and popped his back.

Yeah, it was time to get down to work. He liked money, but the party was over, so it was time to get back to business. His father had served as example on just how important it was to focus on making the money. Example was the right word, too. Marc Grog had more than one son, and Kirkland wasn't even his favorite.

Pulse had been.

But the important part of that fact was the knowledge that Pulse had died alongside his father Marc. Kirkland thought of it often but only as a means of learning from his father's example. Marc had worked with the underground of New Orleans too closely to escape having his identity known.

Kirkland had turned his back on the New Orleans section of business. There were too many cameras now. However, the plugged-in generation was still happy hunting grounds for making money. He just had to make sure he was giving those little addicts to their mobile devices what they craved. Which was more, more, and more.

Instant gratification.

He liked it himself.

But he was careful to hold onto his self-discipline. He didn't want to end up becoming one of the sheep most of the population was becoming. He was going to be the man feeding those animals, keeping them happy while they paid up.

But he wouldn't be able to enjoy his money if he got caught. Sure, he might stick to legitimate business, but that wasn't where the real money was. He finished dressing and went into his office.

No, there was profit potential in places that the Feds liked to try and keep him out of. Proven revenue streams that were older than the country itself.

Like people.

The disposable kind.

There was a rap on his office door. Kirkland looked

at the monitor that showed him a picture of who was waiting on the other side of that door before he pressed the release button.

"We have a problem," Mack said as he came in. "Couple of bodies got snagged by the fire department. Our normal pick up failed. Seems some old goat remembered Ji Su, wouldn't let her claim the remains."

"The sale on the mortuary will be final next week," Kirkland said. "Any bodies will go through there in the future."

Mack nodded. His main security man didn't leave though. Kirkland looked up from his computer and eyed the man."Check your backups on the house. Something feels off," Mack said.

Mack was his head of security for one reason—he got the job done.

"What kind of off?" Kirkland questioned.

"The catering staff was flustered and didn't arrive on their scheduled times. I've checked the main system footage but something still seems off," Mack said. "And I know you've got cameras I don't see."

Kirkland did. That was something he'd learned from his mother. Never let the people working for you get better at something than you were yourself or you'd end up cheated. He tapped in a code and pulled up the footage from the night of the party. Kirkland put the display on the wall monitor so Mack could see it.

"Holy fuck!"

Kirkland wasn't sure who cussed and he didn't care. The additional footage showed the arrival of the team and recorded their entrance into his house.

"I love your instincts, Mack," Kirkland said.

Kirkland was furious, and his words were cutting. Mack knew the tone, sharing a look with him.

"I'll find the girl. She'll lead me to the team," Mack promised.

"Good," Kirkland answered. "And make sure you do a better job with her body than the last two girls."

He valued Mack. Really, he did. But Kirkland had learned one thing from watching his father run his vast empire and that was that the top dog had to be the one who showed his teeth. His people would fear him.

CHAPTER TWO

Agent Servant was definitely in the category of hunk.

Jenna snorted and sat up. She'd slept rough, tossing and turning, and had taken more over-the-counter pain-killers than she should have.

Which was why Agent Servant shouldn't be in her dreams.

She rubbed her eyes and crawled out of bed way too early in the morning for someone who didn't have a job to get to.

Okay, fine, he was good looking too.

Her brain was still fascinated with the black hair. Lots of people had dark hair, but Servant was sporting mid-night black hair and eyes. It was a really stunning com-bination, making him look like some kind of midnight marauder.

You need a job . . .

Boy did she! Something really complex to keep all her brain cells busy.

With that goal in mind, she put the coffee on and went toward her laptop to begin checking in on her appli-cations. There were a couple of new projects she read through, making a choice on whether or not to throw her hat in for them.

But Servant still managed to invade her logically arranged plans for the day.

She cried defeat sometime in the early afternoon and spun around in her office chair. Round and around, with her head hanging back so her hair fell toward the floor.

Ridiculous.

Yep . . . and oh yeah.

But it felt good to laugh at herself. She opened her eyes, and Agent Servant was back in her thoughts but for a different reason this time. Looking up at her ceiling, she recalled her first sight of him. She might be a rocket scientist but she knew a thing or two about security cameras and how tiny they might be.

Had they bugged her house?

They put a tracking chip in your shoulder . . .

She contemplated the ceiling of her office, mentally debating where a camera might be hidden. They'd want a view of her laptop screen, which narrowed down the possibilities.

You're playing with fire . . .

Really? It felt a whole lot like taking back control of her life.

And she liked it.

A whole lot.

Greer started snapping his fingers. "You might . . . want to see this . . ."

Dare didn't hesitate. He moved toward his fellow agent's workstation.

"She doesn't know when to leave well enough alone . . ." Dare muttered.

Jenna was standing on a ladder, looking into the vent on her office ceiling.

"Some guys call that spirit," Greer offered.

Dare sent him a narrow-eyed look.

Greer chuckled. "You've gone and drunk the Kool-Aid, Servant." He pointed at the monitor. "The day you can't enjoy the fact that she's giving us a perfect shot down her bra . . ."

"It's called professionalism," Dare said.

"I hope I never get a case of it," Greer remarked. "If a woman is going to be interesting enough to not accept being pressed under our thumb, I'll enjoy her efforts."

"That sort of interesting just might translate into trouble for her," Dare informed his fellow agent.

Greer didn't agree.

But his fellow agent did drop his teasing demeanor to shoot him a questioning look. "Why the stick up your ass? She's loaded in the brain. I'm surprised it took her this long to start looking for bugs."

"Might be smart," Dare muttered tightly. "But she's not very wise."

And that was going to translate into a problem.

He moved away from Greer, but not before the sight of Jenna was branded into his mind.

He didn't need the distraction.

His cock didn't seem to care.

The problem was, he wasn't too sure which part of the situation was stirring his flesh. Sure, Jenna had a great set of tits. They were high and tight, just barely a handful with rosebuds for nipples and he wasn't too sorry for noticing it, but she was the one staring down his surveillance camera.

Thing was, he was reasonably sure it was her tenacity that was sending a buzz through his system.

He liked tenacity.

Too much for where the source was coming from today. He needed to put her out of his mind, but sitting down at his terminal where Kirkland's house was displayed from twenty different views didn't seem to distract him enough from Jenna.

She was going to make herself a problem. One he'd have to deal with.

His temper got the better of him, her ignorance of just what might happen to her making him see red.

"Going to deal with it," Dare said.

If Greer had anything to say about his decision, the Scot kept his thoughts to himself. Dare didn't turn around to discover just why that was.

He had enough frustration in his day.

Her cell phone was buzzing on the bathroom counter. Jenna's wet fingers slipped on the shower door as she hurried to open it. She nabbed a towel on her way across the tile and dried her ear off before answering.

"Good evening."

"You're totally job hunting," Sam snickered on the other end of the phone. "That was perfectly professional."

"So says the man with two cell phones, so he never inadvertently answers a client call in the wrong tone." Jane punched the speaker button and laid the phone down so she could finish drying off.

"Yeah, yeah, it's a living," Sam replied. "I'm taking you to dinner, no argument."

"I'm fine, really."

"That's an attempt at an argument," her friend accused Jenna softly. "I'm buying, too. We're going to Cliffside."

"I can't let you pay for that," Jenna said.

"But you didn't say you weren't going," Sam swooped in for the kill. "See you in an hour."

The line died, leaving Jenna marveling at her friend's ability to twist arms.

She ended up shrugging and heading toward the closet. Cliffside was amazing and Sam knew his stuff. Sunset was two hours away, which meant they'd have a stunning view of it while they ate their fifteen-dollar dinner salads.

Maybe she'd even forget all about Special Agent Servant.

She was going to give it a darn good try.

Working in a combustion lab meant wearing pants.

Jenna dove into her small treasure trove of dresses, selecting one that would suit the warm summer weather. During the day, California was scorching hot but now, as the offshore breeze blew in, everything along the coast was cooling down to that perfect temperature for short skirts, bare legs, and open-toe shoes.

She turned around and decided she needed to dress up more often.

That was the way to get Servant out of her dreams. Fill up the nighttime hours with other guys.

A twinge of regret went through her though. Servant was in the category of man-animal. Sure, the guy was a hard ass, but that just sort of enhanced his overall appeal because he was dedicated to his duty.

Man-oh-man . . . you need a date, girl!

Truth! Solid and undeniable.

Not that she wasn't trying. In fact, she leaned over and made sure her lipstick was perfect before pushing off the counter and twirling around to take a last look at herself.

The fact was, she was going out . . . dressed to kill.

And her heart stopped when she made it down her stairs.

Sweat popped out on her forehead as she looked straight into the midnight colored eyes of the man she'd been determined to erase from her mind.

"I thought you would be a little happier to see me, Jenna," Dare began.

Special Agent Servant was smooth and his tone too mocking for her taste. At least while she was fighting back a wave of panic over discovering him in her living room. When it came to power plays, the guy knew how to pull the carpet out from beneath her feet sure enough.

Well that wasn't going to work.

Nope.

She drew in a deep breath and forbid herself to crumble.

"Really?" she asked. "Maybe this thing in my shoulder is malfunctioning because I didn't send you a text inviting you into my house."

He'd sat down in her favorite recliner, facing the stairs. It was insane how exposed he made her feel.

Of course, that was exactly what he wanted. He'd invaded her space, to make sure she knew he could.

And it pissed her off.

"There's a few things you need to understand," Dare began as he stood up.

Fuck he was tall.

And she hated the fact that she was so aware of it.

"You will be watched."

She let out a snort. "I got that part when you shot something into my flesh. Thanks. Good night."

"Yet you were looking for surveillance leads in your office." He didn't budge.

His tone made it clear he wanted her contrite.

She ended up flashing him a grin instead. Just couldn't help it. He wasn't the sort of man anyone got the jump on very often.

His pressed his lips into a hard line. "That wasn't a compliment."

"Actually, it was."

His eyes narrowed, and she suddenly really regretted the circumstances of their meeting. He was deeply committed to his work, and that made him a definite "good guy."

Suddenly, being flippant wasn't working for her. She drew in a deep breath and started over.

"Look . . . I'm nobody in your world." She decided to try to fend off hostility. "And as much as you're asking for it, I really don't feel like showing you my bitch mode. You are doing your job, and I was helping out a friend. Call it even and the door is behind you. I've got my own life to get on with."

"So why are you playing with fire?" he demanded in an ultra-soft voice that sent a tingle down her spine. "My world will burn you."

She believed him and yet, it bothered her to see he'd judged her so incapable of being anything beyond a soft civilian.

There was something about him that made her want to measure up better.

Or maybe prove her worth was a better way of putting it.

"Excuse me?" she asked, managing to stand in place as he came closer. "Looking around my house . . . is sort of my right. No reason for you to show up and unleash your intimidation tactics."

"I haven't even begun to try to intimidate you, darling."

His lips twitched, giving her a flash of teeth. It was a menacing look to be sure, one that chilled her blood but also sent a twist of sensation through her insides.

Damn, man-animal was the perfect description for him alright. There was a hint of savageness in him that made her believe he could hold the line against . . . well, against whatever sort of bad guys he went after.

Bitch mode was looking like a great option.

She still didn't want to go down that path.

"Okay." She walked past him toward the door. "Thanks for dropping in. Next time, don't be shy about texting me. I'm sure you have the number."

She was sort of proud of the way she managed to pull off a steady tone of voice and open the front door while looking back at Servant.

"Who's been shy about texting you?"

Jenna jerked, turning her head around to find Paul and Sam on the front walk. Her friend took in the startled expression on her face and shook his head.

"It really pisses me off that you can't tell me why you're so jumpy . . ." Sam started in on her.

"Sam . . . stop . . ."

Sam was shaking his head and breezed right by her on his way inside the house.

"I know, you said you can't talk about it . . ."

Sam stopped as he got a good look at Special Agent Servant. "Hello . . ."

"So this is the someone who has been shy about texting you?" Sam inquired. "I'd write you a formal invitation."

Sam stuck his hand out. "Sam Griffith, very pleased to meet you."

There was a half second of silence as Jenna tried to decide what to do.

"Dare Servant."

He was shaking Sam's hand with an easy grin on his lips that transformed his face. Agent Servant was missing and in his place was a drop-dead gorgeous hunk.

Fuck.

"You didn't say you had a date, Jenna." Sam was beaming at her, suggestion written all over his face.

"Well . . ."

"She's too worried dating someone from work will compromise her project opportunities," Dare supplied smoothly. "I came over in person to make sure she knows how committed I am to changing her mind."

He was smooth, talking Sam over like a kitten standing in a rain puddle.

But the look Dare shot past Sam's head was pure promise.

In the hard and unyielding way.

It pissed her off, and she made sure he saw it before Sam and Paul were looking at her again.

"Great," Sam declared. "I made the reservation for three but you know that means a four-person table, so now were all set."

"I don't think Dare was planning on making an evening out of it." Jenna enjoyed being able to use his name.

"Do I look like a fool?" Dare ask silkily smooth. "If going to dinner is the price for making it so you put that dress on for me"—he swept her from head to toe— "count me in."

Sam let out a little chuckle. "I want to keep him, Jenna."

Dare picked up her purse and held it out to her with a wink.

A wink.

Something shot through her that she refused to name. It was hot and tingly and everything she would have welcomed if it weren't being triggered by Dare Servant.

She couldn't be attracted to him.

How can you miss it?

Okay, fair enough. The guy oozed charisma. That wink, combined with the way his lips were set into an inviting grin, well, perfect combination for her hormones to do something . . . impulsive.

Warning . . .

Oh yeah, she heard the red alert sounding through her brain even as her body was ignoring it in favor of responding to Dare.

She just wished he wasn't so bloody good at it.

The game that was.

He held the car door open for her and slid into the driver's seat beside her. While Sam and Paul piled in the backseat.

She noticed way too much about him but decided to enjoy it. After all, she'd wanted to indulge in being more than a bench warmer.

Looked like life was taking her challenge.

That made her smile, even if the man sitting next to her kept her pulse going faster than normal. There was a buzz to it, she wouldn't deny that. In fact, it was sort of fun.

You're playing with fire . . .

His words and very, very true.

The problem was, fire was fascinating. Oh so tantalizing. Just like Dare Servant. Was it his real name? She found herself pondering that question as he pulled up to the Cliffside restaurant and the valet opened her door.

It would be nice to think she knew something about him.

Dangerous, too.

Yeah, well, bench warmers never were the life of the party.

Paul and Sam moved ahead to talk to the host.

"What are you doing?" she asked.

"You wanted to see if you had my attention," Dare replied.

He'd eased close, playing his part perfectly. It was a tad disappointing because there was part of her that didn't want him to be fake. He noticed, too, and looked like he read her thoughts right off her face.

Maybe he did, it wasn't like she had a whole lot of experience in playing cloak-and-dagger games.

He did though.

Dare recovered in a flash, gently settling his hand on the small of her back as he guided her toward the table.

Her heart rate tripled.

She likely should have been offended over how easily he touched her. There was just one tiny problem with that.

She liked it.

Sure, there were a few unflattering things that might be said about her in response, but she'd always been a realist. One plus one equaled two and she found the guy hot. Overbearing men had never struck her that way before, but Dare, well, her hormones were having a field day at her expense.

He even smelled good.

She caught the hint of his scent as he settled down next to her. Sam was already signaling the waiter.

"We need wine," Sam declared in a jovial tone. "Really good wine."

And she needed a prayer, because divine intervention was really the only thing she might count on to shield her from Dare's effect.

But the wine was a pretty good alternative.

It left her more relaxed as the evening progressed. Sure, she was more susceptible to his charm but there was a point in every great adventure where you just grabbed hold and hung on while you enjoyed the ride.

By the time they made it home, she was sure restlessness wouldn't be a problem tonight. Sam and Paul hightailed it to their car with very poorly disguised intent to leave her alone with Dare. The smiles her friends' faces sent her behind Dare's back were more than suggestive. They were almost a shove toward him.

Under different circumstances, embracing her impulses might have been an option.

But hard reality cut through the wine, leaving her facing a man who had spent the evening with her with the sole intention of intimidating her and undermining her sense of security.

That sucked.

She really didn't like to think about him like that. Jenna turned and unlocked her door. She left it open behind her as she went into her living room.

"Not finished pressing me beneath your thumb special agent?" she asked when he followed her inside. "I rather hoped you were. It's disappointing, but you have my attention. So say what you think you need to."

Jenna tossed her purse down and faced him squarely. She wasn't sure if it was her wording or the sound of her voice that gave him pause. Something did though. He'd closed the door and turned to face her, his expression warning her he was making ready to try to squish her.

It wasn't that she doubted he could. The night spent in his custody had proved it to her. He froze though, fixing her with his dark stare as he contemplated her with eyes she had no doubt saw a whole lot more than most men did.

The guy was just off the scale in every department.

"Disappointing?" he asked. "Why does my behavior matter to you?"

He sounded sincere, and she shrugged, uncertain how to proceed.

A conversation.

A sincere conversation, now that was something she hadn't seen coming. She didn't have a plan for dealing with this part of his personality, but she realized she felt privileged to glimpse it.

"Call me old-fashioned, but I still actually believe men who earn badges want to be good guys."

He liked what she said. There was a flash of approval in his eyes that he covered pretty quick.

"Well, do whatever floats your boat, just don't . . ." She ended up biting her lip as she contemplated whether or not to finish her thought. She lost the battle though because no matter how exposing it might be for her, part of her really wanted him to hear what she had to say.

"That was for all intents and purposes my family you just inserted yourself into. Don't be a dick," she said and looked him straight in the eye as she spoke. She didn't think she'd meant something so much in her life.

Or wanted someone to not disappoint her so much.

He didn't brush her words off either. For a moment, she watched him absorb them, like her opinion actually mattered. "I don't work with the run of the mill bad guys, Jenna. Being a dick keeps me alive. It also helps me hold a line that ensures you get to have the life you do."

A strange little shiver went across her skin, like she was getting a rare glimpse at his personal nature.

"There's a difference and you know it." She opened her hands up wide. "Right here, it's just you and me. Fine, you came over here to make a point, one you feel justified in making for my own good. I get it. I'm never going to know just what motivates you, and I'm better off understanding that ignorance is bliss."

His lips twitched, curving up into a grin. It warmed her insides, and that was a fact.

She savored it. Letting it burn away the tension that had kept her in its grasp most of the evening. Of course, that just left her prey to the flood of hormones she'd been attempting to ignore. She indulged in a long look at him, knowing it was going to be her last.

Like everything else, he noticed.

She watched the way his keen stare picked up the fact that she was looking at him, his eyes narrowing as his complexion darkened. A twist of sensation went through her insides and she realized it was anticipation.

Of what?

Hell if she knew, but she was breathless.

That word had never really held any true meaning to her before. Now? Dare Servant somehow managed to embody it.

Tall, dark, dangerous . . .

Everything a girl dreamed about in those hours after midnight and before dawn when reality arrived to make her realize the sensible guy sleeping next to her was the best choice. Like he'd said, he didn't work with the run-of-the-mill bad guys, and work followed everyone home from time to time.

"Ignorance is bliss, darling . . ." He moved toward her, freezing the breath in her chest. "I don't suffer ignorance very well though . . . always have needed to try things myself . . . like you . . . I want to know what you taste like, Jenna Henson . . ."

He caught her nape with a grip that was soft enough to spare her pain but strong enough to remind her he could hold her.

He was going to kiss her.

She recognized that fact a moment before he angled his head and pressed his mouth to hers. There was a hint of wine on his lips as he pressed his against hers, insisting on more than just a compression. He took her mouth, and she opened hers out of sheer need to taste more of him.

Insanity . . .

Another word she was learning the true meaning of with the help of Dare Servant.

Reality melted away as she reached for him, pushing her fingers into his hair as she kissed him back. She needed more of his taste, more of his scent, more of his skin. It was a frantic urge, beating at her from some place deep inside her that she'd never really realized yearned for freedom.

But he pulled back. Muttering a soft word of profanity beneath his breath.

"You're right . . ." his voice was a mere rasp. "I shouldn't be a dick, but I'm not sorry I kissed you."

He was gone a moment later, leaving her alone as he covered the distance to his car with strides that showed her how powerful he was. He didn't do anything like the men she'd known in her life. Nope. Nothing. There was a rawness about him, which captivated her. An ease with the darkness, which was hypnotic.

Jenna watched him go. Her entire body was tingling long after he'd cleared out of her driveway.

There's your lesson, girl . . .

A man like Dare Servant wasn't going to stick around.

Yeah? Well in that case, she was glad she'd kissed him back.

Life wasn't meant to be a spectator sport.

Mack knew how to go unnoticed.

He melted back into the kitchen, listening to the conversation between Dare and Jenna.

When they started kissing, he shook his head but turned and slipped through the open back door before he was discovered.

He knew special agent Dare Servant.

Or at least he'd seen pictures of the man and knew what he was.

A Shadow Ops agent wouldn't go down easily. Mack wasn't going to make the mistake of trying to drop him alone.

Or without permission from his boss.

So he moved through the tiny backyard and jumped the fence to avoid the motion-detecting security light Jenna had on the side of her garage.

At least they were busy getting naked. That was the sort of distraction he needed. Just enough time to call for a couple of back-up buddies if Kirkland decided to go for a kill.

Mack wasn't a killer.

No, he was a man who did his job, which happened to include getting rid of people Kirkland wanted to disappear.

It was nothing personal.

Mack dug a burner phone out of his pocket and

looked around to make sure no one was listening. Kirkland answered after a few rings.

"Our problem is big," he informed his boss. "Agent Dare Servant is on the case."

Kirkland cussed.

Mack listened to him, letting his information sink in.

"And the girl?" Kirkland continued. "Does she know anything of value?"

"Looks like he's dumped her back into her life with a warning to keep her mouth shut," Mack responded.

"Good," Kirkland bit out. "She'd be buried in witness protection if she'd seen anything of value while she was here."

"What she saw was Servant and his team bugging the house," Mack replied. "I have eyes on them. What do you want me to do?"

Kirkland was silent for a long moment.

"Wait for help," he said at last. "Take both of them down to the docks. I don't want there to be any evidence for Servant's shadow team to find. We'll ship them out in a container. Dump the remains far out at sea."

Kirkland ended the call. Mack cocked his neck to one side and heard it pop. It was time to work.

But it was nothing personal.

He'd given in to an impulse.

Dare hit the accelerator and went around slower traffic.

He was heading away from what he wanted.

Hard to admit, yet true. There was one essential component to every Shadow Ops agent.

Honesty.

Or maybe it would be a little more precise to say that an agent had to know himself, accept who he was, or

there were going to be times when it just might get him
killed because reactions were honest.

He'd wanted to kiss her.

Hell, the throbbing in his cock made it clear he
wanted to do more than swap spit with her.

Blunt . . .

And a tad of a misrepresentation. It had been a kiss.
In fact, Jenna had met him right there in the middle,
taking as good as she got.

Fuck, he liked that sort of thing in a woman.

His cock was stiffening, making him grip the steering wheel harder.

He wasn't going back.

Not a chance. She was part of a case, even if it was
remotely.

Now you're being a dick. Just like she'd called you.

He should be glad she was only slightly involved. It
meant she could stay in her life. Jenna had no idea how
easily her little mercy mission could shred her life and
dump her in relocation. With the nice little restriction
of never being able to return to her life.

He sure as shit didn't want to be the man to haul her
into custody.

Because you'd rather get into her bed . . .

True, and he didn't shy away from the thought. No,
he knew the logic of his job. Jenna was alive, and he was
still seeing the faces of the two girls from the morgue.
He was just reaching for life.

Bullshit . . .

Dare grinned at himself but kept driving away
from Jenna. He was no good for her. It had been reckless to show up at her place, a dick move on his part all
the way. Truth was, he'd wanted to impress her with
his . . . well . . . with something about him.

He'd wanted to get personal.

That admission took him by surprise.

He should have quelled the urge. It had never been a problem before, which accounted for how long he was thinking about Jenna. He was enjoying the buzz of knowing she'd pushed his buttons. More of them than sweet Jenna Henson would ever know, because he was never going to see her again. Not in the flesh anyway. Jenna might be the sort he craved, but he was addicted to his job.

One addictive habit was all any man could afford.

Dare Servant could kiss.

Honestly, Jenna knew she was obsessing a bit, but she decided to let herself linger in the memory of the way Dare had . . . tasted her.

Man oh man. . . . those were certainly the words to describe it alright.

Made her wonder how good he'd be at tasting more of her.

Okay . . . warning girl. . . .

Jenna laughed at herself before taking a final pass with her toothbrush and turning off the bathroom light for the night.

Yeah, she needed to keep her thoughts out of the . . . bedsheets or she was going to have another restless night. Somehow, she got the idea that B.O.B. was going to come up mighty short as a substitution for Dare Servant.

Are you seriously saying you'd have let him sleep with you?

Jenna settled back into her bed with a little huff. In the dark, it was sure a lot easier to be brutally honest with herself.

The guy intoxicated her.

Turned on was an understatement of the way he'd left her feeling.

She was dwelling on it simply because it was so intense. Part of her was honest enough to admit she'd never encountered a man quite like him before.

Well that's the understatement of the year . . .

Oh, was it ever. Maybe everything was more intense because she'd never been so frightened.

Or so alive . . .

That thought was a little unsettling. Like she'd been squandering her days, taking it for granted that the sun would rise in the morning and she'd be there to see it.

She needed a date. And it wasn't just because of the way Dare had kissed her.

No, it was because she'd gotten so caught up in making sure her job was secure, she'd forgotten life was made up of the moments that took one's breath away.

It was time to get out and live.

Jenna drew in a deep breath and let it out. She shifted, finding her spot for the night. Her eyes drifted closed and something slammed down on her face.

She fought, straining away from the hold on her, but whatever was on her mouth got shoved between her teeth. Her mouth was stuffed full of it, dry cloth of some sort.

Stupid . . . scream!

She drew in breath but whoever was there flipped her over, shoving a knee into her back as they tied something around her head so that the wad in her mouth stayed there to keep her from letting out the cry she'd ordered herself to make.

Her own bedding was trapping her, making it too hard to fight. She was pinned and her wrists tied behind her back while she withered.

"Get her feet already."

The guy on her back was grinding his knee into her spine. Pain went shooting down her body, but it didn't stop her from kicking at whoever was trying to grip her ankles. More pain was her reward as he wrapped one ankle with a thick rope and used it to control her.

She kept fighting.

The pain was different, it was a reassurance that she was still alive.

"Fuck . . . bitch is strong. Knock her on the head or something."

Action was instant. A hard blow landed on her skull. She felt like the pain was moving through her brain to the front of her forehead, and when it did, all she saw was a flash before she was lost in a black wave of unconsciousness.

Kirkland picked up his phone.

Well, one of many. This was a burner phone, a prepaid one he'd trash as soon as he finished his business.

"You get my order?" he asked.

"Hot and bagged" was the reply.

Kirkland ended the call before cracking the plastic case and pulling the SIM card out. He crushed it and tucked it into his pocket to be disposed of someplace where it couldn't be traced back to him. Moving through his house, he passed through the living room. There were always a few women hanging around. They knew their place was to be ready when he was.

"Rene," he spoke on his way to the garage. There was a scamper of heels on the polished marble floor behind him as his choice followed. She slid into the passenger side of his car without a word. Primped and done up with style, she looked like a couple thousand bucks. Likely she'd spent that much of his money on herself over the last week.

Kirkland didn't sweat the small stuff. It was money well spent because they looked like they were heading out for a date. Image was key. He'd learned that from his father. Always fit the picture the public had of you and people wouldn't question what you were up to.

Tonight he was a player. A rich man with a pet and an expensive toy car.

Let people dismiss him as shallow.

He enjoyed knowing he had more to him than what people thought.

Dare Servant wasn't dismissing him.

Kirkland took a turn and ground his teeth as he hit the wall of traffic cruising along Pacific Coast Highway. It was a mixture of super cars and BMWs.

Dare Servant was a serious problem.

Kirkland had learned business from the Raven. His sire had been a major underworld figure, and there was only one way anyone kept a reputation among those who ran the darker side of business.

He knew what the night would hold for him. A clashing of Titians so to speak. Shadow Ops were the elite. Men who lived on the edge like he did himself.

Kirkland slowly smiled.

He like a good fight.

This one promised to be bloody.

It worked for him.

Jenna was dropped.

She groaned as she landed on the floor, her bound hands making it impossible to keep from knocking her chin into the hard surface. The smack sent pain through her, but there was already so much swirling around in her body, she didn't really get distracted by it.

Someone was yanking the sack off her head. Being able to see was much more interesting.

Wherever she was, it smelled wet. She heard the water, a sort of low, constant lapping and realized she must be down on the docks. There was a huge metal shipping container next to her, the side of it forming one wall of her prison.

She rolled over and gasped.

"Yeah, got you a little company," one of her captors snickered.

Jenna was fighting the urge to throw up. Still gagged, she knew she had to succeed. But gaining control over her emotions only gave her more clarity to see the details of the girl facing her.

She was dead.

Jenna knew it as a fact as she stared into the frozen, lifeless eyes. Life was gone from them, the face motionless and so damned hopeless. Jenna felt tears sting her eyes for how young the girl was. She hadn't had enough time to do all of the things a life should be full of.

Neither had she . . .

Her own plight hit Jenna hard as she looked up and got her first look at her captors. They were sitting on a couple of chairs, kicking back, clearly waiting for someone.

What sickened her was the way they looked at her. Like she was of no more concern than the dead girl next to her. Bodies didn't bother them, so killing wouldn't either.

"Trouble."

Dare didn't remember falling asleep. He'd been wrestling with the memory of Jenna and somehow dropped off into a deep sleep where he ended up dreaming about her.

Greer McRae startled him by pushing the bedroom door in and slapping it to make sure Dare was on his feet.

It worked.

Not that his fellow agent noticed anything out of the ordinary. Greer expected Dare to jump and was already halfway down the hallway. Dare cussed but admitted being grateful for the moment of privacy. He ran a hand across his face and through his hair. It was enough to help him clear his mind and focus on the case.

Greer was checking his gun instead of looking at the computer screen. Dare felt his body tense. His fellow agent was preparing to go into the field.

"I checked in on the girl and she was gone," Greer explained. "Someone grabbed her within an hour of you leaving. They were there when you kissed her."

Dare grabbed a tablet and punched in his clearance code. He jabbed at the link to the video feed of Jenna's townhouse and scanned the images. The fact that his fellow agent knew he'd kissed Jenna wasn't important.

He didn't have time for his personal embarrassment.

Just for the guilt that punched him in the gut as he realized he'd avoided checking in on her when he returned.

"Shit." Dare grunted as he watched the two men lingering outside the kitchen. They kept tight to the wall, moving around and checking the driveway to make sure he'd left before they reentered the house.

The sight of her being carried out of the townhouse was the only thing that gave him a measure of release.

"The tracking beacon is working." Greer fed him information right on time. "They've taken her down to the docks."

Dare caught a vest Greer tossed him on his way toward the door. "Recall Thais and Zane."

"No need to." Greer was sliding into the truck next to him as Dare started the engine. "They're tailing Kirkland." Greer looked across the cab at Dare. "He's heading towards the docks. I only noticed the girl was missing because I was looking at Kirkland's feed and you had her still up on one of the screens."

It was an inexcusable lapse.

Part of his brain tried to argue Jenna wasn't a primary as far as the case went but Dare shot the argument down cold.

The cases Shadow Ops took weren't normal. A good agent never dismissed any player as insignificant.

It was the break he needed. Kirkland being on the move at the same time wasn't coincidence. No. Something about Jenna had flushed him out.

He should have been elated.

Instead, his muscles tightened as dread became a pounding force inside his brain. The detachment he relied on was eluding his grasp as Greer pointed them toward where the beacon in Jenna's shoulder was sending out a signal.

Problem was, the thing would work even after she was dead.

Jenna cried out.

She really wanted to be stronger, but one of the men grasped her bound feet and dragged her along the ground and up into a shipping container. He didn't give a damn for the way her hair was being torn out of her scalp or the agony being inflicted by the handcuffs locked around her ankles as they bit into her flesh.

Nope, he pulled her up a ramp and into the empty interior of the metal shipping container, dropping her feet once she was halfway inside it.

"Boss won't be here for another half hour," the man said looking toward his companion. "There's still a few of her friends left alive. Let's enjoy how desperate they are."

The "her" was the body. The second man had hauled it into the container while his buddy was dragging Jenna.

"Sounds good," the second man said. "Boss said he wanted this one alive to make her talk. We'd better enjoy our time now. Won't be much left of this one when he's done with her."

They talked as they went back down the ramp. There was a squeal and groan from the large metal doors as they swung them closed and locked her inside.

It was dark.

The container was water tight, made for being transported on huge cargo ships across rough seas. Jenna felt her eyes straining to adjust, even as her brain knew it was a lost battle.

Fuck, she wasn't ready to die.

She latched onto her anger, using it to float above the fear trying to drown her. It was a fight for survival, making her reprioritize everything. The pain in her body was insignificant compared to keeping a handle on her wits.

If she wanted to survive, she'd have to be able to think.

Jenna couldn't see her, but she knew the dead girl was there, too. The knowledge was sitting there like a huge tarantula, waiting to jump on her and kill her with its venom.

No . . .

Just . . . no . . .

She wasn't willing to give up. Wasn't willing to miss out on everything she hadn't experienced yet. Half hour?

Not nearly long enough.

And yet, all the time she had.

Jenna struggled, fighting to slip her arms around her hips and down her legs. She ended up rolling around but managed to bring her hands up in front of her.

The handcuffs held though.

She was straining to see them, to find a way to free herself when she heard the door grinding again. Tears filled her eyes as she listened to the door opening, knowing her time was spent.

Fuck . . . she hated reality!

A meager amount of light filled the space, granting her a glimpse of who was coming at her. She raised her hands, the urge to fight so strong she was lunging forward before she recognized anyone.

The first man caught her. "Jenna . . ."

Her brain was locked into survival mode. The man holding her clamped his arms around her to still her struggles.

"Jenna," he repeated more sternly. "It's Dare."

She froze, trying to believe what she'd heard.

It wasn't possible.

And yet, once she stopped fighting, she felt the difference in his hold. It was solid and hard, but without the callous disregard for her pain that her two kidnappers had employed.

In short, she wasn't just meat.

"Good girl . . . listen to me, I'll get you through this,"
he said.

There was a confidence in his tone she drank up like
the desert did with rain. It was so thick, she would have
sworn she could taste it. She started shaking, relief beating inside her like a trapped bird. He smoothed a hand
along her back, feeling her reaction.

Damn . . . it felt perfect.

His touch that was.

Some of her hair was pulled when he released the
gag, but she didn't care. All that mattered was freedom.
Her jaw ached as she worked it, watching as Dare unlocked her hands before he moved toward her feet.

"I thought you'd be okay," he muttered as he fit the
little key into the lock and turned it. There was a thick
coating of self-loathing in his tone.

"What . . . do you mean?" She had to swallow
because her tongue was so dry it stuck to the roof of her
mouth. Looking over to where the gag was laying on
the floor, she realized her captors had shoved one of her
dirty ankle socks into her mouth.

She really hoped Dare shot them.

The second cuff released before Dare was raising his
head and making eye contact with her. The stern expression she'd encountered the first time she'd woken up in
his custody was there on his face.

"All that matters is we have you, Jenna, and we'll
keep you safe."

It was exactly what she wanted to hear. For a moment,
she was happily drowning in relief.

"Guess I have to apologize for being pissy about you
putting that beacon in my shoulder," she muttered.

He was helping her to her feet with a solid grip on
her bicep. He left her for a moment to take a closer look

at the body lying on the floor near them. She watched his jaw tighten as he pressed his fingers to the girl's throat.

"At least we can tag the body and catch some hard evidence when they dump it."

The second agent was watching the open door. The dock lights illuminated the gun in his hands. He had the weapon pointed out the opening, his position making it clear he wouldn't hesitate to shoot anyone who came too close.

They were more than cops.

She liked knowing it, too. There was a sense of justice in the way they didn't appear to be worried about killing her captors.

Good . . .

"Wait . . ." Her brain clicked on like a light.

"No time." Dare was rising up, the motion effortless. He reached out and caught her arm. "Got to get you clear before . . ."

He just shut his jaw. Jenna realized he was keeping the details of the case from her.

"Before the boss shows up." She filled in the blank.

Dare stopped, one dark eyebrow rising.

"They said the boss was coming down to deal with me," Jenna said.

Dare's jaw tightened.

"But he isn't here yet," Jenna continued.

Dare was taking her toward the door again. Jenna dug her feet in, earning a frustrated sound from him.

"Which means I still don't have anything to add to your case," she insisted.

Dare cocked his head to one side, sending her what she supposed was a get-real look.

"Is getting a look at a man who has no qualms about

killing you really on your bucket list, Jenna?" he asked her.

"Not this morning it wasn't," she cut back. But her burst of sarcasm only left her with an empty feeling. Her home was no longer safe. Her life was no longer secure. It was like being stripped down to her skin and tossed out of a moving car into noonday traffic. The only thing left to clutch at was her dignity. "But it doesn't look like much of anything is up to me at the moment."

"I'm sorry, Jenna."

He was, too. She heard the sincerity in his tone.

"We're going to get you some place safe, I promise you that," he continued.

Not her home though. She didn't have to ask the question because she realized she didn't feel safe returning to the place where she'd been kidnapped from. Her own damned bed, and it wasn't the safe haven she'd worked so hard to carve out for herself.

"I want to matter, be more than a victim," she said.

Dare had reached for her arm again. She'd only whispered, but the metal sides of the shipping container made sure he heard her.

"Jenna . . ." he began.

She cut him off because she just couldn't take being pitied.

"I want to do something more than be a casualty of the situation."

He started to argue with her. She watched him clench his jaw tight as he thought through her comment.

"If I see the guy, it will help your case," Jenna looked back toward the body of the girl. "Maybe get justice for her."

"That would mean leaving you here," Dare muttered.

"I got that part," Jenna replied as she tried to keep her confidence from deserting her.

"Can't do it." Dare gripped her arm. "Too dangerous. This case isn't the type you toy with."

Jenna refused to walk, her feet slipping before Dare grunted and faced off with her.

"What is your plan, Jenna? Just going to stay here and hope you don't end up like her?" He jerked his head toward the body. "This guy has no problem laying you out next to her."

"I know," Jenna snapped. "But I also get that you were bugging his house to gain evidence on him. Only he's coming down here to do his dirty work. You need a witness."

He knew she had a point. Jenna watched the understanding flash through his eyes. His expression never eased though. "You're leaving."

Dare didn't reach for her arm. He caught her wrist and jerked her toward him as he lowered one shoulder. He straightened up with her hanging over his shoulder like a dead deer.

And that image was just too much of a helpless one to bear.

"I am not a coward," she hissed, turning her head so he could hear her.

He carried her outside and behind a stack of shipping containers before he set her on her feet. His jaw was locked, making it plain he was done discussing the matter.

Jenna reached out and hooked her hands into the vest he wore.

"Listen to me."

He clamped his hands around her wrists. "I heard

you, Jenna, but you don't understand what you're dealing with."

"I understand I can't go home. Ever," she said.

He drew back.

"What? You think I don't understand what happens to the people you save from mega bad guys like this one?" she offered. "Maybe I don't know the terms, but I'm pretty sure I'm never going to sign Jenna Henson as my legal name again."

"Relocating you is the only thing that will safeguard your life."

He didn't like telling her that fact either. There was a cold detachment in his tone, which drove a spike through her heart.

But it also fueled her determination.

"So let me make it worth it," Jenna exclaimed softly. "Put me back in there. Let this asswipe show his face to me. Whoever that girl is, she deserves more than me letting her killer go when I can do something about making sure you and your team can keep him from killing again."

There was a pause. She got the feeling Dare didn't rethink his position often.

No, the guy oozed confidence.

"He's shredded my life," she finished. "If my only option is to take the opportunity to strike back and make some sort of difference, don't deny me that. I've got to have something to build a new life on, and pity isn't my style."

Dare let out a soft grunt.

"She's got a point," his fellow agent muttered. "Much as I don't care for the circumstance, I can't much blame her for wanting a shot at . . . him."

"This isn't going to be pretty, Jenna." Dare gripped

her chin and raised it up so their gazes locked. "I can't promise to protect you. This situation is unpredictable, too many variables. You go back in there, you might die."

"Guess you'd better give me a gun," she said.

And she needed to dig deep because she was going back.

The metal container was sitting among a thousand other ones just like it but there was an eerie feel to it.

Yeah? That's because you know there's a dead girl inside it.

Jenna shied away from thinking about just what her chances were for joining the unknown girl.

The facts weighing on her mind were the ones that included starting a new life knowing she might have made a difference but chose the coward's way.

Fine, it might be safer but life was measured in the moments that stole your breath.

"Let's do this," she said as she held her hand out for the gun.

"I don't like it," Dare said, glancing back toward the container.

"Good," she replied. He snapped his attention back to her, a frown on his face. "Just a little happy to hear you don't make a habit of using bait."

He grunted and looked around again. She could feel him weighing the situation and coming to the same conclusion she'd already decided upon. His fellow agent was watching him, the expression on his face grim but set.

"It might as well be me," Jenna argued. "He had his goons bring me down here. If I don't go back in there and give you the chance to catch him red handed, you'll be stuck waiting for him to select another victim. One you don't have tagged."

"Jenna, you aren't trained for this."

She lifted one hand in a no-shit gesture that earned her a tiny twitch from his lips.

"But you've got guts." He swept the area again as he closed his fingers around her upper arm. "So let's do this."

She was scared.

Hell, he'd be fucking concerned if she wasn't.

But she wasn't backing down.

Dare liked that . . . too much.

There was a sting of arousal burning through him that he needed to ignore as Jenna moved back toward the container. She was making it up as she went, reaching for strength instead of crumbling into a weeping mass.

No, she wasn't a victim.

He'd give her the respect of not thinking of her with that word.

She'd earned the respect.

He picked up the gag and caught the way her eyes widened before she turned around and stood still for him to tie it back in place.

At least he could do it without pulling her hair.

"I'm leaving the cuffs unlocked," he whispered as he closed them around her wrists. "Just twist . . . and you'll be free."

He reached down and pulled open the small holster secured around his ankle with the sound of ripping Velcro.

"If you use this," he warned her softly as he wrapped it around her upper arm, where her T-shirt sleeve would cover it, "aim to kill. You won't get a second chance. We've got this can wired, he wants you to talk, so talk. Tell him whatever he wants to know. I won't leave you in here very long. Just long enough to prove he didn't just come in here by accident."

Her brain was working strangely.

Jenna clearly heard each step as Dare and his fellow agent left her. They walked lightly, but she would have thought her eardrums were going to burst because her senses were locked into some sort of heightened awareness.

Lying down was almost impossible. She settled for sitting against the wall where she had a good view of the door.

Waiting sucked.

At least this sort of waiting did. She'd never realized how pitiful her frustrations were. Stuck on jury duty? That wasn't really waiting.

Nope, she knew better now.

Ignorance is bliss . . .

No shit.

And yet, there was an undeniable sense of satisfaction moving through her. It came from the hard surface of the metal beneath her and the knowledge that the girl was lying there still.

Whoever the boss was, Jenna was going to fight back.

Dare forced himself to hold position.

It wasn't the first time he'd had to melt into the shadows and wait for his case to develop.

That was the official way to phrase it.

Case . . . develop . . .

Fuck.

Jenna wasn't an agent. She was who he put himself on the line to protect. He was tormented by the circumstances, feeling like he was being frayed alive.

But she was fighting to control the crash and burn her life was enduring.

He had to let her salvage something from the mess. Some measure of accomplishment.

So he'd wait.

No matter how much he hated it.

CHAPTER THREE

Someone aimed a spotlight into her face.

Jenna withered as the bright light sent pain through her optic nerves like acid. Her feet pushed against the floor as she tried to escape because closing her eyelids was pitiful protection against the light.

Whoever was arriving, they came closer as they aimed the light straight at her face. It was so intense, it warmed her chilled skin.

But she still shivered as she heard another set of footsteps crossing the distance from the door to her. These were unhurried, and someone was closing the door behind whoever it was.

"Want me to take the gag off her?"

Soft steps.

Measured ones.

One . . . two . . . three . . .

Pause . . .

"Break one of those toes first."

Shock flashed through her at the cold-bloodedness of the command. Sure, movie villains said shit like that. Not real people.

This one did though and his thugs were quick to comply.

The crack of her bone being snapped bounced off the walls of the shipping container. Jenna was fighting to escape, even though it meant using her feet to push against the floor. The level of pain was off the scale she'd known until that moment in her life.

So hot . . .

Throbbing pain . . .

Bone deep.

She reeled and snarled through the gag.

"That's right," the boss informed her in a husky tone. The guy was hanging out somewhere behind the light, where she couldn't see him because her night vision was so blitzed by the spotlight. "You know I mean business now."

One of the thugs reached out and ripped the gag off her.

Jenna sucked in a gulp of air, determined to grasp her composure.

This guy was going down.

"Where is Dare Servant?"

"What?" she exclaimed, the question catching her by surprise.

The thug responded by lifting his foot and stomping on her unprotected shin.

Jenna yelped and rolled away.

"Get the fucking light back on her."

The boss man had raised his voice, forgetting to hide in the husky whisper he'd been using. She concentrated on it as one of the thugs worked the light, aiming it at her again.

"Dare Servant," the boss man repeated. "You were fucking him about two hours ago. Where is he?"

Jenna had to catch the handcuffs because they were trying to fall off. She settled in the corner of the container, the light in her face again.

"He's not the sticking-around-for-the-sunrise sort of man," she said.

"What is he looking for?"

Jenna squinted, but her sight was still useless. "I've got no idea what you're talking about. Now why am I here?"

There was a snicker from one of the thugs.

"You're going to tell me where to find Dare Servant and his team."

"Who are you?" she demanded.

"Break her leg this time."

To hell with her plan. Jenna dropped the cuffs and grabbed the gun.

"What the fuck?"

She wasn't sure who asked the question because she was struggling to get to her feet while aiming the barrel of the pistol at the man hiding behind his thugs.

"Aim to kill . . ."

She heard Dare's words and acted on them, the pain throbbing in her foot and shin fueling her determination.

The sound of the gun firing was earsplitting, the bullet hitting the far side of the container with a harsh sound.

"Fuck!" the boss yelled. "Servant set us up!"

Dare's advice had been sound. She'd missed her target, and, in a split second, the man hiding in the shadows crossed in front of her and grabbed her by the neck. He pressed a gun into her throat as he pushed her toward the door.

"Servant will be waiting for us . . ."

Dare wasn't planning on waiting.

The gunshot was his cue. He surged forward, Greer

on his six, as Thais and Zane moved in from the opposite side of the dock.

The door of the container came open, the men pushing Jenna in front of them.

"Federal agents," Dare called out. "Hands up!"

Dare was looking down the sights of his gun, his finger caressing the trigger.

A moment later, the night erupted in a flash explosion. The shock wave sent him reeling as he instinctively flattened himself against the side of the metal container.

Jenna was reeling.

Something exploded, but it was a flash of ultra-bright light. Somewhere in the back of her mind she recalled flash grenades. But her brain was too affected by the blow to really grasp anything. She staggered, her knees buckling.

"Dumb fuck!" someone growled behind her. "Now I have to drag her."

Someone grasped her by the back of her shirt, and the fabric drew tight across her front, digging into her breasts as she was hauled by it.

"Stay back or she's dead!"

One thing penetrated the disorientation gripping her and that was the hard, cold presence of a muzzle being jammed into the side of her neck. Her captor pressed it up into the soft flesh beneath her jaw as she struggled to regain her wits.

And then the gun was gone.

Jenna felt herself flying through the air, a hard body hitting her from the side and pushing her sideways. She was flailing, falling, and then rolling as she hit the ground.

But she wasn't alone.

Dare closed his arms around her, encasing her as he rolled with the momentum of the tackle he'd used to move her away from her captor. They started to slow, giving her a chance to drag in a deep breath, but a sharp popping sound hit her ears and Dare sent them rolling once more.

Pain was a constant presence now. Jenna couldn't distinguish different points. There was just the constant agony as she realized the sound was gunfire. She caught the scent of the gunpowder, felt a new wave of fear sweep through her before they were free-falling once more.

"Fuck."

She heard him grunt a moment before they splashed into the ocean. Jenna struggled to swim, fighting against Dare's hold so she could use her arms.

A new wave of agony went through her shoulder.

This one was precise and focused, like the stupid tracking beacon had turned red hot.

Her lungs began to burn, but Dare dragged her deeper, pulling her through the dark water and leaving the lights of the dock behind them.

Drowning was better than having her bones broken one by one . . .

And yet, she wasn't ready to quit. She struggled to swim in the same direction, succeeding in kicking. With her help, they moved faster, flowing with the current. When he let them surface, she gasped for air, tasting salt water as she struggled to get her head farther out of the water. She dragged in air, opening her eyes to gain a glimpse of men standing on the edge of the dock, looking down the barrels of their guns.

"Deep breath," Dare rasped beside her. "We have to swim farther out."

Ready or not, he took her down beneath the dark surface of the water once more.

Jenna went, the need to survive fueling her like a double serving of an energy drink. She fought to move through the water, desperate to place distance between the dock and herself.

At least the current was in their favor. She felt the motion of the ocean helping them escape. They surfaced for breath and dove again. Her heart pounding, demanding more breath, even as Jenna dismissed the need in favor of making it farther away from the men trying to kill her.

Escape was the only need she could answer.

Time was being cruel. Slowing down so she could live every moment like it was an hour. Somewhere in the back of her mind, she recalled a lecture on how shock made the human brain perceive time differently as it tried to compute massive amounts of data during crisis.

"Here." Dare's tone was harsh as he panted, pulling her closer to something.

Whatever it was, Jenna knocked her nose against it before getting her arms up and out of the water.

"Up," Dare ordered her with a hard hand on her bottom.

She didn't have time to care too much about the lack of propriety. Getting out of the water was more important.

"Grab the ladder."

Jenna managed to close her stiff fingers around a length of metal that felt even colder than her digits. She groaned as pain snaked through her hand but reached for the rung of the ladder above as Dare shoved her over the side of the boat.

It rocked as she landed in a heap. Dare came over the

side with a lot more skill, landing on his feet in a crouch as he scanned the small cabin sitting on the front of the vessel.

"Stay here," he muttered. "Going to see if anyone is home."

The boat had settled into a soft rocking motion. Jenna sat still, her heart rate slowing enough to let her stop worrying about the organ bursting. Which granted her the clarity to watch the way Dare approached the doorway of the cabin. He came at it from one side, looking inside before he exposed his body to anyone who might be inside. She heard the lapping of the waves against the side of the vessel but never his footsteps.

"It's clear."

Dare was back, reaching down to hook her bicep.

"It's no palace, but you need shelter from the wind."

"I'm really ok," she said.

A moment later she was crying out. Dare had lifted her by her arm and pain went shooting through her shoulder. The intensity of it stole her breath. She landed on her backside as Dare released her.

"How bad is it?" he asked.

Jenna was busy dragging a breath of air into her lungs to fend off the darkness threatening her with the ultimate humiliation of passing out while her companion was dealing with their circumstances so very adeptly.

Seriously, she needed to dig deeper.

"I'm fine."

"You're hit," Dare announced. "Come on, I need to see what we're dealing with. Inside, where I can risk a light."

He wrapped a hand around her waist this time, hauling her to her feet with that incredible strength of his. It made her feel inadequate. Jenna fought to get her legs to function, succeeding in stumbling along beside him as he moved her toward the opening of the cabin.

Once inside, she caught the scent of pot.

"Whew . . . seems we found the party boat."

She thought she heard a snort from him as he released her and ripped open one of the pockets on his vest. The sound of the Velcro tearing bounced around inside the little cabin.

"Don't let your guard down," Dare advised with a thick coating of experience in his tone. "The smugglers who own this heap are either on their way to the shore or coming in from the open water to get it."

There was a flash of red light. Dare leaned over behind her, aiming what looked like a pen light at her shoulder. He grunted.

"It doesn't feel bad," she offered, still trying to absorb the fact that she'd actually been shot.

Seriously, things like that didn't happen in her world.

But they did in Dare's.

He was aiming the light around the interior of the cabin, giving her a view of the lack of furnishings. The entire space had been cleared out. Only a single pad was left against one wall and a dusting of marihuana was scattered across the floor like straw on the floor of a stable.

Dare moved toward a hatch, pulling it open. The red light kept their night vision intact. He peered inside before pulling the contents outs.

"Get out of those wet clothes."

Her pajamas were sticking to her like a second skin but she still recoiled from the idea of stripping. Dare was shaking out a sweatshirt. He turned and contemplated her.

Don't look like a startled nun . . .

Jenna dug for a handful of composure and sent him an unconcerned look.

His expression made it clear she wasn't fooling him.

"I need to bind that wound," he explained. "And you're slipping into hypothermia. I'll use what's left of your shirt to bind the wound, and you can wear this."

"But," she muttered as she looked toward the door of the cabin. "Isn't your team nearby? I mean, you don't have to deal with me."

The light flicked off.

"Trust me, Jenna," he spoke softly. "We're not out of the woods yet. My team would be here if we were in the clear. There is no fuel in this craft. We're dead in the water and drifting out to open water. Exposure is a serious threat."

He found the hem of her shirt and pulled the wet fabric off her. She ended up hugging herself, another one of those instant reactions she seemed to have no limit of when it came to Dare Servant.

"But . . . the tracking thing . . . you put in my shoulder . . ." she said.

He was ripping her shirt into strips.

"The bullet took it out."

Jenna laughed. "That takes horrible timing to the max."

"Yeah," Dare agreed with a hint of humor in his tone. "Seems the joke's on me."

He leaned around her and she felt the touch of wet fabric against her skin as he looped the strip around her body and pulled it tight across her back.

Jenna sucked in her breath as pain went through her like a train.

"Easy," he cooed, knotting the strip over a piece of

her shirt that he'd folded up and laid over the top of the wound.

"It's not so bad," she said.

He turned and grabbed the sweatshirt. It landed next to her on the floor. "Get out of those wet pants."

Dare took the moment to look over the steering wheel and gear shift. He used the little red light again, illuminating the dashboard where a few battered gauges were.

Jenna struggled with her wet pants. She was shaking, her fingers so stiff that trying to use them hurt. The sweatshirt was a man's and came down over her hips to her thighs. With nothing to dry off with, she was left with wet skin, covered in goosebumps, that made the cotton feel as rough as burlap.

"You're wet, too," she muttered.

Dare turned and sent her a raised eyebrow.

Jenna sent him a narrow-eyed look in return. "Fact is, females have more insulation. Higher body fat percentage."

"My pants are wool," he responded as the little pen light turned off and she watched him replacing it in his vest pocket. "Wool retains ninety percent of its insulating factor when wet. Which is why I wear it. Even in warmer climates."

He'd always be prepared.

Jenna smiled. "Go easy on me, Agent, it's my first day. I'm used to needing water to put out the fires I start." She poked at her wet pants. "It seems water has turned on me."

His lips twitched. She shrugged and instantly regretted it. Focused on the pain, her teeth started chattering while she was distracted.

"It's more than the water," Dare said as he reached down and picked up another item he'd pulled out of the compartment. There was a crinkle as he broke it open and shook out a thin sheet. "Shock is taking a bite out of you as well."

He came closer, lifting the sheet high and lowering it over her.

"Emergency blanket," he explained.

The consistency of the blanket was less than comfy. Jenna gathered it around her, hoping it would make up in function what it lacked in comfort.

"I'm stepping outside," Dare said. "Stay down."

"But, the wind will freeze you."

Her teeth were chattering again. He was watching her and even in the dark, she got the impression he wasn't missing anything.

"The wind will dry me off enough to keep me warm."

He was gone a moment later, approaching the door-frame the same way, from the side and looking out onto the small deck of the boat before he moved into the open. There was nothing to prove he was even still on the vessel, well except for the feeling she had of his presence.

The guy had that in spades.

And she wasn't going to measure up short.

Tightening her jaw, Jenna fought to control her shivering. It was cold, yes, there was no point in dwelling on it.

She had Dare Servant after all.

Yeah? Better hope you don't get him killed.

"Tell me you have something."

"I've got shit," Zane answered Greer. "Damned flash grenade blew all the footage, even the infrared."

Greer looked toward Thais. She shook her head, the set of her lips telling him she was as pissed as he was.

Greer looked back at his phone, trying to establish contact with Dare. "Damn it."

There was a ring of local police waiting nearby. The flash grenade and gunfire had brought the civilian law enforcement down on them but not fast enough to trap Kirkland. Thais had followed him, but without a witness, they had no reason to haul him in.

Greer fought the urge to do it anyway.

The body lying in the shipping container was a blister on his heel. Every damn motion made him recall how much he wanted to deal with the cause of it.

But hauling Kirkland in would only make the guy cover his tracks that much better.

"Make the call." Thais shot him a look as she spoke.

Greer held her gaze for a long moment. "Clear out."

It wasn't what he wanted but there was one thing he knew for certain, Shadow Ops cases never closed easily. If they wanted to take Kirkland down, they'd have to make sure they had enough evidence to keep him pinned.

Zane reached out and caught Greer by the bicep. "Don't you want to send the Coast Guard after Dare?"

"Yes," Greer answered.

"But it would tip Kirkland off, too," Thais added.

"I have other resources," Greer mentioned. "First we have to clean up this scene."

"And hope Dare can handle what he's up against," Zane responded.

Greer cracked the first hint of a grin that anyone had seen in hours. "Dare can handle anything. Even a spunky civilian."

"Jury is still out on that one," Thais informed him. "The civilian that is. I think Dare might be in over his head with her."

Greer shook his head, but their female agent dismissed his opinion. Not that Greer was any stranger to Thais choosing her own path when it came to what she thought. Truth was, he had no idea what went through her head most of the time. A wise man would learn early on to admit that when it came to Thais Sinclair, it was best to avoid direct confrontation if the man didn't want to feel the femme fatale using her claws on him.

She knew men too well and didn't have much compassion about making sure anyone foolish enough to challenge her learned that truth the hard way.

A crack of thunder split the sky open.

Jenna jumped, letting out a startled sound as she realized she'd started to fall asleep.

"It's going to get a little wild."

Dare was back inside the cabin. He closed the door but it rattled, proving how flimsy it was against the brewing storm.

He reached up and secured the small window before giving the twin size pad a good shake.

Lightening flashed, illuminating him as he stood over her, feet braced wide against the roll of the waves.

"Because we haven't had enough excitement for one night . . ." Her teeth chattered again, but her voice came across in a nice sarcastic tone. At least she could still manage to spit in the eye of fate and its rather twisted sense of humor.

"I hate boring nights to be sure" was his response.

Jenna smiled as the thunder crashed and rain started to pelt the side of the cabin. She looked up but there wasn't any water leaking in, so she'd count her blessings.

"You're still shivering," Dare said.

"It won't kill me," she answered as she tightened her grip on the blanket.

"Don't be too sure about that," Dare replied.

"I'm sure."

She thought she heard him snort, but the blanket crinkled as he sat down next to the wall.

"I give you points for guts, Jenna, but that's not going to keep you from hypothermia."

He slipped an arm around her waist and pulled her against his body.

"What . . . are you doing?"

As far as questions went, it was pretty stupid. Dare had her against his chest, one arm locked around her lower waist as he pulled part of the blanket up and over her head. It crinkled like he was wrapping her in foil.

"Sharing body heat," he replied. "It's all we have to deal with your shock."

"I'm fine."

He ignored her argument, and her body turned traitor by melting against him. She should have had the resolve to remain stiff, but he just felt too good. Maybe if she hadn't gotten close enough to realize how bitterly cold she was, there might have been some chance of toughing it out on her own.

Now, she was curving toward him. Flattening her hands against his chest and shuddering as his body heat eased some of the agony in her flesh.

"You will be fine," Dare offered as he looked at her before pulling his gun from his chest harness and resting it on top of his thigh. He was on his side, facing the door as he flattened her against his body and covered her head completely.

It was perfect.

Wuss . . .

Yeah, truth, and yet, she discovered herself unwilling to forgo the comfort he offered. She'd had enough of cold reality, and suffering for the sake of her pride just seemed ridiculously short-sighted on her part.

Pride wouldn't warm her.

Dare could.

He did . . .

She seriously adored the way he employed action instead of words. The night's events were rushing through her head, reminding her vividly how much she needed action.

"Thank you."

Dare smoothed a hand over her shoulder in response. "I've got you, Jenna."

She slipped into slumber with his words easing the last of her concern.

"Shadow Ops took out my father."

Kirkland was doing more than telling Mack an essential fact. His head of security was already aware of what had happened to the Raven.

Kirkland was thinking out loud, and Mack was wise enough to keep his mouth shut while his boss was thinking things through.

"I think it's time for Carl Davis to pay up for all the support he's been enjoying from me."

Carl Davis was close to winning the next presidential election. Just a summer away, Kirkland had made sure the man's name was in front of every set of voters' eyes in media bursts.

"Sure you want to press the man?" Mack inquired. "Maybe you should just enjoy the profits from the businesses Carl Davis ensures you can run legally."

"It's a drop in the bucket, and you know it," Kirkland

cut back. "Carl said he'd close down the Shadow Ops teams. One executive order and we'll be free to make billions."

"He's not president yet."

Kirkland sent Mack a hard look. "Remind him I can pull my support if he doesn't get Dare Servant off my ass. Carl needs the money and the access to the media network my father built. His numbers will drop over-night if I don't keep his face in front of the voters. He's only winning because I've got the plugged-in genera-tion fired up on his behalf."

The younger voters were the ones who didn't show up at the polls very often. Kirkland had changed that. Carl was ahead because of new voters who believed the feed they were getting through their tablets and social-media sites. But Kirkland wasn't working for free. Carl was going to make sure the laws favored his business, and he'd better get the dammed Shadow Ops off Kirkland's ass.

Otherwise, Kirkland would happily watch Carl sink like the *Titanic*.

The water was hot.

Carl Davis knew what he'd been getting into, and the temperature was climbing fast now that they were down to the wire.

Kirkland needed to be tossed into a ditch with his throat slit.

Carl wanted nothing more than to crush the phone Kirkland was using to call him.

Not yet.

Staying ahead in the polls meant having his name in front of the voters. It was a media generation. Kirkland was a king of the airwaves.

So Carl would have to appease him.

It was risky though.

Carl grinned and tipped back his glass of bourbon.

He was a high roller and liked knowing the stakes were high. He pressed a button on the side of his desk and waited for Eric Geyer to answer. His new head of personal security didn't disappoint him.

"I have an issue," Carl began.

Eric listened intently as Carl laid out the facts.

"The best thing for Kirkland to do is walk a straight and narrow line. We tell a Shadow Ops team to disengage, and they will know they have a solid case," Eric advised.

"I need Kirkland in my corner," Carl insisted.

Eric didn't alter his stance. Carl glared at him.

"Don't forget that your job is dealing with people like Kirkland for me. The world isn't run by the righteous. You won't be working with me in the Oval Office unless you understand how much I need the revenue Kirkland brings to the table. The untraceable kind," Carl said.

Eric nodded and turned to leave. Carl didn't call him back. Flinching over what needed doing wasn't Carl's style, and he wasn't working with any man who couldn't stomach the darker elements of the job.

He was so close. The ice clicked in the glass as Carl contemplated the fact that his goal was coming into range.

The Shadow Ops wasn't going to steal the victory from him. No, he just had to keep his head down a little longer, and then he'd sign the exertive order disbanding Kagan's little covert teams.

Dare didn't sleep.

It wasn't the first time he'd made sure he was on watch. Alone in the tiny cabin of the boat, he only had his thoughts to keep him company.

And most of his attention was on Jenna.

As his witness, that was spot on, and yet, there was a hell of a lot more to it.

The admission came hard. Dare felt the bite of frustration while he was unable to overlook the fact that he enjoyed knowing Jenna was breathing softly beside him.

The scent of her blood enraged him.

Passion for his job was something he was familiar with.

This was different.

Deeper . . .

More intense.

His frustration spiked. Whatever it was, he didn't need it. His plans were set in stone. The Shadow Ops were the perfect place for him, but the teams didn't mix with the sort of intensity he was feeling for Jenna.

Sure, Saxon Hale, his former team leader might have settled down, but minding a computer console wasn't something Dare had planned for his own future.

The world needed the Shadow Ops teams. Men like Kirkland would continue to build their underworld empires if there was no one willing to risk it all to take them down. Add in the fact that Kirkland was making sure Carl Davis was elected, and there was a combination that chilled Dare's blood. Men like Carl and Kirkland didn't care if they spilled innocent blood in pursuit of their agendas.

Dare didn't crave glory.

No, he wanted to know that at the end of the day, he'd breathed a little life into justice, because someone had to make sure men like Kirkland and Carl Davis didn't kill it off completely.

They could do it, too. His memory was still crisp and vivid when it came to the night his family had fallen at the hands of scum like Kirkland. The name of his parents' murderers didn't matter. Dare's father had refused a bribe and it had cost him his entire family.

"Don't make a sound, my little cub . . ."

His mother's voice still rang in his ears as she'd hidden him. Her eyes bright with fear, she'd found the strength to smile at him as she pushed him into the back of a linen closet, behind fluffy stacks of towels she'd washed and folded for her family.

"You must grow up . . . become a bear before you can right the wrong of this night . . ."

Dare gripped his gun, listening to the storm but paying attention to anything that might hint at them being found. He was wedged in the corner, Jenna curled against him so he had a clear shot at the door.

He would right wrongs.

"Remember you are your father's son . . . always do the right thing . . . no matter the cost."

The cops had tried to spare him the sight of her body. Dare didn't shy away from the memory of her staring up at the ceiling with a hole in the middle of her forehead. He looked straight at her and his siblings while his father struggled to draw his last breaths because the men who had come for him, had sliced only one side of his neck so he might linger in the room and know his family had paid a high price for his devotion to duty.

Dare had a plan for his life.

One that didn't include intense responses to anyone.

He shouldn't have kissed her.

There was a lesson there, one Dare took the opportunity to learn while the night hours ticked away. The scent of Jenna's blood reinforced it, driving deep into his gut with just how dangerous it was for civilians to have any knowledge of him or his Shadow Ops team.

Sure there would be moments when regret touched him.

But that was the cost of dedication.

One he willingly paid.

Sleep had a tighter hold on her than she was used to.

Jenna shifted, feeling pain. It cleared her thinking a bit, and yet she still felt like she was being sucked down to the bottom of a pool, the water flowing over her like a comfy blanket. Her brain just went with it, shutting down while she struggled to decide why she wanted to wake up.

Pain . . .

Waves of it as she was tossed and turned. She heard her name, tried to respond, but it seemed to take too much effort. It felt like her battery was on low, giving her just a trickle of energy but not enough to really do anything more than be half aware of how much she needed to sleep.

It was frustrating.

Knowing she needed to sleep, yet being half aware of everything. There was more pain, and then blackness hit her like a gust of wind.

"Kagan."

Thais Sinclair offered Dare a phone. He took it as he forced himself to take his eyes off the doors Jenna had been taken through on her way to surgery.

"You need a checkup as well," Kagan, his section leader, began. "Before you leave the hospital."

"Is that really the top of the priority list?" Dare asked.

"I brought it up first, so you'll know I mean it," Kagan replied.

Dare headed for a coffee station. The Coast Guard

chopper crew who had picked them up was clustered around it. One of them poured a measure of the brew into a mug and offered it to him.

"My witness is in surgery," Dare offered before taking a sip. "I won't know what we have until she's out."

"According to Sinclair, it won't be much. Kirkland learned a lot from his daddy, put a spot light in her face. She won't pull him out of a line up."

"Kirkland was still there," Dare said confidently. "We saw him enter the container."

Dare enjoyed the way the hot beverage warmed his insides as he swallowed it. "Kirkland wouldn't have shown up himself if he didn't have something to hide."

"We know he's dirty," Kagan responded. "I want him on the human trafficking charge. That's how to cut the flow of money to Carl Davis. Just being there isn't enough to convict him of running the operation. Kirkland will be interested in your witness now that he failed to silence her. Keep her close and don't raid his house. Tax fraud and underground brothels aren't the case you're down there to solve."

"Yes, sir."

Dare ended the call. He drew off another sip of the coffee. Keeping Jenna was something he still liked the sound of.

She had to be only a witness.

He'd dealt with them before. Found the detachment necessary to keep them just faces, which didn't rise from his memory unless he was actively thinking about a case.

Mental discipline.

He needed to find more of it.

And fast.

Thais was watching him. Greer and Zane both leaning

against different points in the hallway. The hospital was a private, military one. The walls were basic, flat white. No soothing music filtering through the air.

There were also no prying eyes.

Everyone in the place knew to seal their lips.

Which got him thinking about the press. The rescue at sea had been noticed. The California coast line was too populated to avoid someone catching sight of the Coast Guard helicopter bringing them in. Zane had people making sure cell phone footage disappeared from social media sites, but maybe that was the wrong approach.

Thais noticed when he came to a conclusion. She shifted closer, ready to get their case moving.

"Let's toss the media a bone," Dare began. "Kirkland likes to run his media empire. Let's see if he rises to some bait."

Greer and Zane clustered in close to listen.

"Let some footage out," Dare continued. "Let's see what Kirkland does when he realizes Jenna is alive."

Jenna didn't like sleeping on her belly.

She rolled over and yelped before rolling another time and ending up going over the edge of the bed. The only problem with her landing was the fact that her knees felt like Jell-O. She opened her eyes wide as she waited to see if they were going to hold her up.

The shag carpet she was standing on kept her attention on her feet. It was long shag. The type that screamed seventies. Her toes were sinking into it, and she looked around the room to find it just as dated. The walls were an avocado green with wood paneling on one side. There was still a popcorn textured ceiling complete with gold colored light fixture.

"Vintage is the kind word to use."

Jenna jumped. She blinked at the man in the doorway. He held position, waiting for her to clear more of the fog from her mind.

"You're . . ." Jenna hesitated as the fog clung, but her attention focused on the badge clipped to his belt.

"Agent McRae," he offered, moving forward and clasping her bicep. "You might want to take it slow. You had a wound that needed surgery."

"Oh . . . right." Her memory rushed back in like a wave crashing on the sand.

The impact sent her down onto a padded footrest as she recalled the gunfight and swim. There was a piece of white medical tape across her toe and a huge bruise on her shin. "Now that—" she lifted her leg and peered at her skin—"is some serious color."

She heard a soft sound from Agent McRae and lowered her leg. "Sorry. My sense of humor is a little twisted at times."

"Don't be," he offered as he pointed to the bedside table. "I'll take a witness with humor over a weeping one any day. There are some painkillers sitting there for you. I suggest eating something first." He pointed behind him. "Kitchen is that way."

"Thanks."

He turned and left. Now that her brain was awake, she realized she was in a hospital gown, the back of the thing being held shut with two ties.

But there was a neat stack of clothing on the dresser. She crossed the expanse of shag carpet, her toes sinking into it, and sorted through what was waiting for her. Jenna peeked around the doorframe before moving into it in search of a bathroom.

The fixtures in the shower weren't any more modern

than the rest of the hospital, but hot water was hot water and it made up for the calcium encrusted faucet.

Okay, not having her ass on display was a big step up, too.

A full-length mirror attached to the door gave her a good look at the bruise on her shin. It had plenty of friends, too. Her elbows were sporting scabs, and there were scrapes along her forearms and cheeks. The bullet wound actually looked pretty tame considering it had been made by a bullet.

You've been shot.

Welcome to the secret-agent club.

Okay, special agent.

Jenna rummaged through the drawers and found a hairbrush. Greer had been wearing a badge and a gun. What she'd realized on that dock was slamming into her now that all the excitement was over. Sure, she'd survived, but now? Well, that was the question alright.

What now?

Her belly rumbled, making her realize how hungry she was. Jenna caught the scent of toasting bread as soon as she opened the bathroom door. Her belly contorted with a demand to be filled.

Well, at least some things were just normal and fine.

She realized how undervalued those words were. Normal was really a lot more precious than she'd ever given it credit for being.

"Eggs and toast." Greer slipped a plate in front of her. "Servant needs some rack time. Took us a good twelve hours to find you, another ten after that before the doctors released you."

Jenna was distracted by the salt shaker. It was a little hen, the markings on it mostly rubbed off from use. "This is someone's home."

"The owner passed on two days ago," Greer provided the information.

Jenna dropped the salt shaker.

Greer shot her a stern look. "It's just a building. The stepson is itching to toss it to the house flippers so he can rake in the cash. He isn't interested in the memories attached to that little shaker. Our team uses property like this because it's harder to track us."

"That's sad," Jenna muttered.

But she was starving, so she picked up the hen and used it before her eggs went cold.

"Everything ends," Greer said.

There was a touch of remorse in his tone. Jenna concentrated on her meal because she didn't want to think about the guy feeling sorry for her plight. Sure, it wasn't fair but that didn't change anything.

"Thanks . . ." It was an afterthought, that made her cheeks heat as she realized she'd been rude.

Greer shrugged. "Don't sweat it. Your world is off-center at the moment."

And he'd seen it before.

There was an ease in his actions, almost a bored acceptance of the situation.

Right, because he was babysitting.

"Servant will fill you in. For now, I'm on point. You need to stay out of sight, that's why all the drapes are closed," Greer said.

Jenna looked at the kitchen window.

"Stay away from the glass," Greer warned her.

His tone was congenial enough but she still heard the warning to not test him. Her first encounter with the team flashed through her mind.

"I think we can skip the handcuffing to the bed part this time."

Her comment was less than professional, but it earned her a flash of teeth from Greer before he turned and disappeared into the living room.

Eating took little time, giving her plenty of opportunity to realize how many little things in life she'd taken for granted.

It would seem that today, looking out of windows was something she wasn't allowed.

Well, you're not dead . . .

There was a definite positive core in that thought. It helped Jenna put a smile on her face even as her shoulder started throbbing.

She hurt . . . What a surprise to discover pain to be something to be thankful for.

"The girl is still alive."

Kirkland faced off with Mack.

"It's your call," Mack informed his boss. He sent Kirkland a solid look.

Kirkland was thinking the matter through. "What do you think?"

Mack didn't hesitate. "Leave her alone. She didn't see you. The Feds would have already hauled you in if they had anything solid to tie you to their investigation. Keep your head down until after Carl is elected and can disband them."

Kirkland looked at the YouTube video playing. It was popular with the viewers, the footage of the Coast Guard helicopter as it lifted two people off a small boat bobbing in the water. A real feel-good moment that kept people believing in fairy tales and happy endings. A real man made his own luck and never apologized for climbing over the bodies of the men who got in his way. They'd do the same if he wasn't smarter and faster.

Life was a competition sport.

"Maybe Davis is doing what he promised," Kirkland added. "Keeping that team off my ass. Keeping my head down will kill our profits."

"He isn't in control of the Shadow Ops yet," Mack responded. "Better to play it safe."

Kirkland grunted. Playing it safe was for pussies, men content to live their lives chipping away at a mortgage while they sat in rush-hour traffic, sucking the exhaust fumes of the rest of the slaves.

Kirkland was a king. He didn't play by the rules, he made them.

"Carl Davis knows a lot of powerful people," Kirkland replied. He moved around his desk and sat down. "Know something? That's the only reason I put up with that cocksucker." He tapped the top of his desk. "Let her be. At least until after the election. We'll own the mortuary by then and can clean her up once we know Carl Davis has disbanded to Shadow Ops."

Dare Servant was just as much of a hard-ass as she recalled.

Somehow, Jenna had eased up on her thinking about the man.

Well that was a dumb-shit move to make . . .

He was back in command, somehow managing to transform the vintage living room into an interrogation cell. Jenna found herself looking at the sofa with its plastic covers and wondering about the family that had enjoyed it as a media hub.

"Ms. Henson?"

Dare cut through her distraction.

Actually, it was an attempt to avoid sharing the details of their evening with his team. Greer was watching from across the room, and there were two other agents eyeing her from different vantage points. She turned and shot both of them a look.

"This is unnerving." Jenna decided to just say what was on her mind. "I feel like an exhibit at the zoo."

"You didn't seem to have a shortage of courage on that dock," Dare remarked.

Jenna snapped her attention back to Dare. He was testing her. Tugging on her hair to see how she'd respond.

That's nothing new . . .

"I don't know what time it was when they attacked me," She answered him. "Honestly, you had my house bugged, don't you know?"

Dare was dressed again in slacks and dress shirt. He had a chest harness buckled over his torso.

She recalled him withdrawing that gun . . .

"We're recording your testimony, Ms. Henson, not my mission statement," he explained.

"I get that part," she muttered. "But the only part that matters is when we left my house and you don't know what happened. Why all the focus on what happened when you have video evidence?"

Her brain offered up the answer. They were testing her memory as well as her honesty.

"Fine . . ." She sat forward. "You . . . Agent Servant . . . arrived without invitation at about six in the evening. My friends accompanied us to dinner and then high-tailed it out of my townhome because you"—she pointed at him—"employed deception in the form of verbal language, telling them you and I were dating. Playing on the fact that my friend Sam is a hopeless romantic."

Dare didn't flinch. He was in complete control, facing her with a mask on.

Well . . . give as good as you get . . .

"You proceeded to take physical liberties, which crossed the line of professionalism as well as being immature enough to tell me it was my fault," she finished up.

His lips thinned. "You kissed me back."

"You started it . . . I finished it." Jenna shot him a hard look. "And I wasn't flashing a badge in your face, but if you're saying I intimidated you . . . well . . . fine by me."

He was back to undermining her foundation once more. His presence melting everything else beyond the pair of them and making her entire focus be only him.

"I took a shower, gave myself a stern lecture on not thinking about you, and went to bed."

Jenna folded her arms over her chest and shot him a solid stare. The rest of his team was silent, waiting to see what he would do next. The fact that he was hesitating struck her as some sort of victory because Dare Servant wasn't exactly the sort of man who suffered having his composure shaken very often.

He's not shaken . . .

Well, maybe not, but he was at least thinking things through. She'd take what she could get.

"Let's move to the docks," Dare decided.

As far as a peace offering went, Jenna decided it was good enough for her. She turned her mind to the events of the night, feeling her heart rate accelerate.

That was stupid.

There was no reason to let it bother her.

Right . . .

"Would you recognize the man's voice if you heard it again?" Dare asked.

Part of her was certain the sound of "the boss's" voice was branded into her memory. The more logical response though was to question if she really could distinguish it from other men.

"Honestly, I can't be sure. At least not sure enough to condemn someone on my say so. The spotlight was too bright," she answered.

It sounded pitiful.

At least when she stacked up her gains against what she'd lost.

Which was still a gray area. Jenna sat forward. "My turn."

Dare cocked his head to one side. "For what?"

"Questions," she answered.

"You're in custody," he replied. "We ask the questions."

"For how long?" She decided to just ignore his warning.

One of his dark eyebrows rose. "Need me to repeat myself?"

"No," she said. "I need you to understand that I'm not going to just sit in my place. It's your fault I'm here."

"You're not the first civilian to walk into the line of fire, Ms. Henson." Dare had straightened and was facing her with his feet braced shoulder-width apart. "My team is not responsible for your arrival at Kirkland's home. We were there in an attempt to keep a criminal off the streets you live on."

"Right."

Jenna stood up and turned her back on him. Sitting was driving her crazy, so at least the walk through the hallway kept her from screaming. The little vintage room didn't offer her any further solutions though.

Not a single one.

* * *

"Being a little hard on her, aren't you?" Greer spoke the obvious.

"That's my opinion," Zane offered before he turned and tapped in a line of passcode on a keyboard that was connected to a large portable screen.

"In case the pair of you don't get it, our job is hard," Dare responded.

Dare turned his back on his team but discovered himself facing Thais Sinclair. She had a habit of shifting into the shadows, one he was fairly comfortable with because it made her so very effective and he was one-hundred-percent convinced of her dedication to the team.

But her ability to appear like she could see straight into his thoughts? That was something he was having trouble dealing with.

Her eyes narrowed as she caught his guarded expression. "The job is hard . . . yes . . ." Thais shifted closer. "You're reacting emotionally."

Dare shot her a hard look of denial.

Thais only turned away, heading back to her workstation. Dare was left looking at her trim backside, the one that made men drool but for some reason left him cold today.

That was a new devolvement.

He didn't care for noticing the detail and yet, wouldn't let the fact go unnoticed.

Okay, he couldn't ignore it.

Dare ended up grinding his teeth, frustration bothering him a hell of a lot more than it ever had.

He didn't do personal.

That wouldn't be changing, and Jenna wasn't the type of girl to deal with friends with benefits.

Which was likely a good thing, because he was having far too much trouble detaching himself from his witness.

Miranda Delacroix had been raised with the press hounding her. She knew how to smile, the way to lock all her true feelings inside. And yet, she hadn't allowed her political family to carve out her heart.

They had certainly tried.

Today she held her feelings on a tight rein. Carl Davis was edging closer to winning his bid to become President. Which meant she'd have to suffer him during certain events because she was also doing well in the voter polls.

"Miranda," Carl Davis said warmly as he stopped next to her. He captured her hand and turned so the press got a good shot of them together.

He held her hand too tightly.

"So happy you could make it today." Carl was looking at the press, using her popularity to plow his own path.

It was a facet of his personality that she was well acquainted with. Carl had tried to force her only daughter to marry him with the help of Miranda's husband. Well, she'd seen to it that Damascus was free to marry the man she loved.

Not that Carl seemed any wiser when it came to trying to bend her into supporting his ambitions.

"Of course I'm here," Miranda purred. "It's so good of you to join us at last. Arts in our schools is a longtime passion of mine."

Carl's grip tightened as he turned his head to send her a warning glance. "I've brought along a special guest

who exemplifies the qualities your program aims to in-
still in our youth."

"We cultivate creativity." Miranda pulled her hand
free.

The outdoor event was brimming with school-aged
kids. They were clustered in groups wearing the same
T-shirt as they enjoyed having a rare field trip. A huge
stage was set up, the lights beginning to flicker as Carl
sent Miranda a smug look.

"It's my pleasure to present Kirkland. A creative
genius."

There was a cry from the kids that cut off Carl's
words. They surged forward, eager to greet the music
artist as he arrived on stage with a flash of lights and
blare of music. The press turned, moving toward the
stage.

"Watch yourself, Miranda," Carl warned her in a low
voice. "Get in my way, and I'll go through you. No one
survives in Washington without playing the game, and
I have a card in my hand you don't want faced up on the
table."

It was a threat.

Miranda was used to them. Carl waved as he moved
off to find more people to mingle with.

The right kind of people of course.

Miranda went on with making sure the program went
on. Carl's efforts would only help, even if she wished
he'd stayed away. Unlike Carl, she was truly committed
to making the world a better place. Her family might
have been political royalty but she'd managed to keep
her heart intact. Of course she'd had to keep it locked
away where no one really knew her secrets.

Carl knew one secret though. He knew she'd fired

the shot that had killed Jeb Ryland, her late husband. The Shadow Ops teams had sealed it all deep inside some file where no one would ever know.

Unless Carl became president and dissolved the Shadow Ops teams.

He'd still be a fool to do it. Exposing her wouldn't be worth the amount of judgment from the Press.

The problem was, Carl had made rash decisions in the past when his temper got the best of him.

"Keep your witness," Kagan informed Dare.

Dare's fingers tightened on the phone. He rocked back on his heels, nearly giving into the urge to pace.

He hated showing his feelings.

Keeping the world guessing was a skill, one that helped keep Dare alive and effective. Kagan was a master though. A man who never raised his voice and made a man wait for him to decide what was going to happen. Dare had no idea if Kagan was his name or a cover label. Not that it mattered. Kagan was his section leader and possibly other things Dare wasn't aware of. It was a sure bet Kagan had roots that ran deep in the Shadow Ops world.

"There is going to be a nice little medal ceremony for the Coast Guard boys who pulled you two in. Take your witness to it and make sure the press has an open shot at her." Kagan stopped and drew in a deep breath before letting it out. "Your witness wanted to help, get her on board."

"An impulse which nearly got her killed," Dare reminded his section leader.

Kagan grunted. "Almost doesn't count."

"She's a civilian."

And he was being defensive.

As far as plans went, it wasn't a bad idea. Thais was right, he was taking things too personally. The problem was, he couldn't seem to change his responses. Logic was failing to have the effect it normally did.

Kagan ended the call. Dare tucked his cell phone into his vest pocket. It was a habit that served him well. Making sure his phone was on him in the event they had to bug out fast. Communication meant being able to reach his resources.

He also needed to fill in Jenna.

Dare glanced toward the hallway but went toward Thais first. It made sense because the team was his life.

His choice.

His family.

Logic would prevail.

She was bored.

And yet, Jenna was resisting the urge to nap halfway into the afternoon because she was drawn so tight, the stress was burning through her energy.

Well, you don't have anything else to do . . .

She scoffed at herself, finding a thread of humor in knowing she had all the time in the world and now, all she longed for was an inbox full of stuff to keep her busy.

Okay, lab. She really missed her lab time. The emails were just a necessary evil. What she really craved was a nice batch of new samples to test.

"What put that smile on your lips?"

Jenna jumped, whirling around to find Dare a step inside the door.

"Don't you knock?" she asked.

Dare shook his head and strode another couple of steps into the room to elucidate his point. "If you can't anticipate my movements, neither can a bad guy. There is no personal space in safety."

She felt him.

In that insane way he affected her, like flipping on every light in the house in the dead middle of a moonless night. If she was being honest, she'd admit the reaction fascinated her.

"Don't look at me like that, Jenna."

She lifted a hand. "You might have to be a little more precise in explaining exactly how I'm treading on your space here."

His dark eyes flashed. They really were black, which suited his black hair and part of her was über-curious as to his ancestry.

Yeah, he'll likely think you're being nosy if you ask . . .

Jenna felt herself grinning, which earned her a scowl from Dare.

"Cases like this," he began, "cause a surge of hormonal response. It's a survival instinct. You can't trust it, Jenna."

He clearly wasn't.

That ticked her off because he looked so damned composed while she felt like she was sliding down a sandy cliff face.

Well, life wasn't fair. No news flash there. At least she could give him back the cold shoulder he was trying to introduce her to.

"Fine by me." She pointed at the doorway behind him. "Shove off."

His expression tightened. "It's not personal."

"Well hell," she exclaimed. "I guess you should have thought about that before you kissed me."

His eyes glittered.

"I did," he rasped. "I thought about it and lost the argument."

He'd closed the distance, filling the room with his presence. There was a whole lot of logic in his words, and yet Jenna admitted she was far more fascinated by the way her body was reacting.

She let out a little sound of mirth.

His eyebrow rose in question.

"Trust me, you don't want to know," she offered as she waved her hand in the air between them.

"Let me be the judge of that," Dare insisted.

Red alert . . .

Temptation was flaring up inside her, like a log drenched in lighter fluid. All she needed was one little spark and Dare Servant was playing with fire.

"You enjoy playing chicken, know that?" she said seriously.

"What part of me strikes you as safe playing, Jenna?"

"None of you," she answered honestly. "But you're the one whining about the lack of barriers."

He slowly smiled and there was nothing friendly about the expression. "Sure you want me to unbuckle my collar?"

Oh yeah . . .

She felt like the wind was knocked out of her with his question. He was warning her, and she felt like there was a bone deep recognition of just how wild he was when he wasn't forcing himself to toe the line.

"I'm a combustion expert," she muttered, more for herself than for him. "Watching things blow up is a personal fascination."

His lips twitched. "I've noticed."

"And you like it . . ." she shot back.

Honestly, she'd meant that as an inside comment.

Her eyes widened as she realized she'd spoken. His eyes narrowed, warning her she'd scored a direct hit.

She wasn't sorry.

He caught her wrist and pulled her forward.

"Yeah, I like it too much."

He smothered her response beneath a kiss that was hard and slow. Dare took his time, pulling her hand around him as he turned so she was locked against him, completely immobilized while he caught a handful of her hair and used it to keep her head in position.

It was bliss.

And a storm of insanity.

She shivered, enjoying every second of the intensity as she indulged herself in smoothing her hands along his chest. Up to his collar bones and onto the warm skin of his neck.

He shuddered, the reaction fueling her need to kiss him back.

It wasn't her first rodeo, and yet there was something vastly different about the moment. Everything she felt was off the scale, like the first time she'd drank shots. It was fast, blistering hot, and so quickly done, there was no time to second-guess herself.

Not that she wanted to.

No, she wanted him. Jenna stretched her head up as he trailed a line of kisses down her neck. She'd never realized how sensitive her skin could be or how impossible it would be to contain the little sounds of delight bubbling up from inside her.

He drew back. Frustration drawing his lips thin. "Door's open."

She bit her lip because she wanted to protest. The glitter in his eyes told her he was just as interested in continuing as she was but reality was a cold bitch.

"You're one hell of a pistol, know that Dare Servant?" Jenna pushed against his chest.

It wasn't what she wanted.

Neither did he.

For a moment, his arms were locked around her, letting her feel his strength, absorb just how hard his body was compared to hers.

Her curves were melting against him and the last thing she wanted was to let him get away before she discovered just how mind blowing the experience might get.

"Are we closing the door or what?" Jenna was on the edge, ready to just throw every last bit of reasoning she had to the wind and take what she could while she had the chance.

Enjoy the ride . . . before the wave crashed.

"You don't mean that," Dare muttered as he released her.

Jenna started to turn away but realized she was likely being way too chicken. So she faced off with him, locking gazes.

It was a challenge.

Dare didn't miss it either.

She watched as his eyes narrowed, his features drawing tight with the same hunger gnawing at her insides. There was a certain allure in toying with the flames flickering in his eyes. Was it dangerous? Only if she thought it through. Which seemed less and less important as she stood there, so close she could detect the scent of his skin.

Man animal . . .

He suddenly grinned and lifted one hand up to his forehead where he cut her a two-finger salute.

"I'm impressed, Jenna," he muttered in a husky tone that sent a shiver down her spine.

He walked toward her, making her tip her head back

so she could maintain eye contact. Time slowed down while her heart accelerated. The thing was pounding against her breast bone as she heard her breath rasping through her teeth.

"You're all woman."

He was pleased with her. She heard the compliment and soaked it up, reveling in the moment of praise. Dare wasn't the sort to hand out idle comments.

"Seems sad to waste the moment." It was almost a confession, but at least her tone of voice resembled a declaration. Jenna felt her nipples drawing tight even as she enjoyed knowing she was standing fast.

Dare didn't miss it either.

He contemplated her, noticing the details of her stance before he reached out and stroked her cheek.

"I'd like to close the door."

Her breath caught, heat teasing her cheeks. He tapped the skin, his lips curving into an arrogant grin of victory.

But there was lament in his eyes.

"But you deserve better from me than that."

He was backing away, the expression on his face determined.

"I know what's going to happen when this case is finished," Dare continued as he made it to the doorframe and grasped the doorknob. "You'll have plenty of reasons to hate me, Jenna. But me being a callous opportunist jerk won't be one of them."

It was her turn to grin. "Careful, Servant, keep talking like that and I might start to like you."

She was trying to lighten the mood, but his eyes darkened. She caught the hint of danger instantly, like a deer who'd been oblivious to the predator lurking nearby.

"Don't . . . like . . . me," he warned her. "You were

dead on the mark. You're here because of me, and there is no way I can let you go back to your life. I will close this case and have something to show for my personal effort, you . . . will be resettled with the stipulation of never being allowed to connect with anyone or place from your past."

"Guessed that all on my own." She sounded pissy but couldn't quell the urge to just stand silent.

"You're sharp," he agreed with a nod. "And in the wrong place at the wrong time. I can't change it, just my personal conduct. My badge is my identity. This team, my family."

He disappeared as he closed the door. She was suddenly more alone than she had ever been. The forgotten décor of the room like some sort of comparison of how she herself was now lost to the passing of time and slated to be revamped in an effort to cover up everything she'd ever been.

Opportunistic jerk?

Truth be told, he'd been in more danger of her jumping him, just to prove she could make a choice.

She flopped onto the bed, feeling like a teenager stuck with a tide of rising hormones while stuck in a body that was too young for action.

Dare was . . . decades older than her in many ways. More worldly for sure, deeply committed to his badge in a manner she'd only ever expected to come face to face with in movies and spy novels.

The face-to-face thing was a major buzz.

Her body was throbbing, her clit begging for attention. In short, she'd never been so turned on.

"My badge is my identity . . ."

His tone had been so determined. Like he was hiding.

Whoa . . . girl, don't go trying to save him . . .

Jenna forced herself up and off the bed. She took a long look at the bedroom door before going toward the bathroom and a cold shower.

She was all for tossing aside the rules she'd lived by before her life went through a shredder, but what she wasn't going to do was be alone in choosing to enjoy the moment. Dare wanted to walk away.

So she let him.

CHAPTER FOUR

Dare's team were very good at what they did.

Jenna stood on a huge expanse of asphalt outside a Coast Guard hangar. The afternoon breeze was whipping her hair around her face as she stood and waited for the official ceremony to begin. The members of the team who had rescued her were lined up next to a podium while she stood on the other side and listened as the Chief spoke about dedication and duty and the fact that she was alive because of the efforts of the men waiting to be decorated while members of the local press watched.

Dare and his team had blended in flawlessly with the people attending. Greer McRae was snapping pictures and sporting a lanyard around his neck with a press badge. In the direct sunlight, she caught the hint of copper in his hair. It suited the hint of Scottish accent that came out of his mouth from time to time.

Zane was looking too sharp in a business suit. More than one female member of the press was sending him obvious invitations. Thais had on a pair of head phones while she sat in a news van and appeared to be working the video feed.

Jenna didn't see Dare.

But she would have sworn she felt him watching her.

Half the people here are looking at you . . .

True. Jenna's smile was genuine for a moment. The crazy way Dare affected her made her laugh.

Maybe she'd tell him so just to see the reaction.

Not done playing with fire?

Clearly not and she refused to be contrite over it. After all, it seemed an extremely poor choice to lie to herself when the only thing she had left was who she was at her core.

Music started up. The press settled down, their cameras raised.

"Ms. Henson is here as an excellent example of what teamwork can accomplish."

Jenna did her part, nodding as the men who had lifted her off the ocean were awarded metals. The press offered up the expected round of applause before the master of ceremonies concluded the official part of the afternoon.

That was when the press swooped in.

Jenna felt her eyes widen and struggled to grasp at her composure as she was surrounded.

Like a loaf of bread tossed in the center of a flock of pigeons.

Questions came at her from all sides as huge microphones were shoved into her face. Zane was watching from just a few feet back but held his position. Greer sent her a wink along with a half grin of confidence in her abilities to survive.

"Going to leave her to that bunch?" Thais asked Dare without turning to look at him.

"She's holding her own," Dare replied.

And she was. After a moment of wide-eyed shock, Jenna drew herself up straight and started answering questions in a clear, firm voice.

"When she calls you a dick again, I'm going to tell you I agree," Thais informed him.

Dare took his attention off his witness for a moment to look at his team member. "Getting her in front of the media is the point of today's exercise."

"You could have warned her what to expect," Thais said.

"It would have altered her reaction," Dare replied.

Thais sent him a narrow-eyed look. Dare turned his attention back to Jenna.

You are being an ass.

Or at least he wasn't making much of an effort to ease the circumstances for his witness.

Ass . . .

Right. It was a solid truth even if he was doing it for valid reasons.

He couldn't let her fall in love with him.

Settling down wasn't something his life-plan included. Even if he thought Jenna was damned cute. She had a pixy hair cut that begged for him to shove his hands into the uneven strands of dark hair.

And she had a butt.

Vulgar? Maybe but he had a weakness for a girl with a little curve on her bottom. Thais was considered prime quality with her slim figure and tiny derriere. Dare preferred the way Jenna's backside would give him something to hold onto. Her love of cooking was likely the source of her curves because she wasn't slow. Her shoulders and arms were toned, proving she was hands-on all the way.

You might have noticed that when she went back into

the line of fire . . . or when she asked if he was going to
shut the door . . .

There were another couple of reasons he wasn't going to become her friend. She was spunky and curvy, and his cock hardened too often when she was around. Better to keep her frustrated with him, better to have her putting up barriers between them because he was losing ground when it came to keeping her delegated to the parts of his brain where witnesses were filed.

So he'd be the hard-ass she called him.

No matter how much more he wanted from her.

She truly hadn't realized how many television stations there were in the world. The press were eager to get their time with her. They offered her business cards with their credentials and her stack quickly grew into such a handful that she longed for a purse to stuff them into. The sides of her cheeks felt sore as she forced a smile, and she was pretty sure the two Coast Guard officers who had framed her were getting ready to strangle her if she elaborated on any of her answers.

The sun was a glowing ball on the horizon, turning the surface of the ocean to ruby red lava. The on-shore breeze made the surface of the water ripple while the waves crashed off in the distance. When they'd started, there had been a steady line of fishing boats making their way into the marina for the night. Now the parking lot was almost empty as the birds swooped in to dine on the trimmings from the fishermen.

"Thank you, Ms. Henson."

The last reporter ended the interview. Jenna heard one of the men let out a grunt of relief. She turned toward him and flashed him a smile. "Could you point me toward a water cooler?"

Her question amused him. He jerked his head toward the hangar. With a quick "thanks" she started toward it.

For a moment, she was more alone than she'd been in a while. Part of her enjoyed the freedom, but there was also the memory of being bound and gagged and laid out next to a dead girl.

Jenna looked at the far side of the base, where the official fence was and the civilian area of the beach began. She knew the area. There was a little barbeque place just two blocks away and an Irish pub across the street from that.

Places she could never go back to.

Dare had said it to drive a wedge between them. He'd pissed her off, and she realized that was exactly his plan.

It was sad.

The guy was pitting his life against the sort of people who killed girls like the one she'd seen in the shipping container. He deserved some happiness. In fact, he'd earned it. Which just enhanced his appeal because it was a true mark of maturity when a person started earning their way instead of waiting for life to give them their fair share.

Life wasn't fair.

Nope. And Dare and his team were content with the fact, too. They loved what they did, expecting to live in obscurity.

He doesn't want to be saved.

No, at least not by her anyway.

Still. The idea refused to be shoved off into the oblivion of "don't go there." Jenna forced herself to look for the water cooler. She spied it just inside the hangar door.

"Jenna!"

She'd only made it two steps when she heard her

name being shouted. Turning back around, she looked for the source.

"Jenna!!!!" Sam was running up the sidewalk from the parking lot.

The sight hit her like a concrete block, sending a jolt of pain through her chest as her pep talks dissolved, leaving her facing what she'd truly lost. Sam was waving with his full arm, Paul coming up behind him with car keys still dangling from his fingers. Jenna felt herself smiling as she lifted her hand to wave back. Relief spread across her friends' faces bright enough to melt the chill Jenna hadn't realized was clamped around her heart.

A second later her wrist was caught in a hard hold. There was a jerk and her arm was locked up.

"What are you doing?" she demanded.

"My job," Dare replied.

She was swung around, helpless to do anything but go where Dare Servant pushed her with the lock he had her arm in.

"What the fuck is your problem?" Sam bellowed behind her. "That is my friend!"

Jenna didn't get a chance to see him again. Dare strong-armed her right into the open side of the news van. She landed on her knees, face first into a seat and heard the click of handcuffs as he secured them around her wrists.

"You . . . prick!" she growled.

Most of the venom in her tone was lost as someone put their foot down on the accelerator and the van pitched forward. Jenna went face first into the pleather-covered seat. Without her hands, it was a hard connection.

Whoever was driving took a turn. The van wobbled

and jiggled, jolting Jenna around like a forgotten soccer ball.

"Keep your head down, Jenna."

Dare's voice was Arctic cold. He reached over and pushed her face-first into the seat with a hand on the nape of her neck.

She wasn't going to win the battle, but that didn't make it easy to stop fighting. The urge was all consuming, flaring up into true rage as she heard herself snarling.

Of course it didn't change how pathetically easy it was for Dare to reduce her to his will. Helplessness was bitter beyond her endurance, and the hold he had on her neck forced her to swallow it while the van took her away from everything she knew.

Her eyes stung with tears.

No! She refused to cry.

But the damned tears flooded her eyes anyway.

"Jenna Henson doesn't exist any longer."

The little seventies-era home was still as death.

Dare had deposited Jenna in a chair while he faced off with her, and his teammates stood on the sides like velociraptors making ready to go for a kill.

Well, she wasn't having any of it.

"You were told no contact, Jenna," Dare continued.

"I was told no such thing." Jenna made sure she enunciated each syllable. Her hands were still locked behind her, but she sat on the edge of the seat, shooting him daggers. "You tossed me out without a single word on what this afternoon would entail."

He wanted to argue the point, but she could see him thinking and accepting she'd won the argument. His eyes narrowed as he switched tracks.

"You're a witness, which means you don't sit in on team briefings."

"Exactly my point, I wasn't told anything about what was expected from me today," she growled. "You wanted a front-line seat to a knee-jerk reaction at my expense." Greer tilted his head to one side, proving she'd hit the nail on the head.

"You're not the only professional in this room, Servant," she continued. "I've seen my share of observation-based, analysis-data gathering sessions. Being the subject of it is a first though. Hope you enjoyed the show."

Silence returned. For a long moment Jenna stared Dare down. She took a great deal of pleasure out of knowing she'd shut him down, even if she didn't expect it to last very long. He decided on action, ripping open a small pocket sealed with Velcro on his chest harness. The sound bounced around the room because of how still everyone was.

Jenna actually heard his steps as he came closer. Her damned insides tightened though, pissing her off because of how responsive she was to him. Sitting still was a torment she suffered only long enough for him to unlock one of the cuffs. Jenna slipped off the chair and out of his reach with the open cuff dangling from her wrist.

"Let me unlock . . ."

She stuck her finger up between them. "You've done quite enough, thank you, Agent Servant."

She needed space.

Or to scream.

Maybe hit something.

Not something . . . *him*.

She felt like her blood was surging through her veins.

Nothing made sense because her instinct was to keep arguing with him while she knew logically he'd never budge from his choices.

And you don't want him to bend . . .

Jenna turned and headed for the bedroom that had become her holding cell. Her stupid hormones were reducing her to putty.

Yeah, there was a truth and a half.

She was pissed off, and all she wanted to do was fuck the hell out of Dare Servant. Jenna sent the bedroom door shut with the help of all her pent-up frustration. The damn thing rattled, proclaiming just how under her skin Dare was.

Fine.

Let him hear it.

And know she'd scrounged up enough dignity to walk away from him. The knowledge was slim pickings as far as compensation went for what she really wanted. Especially when she made it across the room to the dresser. It had a mirror mounted onto it. One that showed her how flushed she was. There were bright patches over her cheek bones, which just made her recall the way he'd stroked her face.

She shivered and watched the soft fabric of her dress rise up when her nipples contracted into hard points.

"Cases like this," he began. "Cause a surge of hormonal response. It's a survival instinct. You can't trust it, Jenna."

Fate was a bitch. Because Dare had been so very right.

At least he was experienced enough to know the facts. Someday, she'd think good thoughts about him and the way he'd left her alone.

Today however, all she wanted to do was get back in

his face and keep at him until he was as worked up as she was.

Wave the flag in front of the bull . . .

Sex had never been such a force of nature in her life. It was titillating the way the urge invaded every aspect of her dealings with Dare. It didn't seem to matter if she was on good terms or spitting mad at him, the answer was still the same.

Get her hands on him.

Jenna forced herself to look at the handcuffs, made herself focus on the hard reality and use those facts to stay right where she was until her body settled down.

One deep breath helped.

But the door was being pushed in before she took the second one.

"You need to hear what I'm telling you, Jenna. You are my witness," Dare started in on her.

"Fine," Jenna responded as she turned to face him.

He was right on her tail, pulling up when she whirled around to face him.

"But that's not why you're following me," she hissed at him.

His expression tightened. He really did have midnight eyes. Jenna seriously could have labeled him a marauder and it would have suited him.

"By all means," he demanded in a husky tone. "Share your opinion with me, Ms. Henson."

"You followed me because you want to nip at me as much as I want to keep at you until we both just give in." She took another deep breath, grinning just a little, as she discovered herself sweeping him from head to toe because he was utterly devastating to her entire system.

"Be honest," she muttered off-handedly. Maybe

that was a challenge, so be it. "You've been quick to toss the psychology facts at me. Well, I walked away because I think you're right. This situation is driving me crazy. Otherwise, I'm left thinking you're a prick for today's little handcuff and face plant into a seat maneuver."

He was looming over her. The door to the bedroom closing with a soft sound as Jenna caught the scent of his skin.

Musk . . .

Her blood started racing through her veins again, the small amount of calmness she'd fought to gain slipping away like it had never been there. His nostrils flared, while her heart accelerated. Time slowed down, allowing her to experience every minute detail.

"I did follow you because I can't drop it," he said.

It was an admission. Dare didn't really care too much for making it either. She watched frustration draw his lips tight.

Lips she really wanted to feel against her own again.

He caught her own admission, read it right off her face as her attention lingered on his mouth.

"We . . . can't do this Jenna . . ." He was hissing at her, a soft sound that seemed to be escaping through the holes in the wall he was using to hold back his impulses.

"I . . ." She jabbed him in the middle of his chest with her finger. "Walked . . . *away* . . ."

His lips twitched. "After throwing down a gauntlet, baby . . ."

She had. Satisfaction filled her as he admitted to noticing it. Their gazes were locked, ensuring he saw it flash through her eyes.

"So pick it up already," she said.

She was daring him.

Jenna opened her arms wide. "I can't change where circumstances have dropped me, but I sure as hell can enjoy the ride. Leave the way you came if you don't have the guts for it."

She was having a breakdown.

And Jenna suddenly understood it was exactly what she'd been needing. A full breakdown of all the walls holding her in position, while fate flung her into their hard surfaces over and over again.

There was a rip of Velcro and Dare was shrugging out of his chest harness. The hard glint in his eyes was as much warning as promise.

It fucking curled her toes.

She stepped back, needing to put more space between the outside world and the place where she could indulge in what she wanted from Dare.

"Second thoughts?" he questioned, his hands freezing on the button of his waistband.

She shook her head, biting her lip as she tried to decide what to do next. Her brain was shutting down, instinct trying to take over, only she kept trying to understand, which left her confused.

"I want . . . you . . ." Another step back and he followed, her insides twisting as her nipples tingled with anticipation.

He reached out. She expected him to capture her nape. Instead he cupped her face. His fingers warm against her cheek. The touch so tender, she shuddered as her eyes slid shut.

"It can be easy . . ." he was cooing. His tone dark and enticing.

She let out a little breathy sound as she opened her

eyes. "Don't be . . . *angry* . . ." Jenna reached for him, her fingertips landing on where he'd opened the first couple of buttons of his shirt. "Don't let me be . . . alone in this . . . *need* . . ."

He stroked her cheek. Sending a ripple of awareness down her spine.

"You're not . . ." He moved closer, slipping his hand into her hair before he tightened his grip and held her head still so he could loom over her. "You're just more honest than I am."

She felt her lips twitching. "It's all I have left. Me. And whatever that really is."

"It's pretty impressive."

The compliment hit her ears a moment before he was kissing her. She gasped, the level of sensation shocking her system. He teased her lips as he took them in a kiss that left nothing between them. Intimacy became a living thing, something that blurred the lines between where he ended and she began.

Which felt perfect.

Jenna kissed him back, tracing his lower lip with the tip of her tongue before he boldly thrust his into her mouth.

She grabbed his hair, trying to pull him closer as he stroked her tongue with his, setting off a need to have him deep inside her.

He pressed her back another few steps, lifting his head from hers as she felt her bottom hit the dresser.

Satisfaction glittered in his eyes as he clasped her hips and lifted her. He sat her on the smooth wood, pushing her skirt up as he stepped forward, making her spread her thighs.

"Impressive isn't a word I use lightly, baby . . ."

"You never struck me as a brown-noser," she answered.

His lips split in a grin, flashing his teeth at her. It was a raw expression, one that gave her a glimpse at just how wild he truly was.

God, she fucking loved the sight.

It made her tremble.

And it made her wet.

Blunt? Sure was.

But truthful.

And she wanted to know she wasn't alone. She reached out, pressing against the front of his pants, a little sound of approval rising from her throat as she encountered his erection.

"I'll rise to your challenge, Jenna, but you're going to wait for what you want."

He pulled back, reaching up to find the sides of her underwear and pulling the garment down her legs. For a moment, her knees were back together. Dare parted them with a sure motion that sent another zip of excitement through her belly.

"I'm going to watch you first . . ."

He'd moved back between her thighs, keeping them wide with his hips.

"Going to make sure you get a taste of how out of control you make me feel . . ." Dare warned her darkly.

She felt her eyes widen as he caught her hair again. He was sweeping up the inside of her thigh, doing it slowly while he watched her.

"You're wet . . ."

She was and he could smell it. Jenna felt her eyes widen. She'd never been so exposed, so very much at the mercy of what she craved.

His fingers reached her slit, skimming the edge of her folds as his lips thinned in enjoyment.

"I did this to you . . ."

Jenna tried to nod but his grip was too tight.

Dare shook his head. "Not a chance baby. You're going to vocalize. I'm not letting you get away with anything less."

"*Yes . . .*" Her tone was a raspy whisper.

He was so dammed commanding, and she loved it too much for her pride.

But her cravings needed him just the way he was.

She reached out and gripped his shirt, curling her fingers into the fabric. He drew in a breath, a hard one that was caught in his gritted teeth. "And you want me, no matter how bad an idea it is."

The hand on her nape tightened, the sound of his breath hitting her ears as she felt it touching her lips because he was so close to her.

"Yes . . ." he growled.

The admission pleased her. She felt the last bits of restraint crumbling as she watched him fumble with his pants.

For a moment she was alone, watching the way he yanked a condom from his wallet and tossed the wrapper on the dresser top. A couple of sure motions and he'd sheathed himself.

And then he was back. A hard arm encircling her back as he guided his length to her folds.

"I want you too damned bad . . ."

It was half growl, half confession.

But all Jenna cared about was the first touch of his hard flesh against hers. She shuddered, her clit giving a crazy twist that made her gasp.

Not yet . . .

It was too soon, and yet her body wasn't interested in

savoring the moment. She struggled against the tide, losing the battle after only a few hard thrusts. Climax twisted through her, wringing her, and snapping through her in a hard jolt that dropped her like a rock.

Dare smothered her cry beneath his lips, holding himself deep inside her as she twisted and strained.

"Fuck . . ." she muttered when he lifted his mouth from hers, frustration clear in her tone.

"We're not done, Jenna." He pulled free and pushed back in with a slow motion of his hips. "Not by a long shot."

A ripple of sensation went through her. His cock stretching her passage as it tried to contract.

Dare clasped her hips, making her flatten her hands on the dresser behind her.

"I'm going to take . . . my . . . time . . ." he promised. There was a warning in his tone.

His eyes were full of determination as he locked gazes with her.

"Going to give you exactly what you crave . . ."

He was making good on his words, working his cock in and out of her with a control that left perspiration on his skin. His hold on her hips sent a crazy little tingle of excitement through her, touching on some deeply embedded instinct she had to be taken.

He was up to the challenge.

Filling her.

Holding still for just long enough for her to feel like she'd die if he didn't start moving.

She was straining toward him, trying to gain just a tiny bit more friction as her clit throbbed for release.

"Not yet . . ."

"You are such a control . . ." He thrust hard, killing

her train of thought. Taking her to the edge of release but leaving her poised when he pulled free.

"Hard ass," she accused him softly.

His lips twitched. "You like that best about me."

She did.

And she didn't want to think.

No, all she wanted was to lift her hips for his next thrust, absorb the way he drove deep, making her feel like she couldn't take him and then staying inside her long enough for her to realize she could.

Pleasure was building inside her, rising up from the ashes of her first climax, burning brighter as this time everything was deeper, more intense.

And he was right there with her when it all broke. They clung to each other as pleasure ripped them apart. It was hard and primal, Dare shoving her face into his shoulder as he smothered his own cries against the top of her head. He jerked, his hip driving into her with a frantic need in those last moments as ecstasy claimed them both.

Kirkland waited for privacy before he growled at Carl Davis.

"What the fuck is going on with this bitch?"

Kirkland turned his cell phone toward Carl, the coverage from the Coast Guard ceremony playing across the little high-definition screen.

"She can cause a whole lot of trouble for me," Kirkland informed Carl. "I need her cleaned up before she fingers me for that night on the docks. Servant set me up, or I'd have killed her then."

Carl shoved the phone down. "Don't be stupid. You know how powerful some of those camera lenses are."

He looked across the lawn to where the concert kids were lining up to get on their buses.

Kirkland flashed a couple of hang-loose signs to the delight of his fans before he sent a hard look at Carl. "If I go down, you do, too."

"Servant and his team are fishing with her," Carl exclaimed in a harsh whisper. "Showing her off and seeing who surfaces. I brought you here to keep your head down. If she had anything of any value to add to the investigation, you'd already be facing a judge. Stay here, smile, and be seen as unaffected by her little press event. Don't be stupid enough to make a move towards her."

"But she knows my voice. Knows I'm involved in shady dealings down on the dock. There was a fucking body laid out next to her. One she knows I knew about," Kirkland growled. "I give you a healthy share of the profits from my empire. When are you going to get these Feds off my ass so I can get back to making real money?"

"When I'm president, I will shut them down," Carl answered.

"That's five months away." Kirkland scowled.

"Servant runs a Shadow Ops team," Carl said under his breath. "As it stands, shutting them down will have to be done carefully or they could darken my reputation."

"I pay you to take the risk," Kirkland shot back.

"And I make sure you stay in business," Carl cut back. "I can find someone else who will pay for my partnership. How long do you think you'll be running those prostitution rings if I don't shelter you? I can make it so you never get another load of girls from overseas in to staff your places. A good percentage of the money you send me is used to keep the Feds off the docks when your shipments arrive. That will leave you with nothing but crackheads and runaways," Carl sniffed. "Don't threaten me Kirkland. We're too deep in bed with each other for one of us to pull out now. Do it my way."

Carl flashed him a smile before he strode out of the secured area where they'd been standing. His security escort formed around him as he waved and made his way to a waiting car.

Kirkland didn't have to smile. His stage persona allowed him to look mean, and he pulled his hat a little lower on one side of his head as he enjoyed not having to kiss ass the way Carl did. When he left, the press leaned over the line confining them to get parting shots of him. He liked the way they strained, showing him that he was a force to be drawn toward.

Carl should remember it, too.

Kirkland settled back into the plush seat of his limo and made sure the privacy screen was up between him and the driver. He pulled a phone from his pocket and typed in the number from memory.

"The chef bitch was on the news."

"I saw," Mack answered.

"Davis says they have no evidence. Make sure there is none to find."

Kirkland didn't wait for a reply. He ended the call and popped the battery out of the prepaid phone. He dropped it into a glass and opened a bottle of water before pouring it into the glass. He pried the data card out and broke it. He scooped up all the pieces and put them back into his pocket before getting out at a nightclub. There was a roar from the people waiting to get inside as he appeared. The rumor that he was in town having sparked a flood of hopeful fans out to some of his favorite spots.

Much later, he dumped the pieces of the phone in different trash cans. In the densely populated urban center, they would never be reunited.

Clean.

Miranda Delacroix smiled.

She was known for her sweet smiles, but this was one of complete contentment.

Victory even.

In her hand was her cell phone. She tapped an icon on the screen and played back the conversation between Kirkland and Carl Davis.

She hadn't imagined the exchange.

It was a victory against Carl and the way he'd hurt her daughter Damascus. No mother ever forgot a wrong done to their child.

Her expression changed to one of seriousness.

Carl had forgotten he'd brought Kirkland to her event and the secure area was not for them alone. Carl was too accustomed to be the highest ranking person at an event.

Carl thought everything revolved around him. Miranda enjoyed knowing she'd managed to catch him with his pants down. Carl hadn't just worked out a deal with her late husband to force their daughter Damascus to marry him for the image Carl wanted to present to the voters. No, Carl had turned nasty and tried to force Damascus to fall in line by having her kidnapped to prove Carl could do whatever he wanted.

But her baby had been in love with Vitus Hale.

Miranda dropped her lipstick into her little clutch purse and enjoyed knowing that going to fix her make-up was the reason she'd caught the two unaware.

Carl Davis certainly didn't know anything about

women and the fact that touch ups were necessary. And doing it out of sight was a must when the press was so very eager to snap a picture of her looking less than her best.

She moved forward and felt her own security people join her. They kept up with her quick pace as she moved toward her car. Miranda waited until her driver had pulled away from the curb before she dialed a number she wasn't even certain would connect her with the man she'd met on the night of her husband's murder. He was a legend in the Shadow Ops world, a man with whom people didn't want to be publicly associated. Kagan was the only name she had for him and in spite of her connections, Miranda had been wise enough to not go looking for any other information.

The line might be disconnected. The number she had might be for a burner phone long since discarded as Kagan moved on to another case. She hoped not. She owed Kagan, and he would be the only one to see that what she had on Carl was significant enough to move on.

Jenna was shaking.

Dare smoothed a hand down her back.

Satisfaction was glowing inside her like a lantern light in the middle of a moonless night. The need to drift off into sleep was only being held back by the fact that she suddenly felt awkward.

Maybe exposed was the better word.

She'd laid it out. Followed her impulses, and she didn't regret it. She had a firm knowledge of what she'd done left and she had no idea how Dare would react now that the moment was past.

His phone started ringing.

He pulled away from her, withdrawing the little

buzzing machine before frowning. It landed on the dresser beside her as he cleaned up and closed his fly.

"Got to take this," he said.

There was something flickering in his eyes that looked like reproach but he'd retrieved the phone and hit the redial before Jenna got a long look at him. He crossed the shag carpet and started to open the door as she scrambled to stand up so her skirt would fall back into place.

She was staring at the door a second later, wondering if she imagined the scent of his skin still clinging to hers.

No, he'd been there.

Of all the dates she'd ever had, Dare wasn't the sort of man she could say she'd been less than impressed by.

He'd captivated her. Bringing a new meaning to the word passion.

The only problem was, she had a bad feeling she was going to be left looking for the same level of intensity for the rest of her life.

Well, it beat regrets.

Or at least that was what she was going to keep telling herself.

Dare hesitated.

It wasn't something he had a lot of experience with. Looking down the hallway toward the closed door he'd left Jenna behind, he was torn between the call he'd just received and the need to tell Jenna what he was doing.

Duty had always come first.

He didn't like the way his emotions were trying to chance his priorities.

Dare let out a whistle as he came back into the living

room. "The firefighter paramedic called. He's got the woman who tried to claim the bodies. Zane, Thais, you're on nest duty."

Dare made a circle with his hand, one his team knew well. He'd already made it out of the front door and into the front seat of the car they were using when Greer looked across the seat at him.

"Sure you don't want to tell Jenna you're leaving?"

He turned a scathing look toward his teammate.

"Do nae try it," Greer bit back, the brogue breaking through to prove the Scot was more than willing to rise to the challenge Dare was issuing.

"Ye're being a dick," Greer advised as Dare pulled into the flow of traffic.

"I never misrepresented myself to her," Dare said.

"Didn't say you did."

Dare grunted, earning a snort from his teammate.

"The timing is less than perfect but I didn't make the call to myself," Dare explained. "Jenna knows I'm working a case."

"If she shoots ye with your own gun, I'm going to laugh until I piss myself at your expense," Greer replied.

Greer gained a half grin from Dare. Greer might feel strongly enough to speak his mind but that was only because they were teammates.

Nothing came between them.

Not even personal privacy.

Dare drove toward a traffic accident. The scene was lit by the swirling lights from the fire engine and the flickering blue and white ones from the patrol cars. He flashed his badge, driving along the shoulder to get ahead of the cars stuck creeping along as people rubbernecked.

Dare and Greer were out of the car the moment he parked it, striding into the mess. Ramos, the veteran firefighter who'd first called Dare, caught sight of him as he moved through the scene. Ramos moved close and turned to look at a woman arguing with a cop.

"Glad you answered. That's her." Firefighter Ramos pointed at a woman standing across the way. "Ji Su Shin. She used to run the massage parlors, and she tried to claim the other two bodies."

The woman in question was arguing with two uniform cops.

"I told you . . . no treatment . . . I am fine," she insisted. "You must let me go now."

There were the remains of three cars on the side of the road, the scent of burnt rubber and flares filling the night air.

"You need to go to jail!" one of the other drivers yelled. "Driving a BMW doesn't give you the right to cut other people off and try to run away from the accident you caused!"

The cops had their hands full dealing with the occupants of the three smashed cars. Ji Su's companions weren't interested in anything but getting her into another car that was waiting with its engine running.

"Glad you got here quick," Ramos continued. "She's not going to let me trick her into going to the hospital."

"Good work," Dare said.

He sent Greer a quick glance, but his fellow agent was already in action. They approached from different sides. The uniform cops saw them first. Ji Su's companions noticed them before she did. In the blink of an eye, the entire scene turned into a brawl. The fight was vicious, taking the cops by surprise.

Dare expected it.

They knew they were dirty and were fighting for their lives.

What surprised Dare was the way one of the younger firefighters jumped into the fray. He was light on his feet and dodged the advanced martial-arts moves being thrown at him, following up with kicks that landed perfectly.

Traffic was standing still when it was over, the person in the car nearest them recording it all on a cell phone. Dare grunted and hauled Ji Su off the ground.

"You cannot arrest me . . ." she sputtered as Dare handed her off to a cop.

Dare didn't argue with her but looked at the young firefighter. One of the uniformed cops was grinning at the kid. "Why aren't you wearing one of these badges?"

The kid cocked his head until his neck popped. "I want to be a paramedic."

"Well someone had you trained," Dare observed.

The kid sent him a grin. "My mom. Pretty sure she's really a Klingon."

The firefighter went back toward his engine crew. The uniformed cops were arguing with the motorists over the cell phone and their First Amendment rights.

"Ever feel like it's getting harder to be a good guy?" Greer asked.

Dare nodded. The problem was, what was on his mind was Jenna and just how much he didn't want the current case to end.

Because it would mean letting her go forever.

"Nice work."

Kagan rang Dare's phone before they'd made it more than a couple of miles from the accident scene.

"It was Ramos who spotted her and called me," Dare

replied. "He's sharp and doesn't like people messing up his city."

"I'll be back in touch when the drill team gets done interrogating her," Kagan said.

"I'm moving my team," Dare said. "I don't want to risk being followed in case one of her buddies made it into the road-side brush before the cops got there."

There was a pause on the other end of the line. "Check in when you're settled."

Dare dropped the phone into his vest pocket as Greer turned toward the local hospital. They parked the car and headed toward the elevators. When they made it to the top floor, a few nurses tried to stop them but they flashed their badges and walked out onto the helicopter landing pad.

A military chopper was heading their way. The pilot wouldn't have any clue who they were, and the guy wouldn't ask questions. As far as being Shadow Ops went, Dare and Greer would live as men who had no identities.

That was why Dare had to stay away from Jenna. She deserved better.

More . . .

As they lifted off, Dare lost the battle to ignore just how much he might enjoy more of Jenna. More of her spunk, more of her in-your-face attitude.

He grinned as he thought about it. The inside of the chopper was noisy, giving him the space to indulge.

Landing ended his reverie. The details of his case flooding back to the forefront of his thoughts.

They'd touched down on a military base. It was the classified side of it. The aircraft they'd been lifted in was a common Black Hawk but now they were among some of the meanest helicopters on the planet. They were all sitting at rest, most of them covered by nets or being pushed by ground crews into huge hangars where they'd be out of sight from the air.

It was a place where hard men were either going to or coming from missions that would never be talked about. A smattering of ground crews were interspersed among them, which made Dare look twice when he spied a female among the group in front of them. Her slighter build was easy to spot, and she turned around looking back at Dare and Greer for a long moment, like she'd known they were there. He felt a tingle across his nape as she locked gazes with him.

"Sorcha?"

Dare turned as Greer suddenly took off across the tarmac. His surge of motion caused a nearby group to turn on him with deadly purpose.

But a woman came barreling out of their ranks, neatly evading the two men who tried to stop her.

"Greer!" She cried out.

Greer caught her in a hug and spun her around, looking like he was going to crush her.

"Step away from my Operative," the officer in charge insisted.

Dare was already moving toward Greer, ready to close ranks as the men who had been accompanying all started to converge on Greer.

"She's my sister," Greer declared.

Dare had worked with Greer a long time and had rarely seen the man lose his temper.

"Greer," Sorcha said softly.

"Well ye are," Greer informed her. "And I never get to see ye. She is not your damned service animal."

"Take it . . . inside . . ."

The officer in charge spoke with a soft voice that

didn't lack command presence. The men around them closed ranks, making it less of a request. Dare ended up waiting while Greer spoke with his sister.

"This never happened."

Dare turned his head to find the commanding officer next to him. A quick glance and Dare realized the guy didn't have a standard name badge on.

"Caxton," the guy supplied. "Major."

Dare lifted his badge up. Caxton considered the markings for a moment.

"That makes it a lot simpler," Caxton said. "Neither of us exists."

Kagan never answered the phone.

Miranda scrolled through her contacts, looking for her daughter's husband. Vitus Hale had saved her daughter Damascus when Carl Davis had thought to force a wedding because of Miranda's ties to the Delacroix family.

"Is something wrong, Miranda?" her son-in-law answered on the second ring and true to his nature, the ex-SEAL cut right to business.

"Damascus is fine," Miranda assured him quickly. "I need to share something with you, for Kagan."

There was a short pause on the other end of the line. "Give me twelve hours to join you in D.C. Do not leave your escort, even for a moment."

"I understand. Thank you."

The line cut, leaving Miranda satisfied. Tyler Martin was dead but Carl Davis was about to get everything he'd wanted and killed to ensure he achieved.

Not while she drew breath.

Well, at least not while Carl was stupid enough to have private conversations at her charity events. Fate was finally delivering power to her after a lifetime of her being helpless against her family and husband.

It felt very nice, the knowledge that she had the means to thwart the way men like Carl got what they wanted when they deserved it the least.

She would make very sure of it.

Someone knocked on her door.

Agent Zane Bowan gave Jenna about two seconds before he pushed the door in.

"You're reading Nancy Drew?" he asked incredulously.

Jenna looked up from the book. "Due to a lack of options, it was this"—she closed the book—"or ask you for some rope so I could practice the knots in the *Boy Scout Handbook*." Jenna rolled off the bed where she'd been lying on her belly while reading. "I decided you'd refuse the rope request on account of being worried I might hog tie your boss and call it even."

Zane cleared his throat in a very bad cover for the snort of amusement her comment drew from him. He flashed her three fingers. "We're clearing out in three."

More fun adventures . . .

Jenna looked at the pair of handcuffs still on her wrist. She'd snapped the second one closed below the first so it wouldn't dangle. She picked up the book and laid it back on the shelf with the rest, deciding they'd been a set for a long time and didn't need to be broken up.

She had new appreciation of things being taken away from where they belonged. Sam's face was still burned into her mind. She was going to miss him so much.

Tears stung her eyes but she wiped them away.

Life wasn't fair.

Sam and Paul were her adoptive family because

her own blood kin had more in common with leeches than humans. She'd learned young that she wanted more from life than what she could swindle out of the people around her. It meant standing on her own two feet and working harder and always remembering that fairness wasn't something she was owed.

Victory, on the other hand, was something she could claim.

And Sam would kick her ass if he found out she was crying over the way life had decided to throw her for a loop.

Yeah? Well he'd also high-five you for taking the chance to have Dare Servant.

Vulgar?

Sure was.

That didn't make it less true.

And she was going to be comfortable with herself, no matter what. It was all she had at that moment, who she was. Strengths, weaknesses, bad habits, and good ones. So she'd embrace it and hug it tight because what really scared her the most was losing her confidence in being able to make her own way.

"We need to talk."

Carl Davis frowned. Eric Geyer waited for permission to cross over the threshold into his private office.

Carl crocked his finger at his security chief, not caring for the way the man made sure the door was shut.

"Servant's team managed to nab Ji Su, Kirkland's associate." Eric turned his tablet around and showed a live feed of the woman sitting shackled to an interrogation table.

"If she breaks, the Shadow Ops will have enough evidence to convict Kirkland on human trafficking and murder—"

"And there will be a nice money trail leading straight to me," Carl finished.

Eric nodded but remained silent, waiting as Carl thought the matter through.

"Five more months and it wouldn't matter," Carl muttered. He leaned back in his chair, the springs groaning. "Five stinking months." He straightened up and looked Eric in the eye. "Bury the entire operation." He pointed across the desk at his security chief. "This is the test of your new position. If I go down, so do your chances of being head of White House security."

"Servant's team have a witness, three bodies, and now the madam," Eric said. "I can send a man in to kill her but if she dies in interrogation, Servant is just going to know he's digging in the right spot."

Carl drummed his fingers on the desktop for a long moment. "Do it. Better a few agents who think I'm dirty instead of a madam who is talking and can be put on a witness stand in exchange for not being deported. After I'm president, I can use an executive order to shut down the Shadow Ops teams."

Eric nodded and stood.

"Eric." Carl stopped the man from leaving his office. "Good job staying on top of my interests. You're just the sort of man I need at my side."

Carl stared at the closed door for a long moment. He enjoyed power, some might say he was obsessed with it.

Pussies . . .

They tried to color him bad because he won, no matter the cost, and life was a competition sport. Had been since the dawn of time. He was just more honest about what he wanted.

And he was going to get it, even if he had to go through Servant's team to do it.

Carl admitted, he'd enjoy the bloodbath.

Victory was best when the cost was high.

The newest location Dare's team delivered her to had a barn.

Outside the dense urban areas of Southern California, Zane and Thais drove her into the Inland Empire to a house that had enough property for horses.

The animals were long gone. The barn was sitting behind the house, painted a brown and yellow combination.

"Same rules," Zane spoke softly as he came back from checking the bedrooms of the house. "Stay away from the glass."

"There isn't a house in sight," Jenna answered. "Who do you think is going to see me? A squirrel?"

"You might not have a location chip in your shoulder any longer," Thais said on her way through the door with a huge laptop case. "And we might think we've done a good job of making sure our gear is clean, but you can never be too sure."

Zane caught Jenna by the wrist and inserted a key into one of the handcuffs.

"Didn't re-tag me?" Jenna waited for the agent to finish the second cuff before moving away. "There's a surprise. I just assumed you had the surgeon put one in a lot deeper while he had the chance."

"It might have been used to track you while we've got you off grid," Thais said.

The female agent was busy pulling laptops out of her bag. There was a focus in her that made Jenna feel more like a third wheel than ever. It wasn't that she was short, it was just clear Thais wouldn't have thought to fill Jenna in if the question wasn't asked.

"I will close this case and have something to show for my personal effort."

Dare's words rose from her memory.

He'd been honest.

And so had she.

Yeah, brutally honest . . .

Heat teased her cheeks as the memory rose from her mind. Not that Thais or Zane noticed. The two agents were completely focused on bringing their tech on line. She might have found it fascinating except the sight made her realize she was just a piece of evidence being kept on ice until they could move on to the next case.

She wandered into the kitchen, peering into the refrigerator with a skeptical look. Zane appeared right on cue.

He plunked a cluster of plastic shopping bags onto the island in the middle of the kitchen. "Provisions."

He winked and headed into the living room to help set up.

Guess you're on kitchen duty . . .

Jenna put the perishables in the refrigerator as the sun went down. A set of wind chimes was jingling outside the back door. She moved toward it, intending to open it and let in some fresh air.

"You were told to stay away from the glass, Jenna."

She stiffened, freezing, with her hand on the handle of the sliding glass door.

Dare's voice punched all her buttons once again, and

the topic didn't seem to matter a bit, only the fact that he'd emerged from thin air and was telling her what to do without asking her what her plan was.

She flipped the lock and shoved the sliding glass door open anyway.

"Do I really need to put you back in cuffs?" he said.

She turned on him. "There is nothing except that barn out there to see me. I'm not going to become paranoid."

Her words came out in a rush because she'd thought she was composed.

Dare undermined that poise in a few seconds. Her body didn't give a fig for her pride or the fact that she was miffed over him leaving the second he finished with her.

Nope.

All her flesh cared about was how damn much she wanted another taste of him.

His eyes narrowed. "You need to work on adjusting to the situation."

"You're just being a hard-ass," she shot back. "Fine, whatever floats your boat."

She walked through the other doorway that led into the living room. Greer was watching her as she walked across the living room toward a door that would open into another bedroom.

Holding cell . . .

The furniture was covered in a thick layer of dust, the blinds closed tight against the powerful desert sun. Still there was a strip of carpet along the wall that had been bleached over time.

"We're not done talking, Jenna. Procedures are in place for your protection."

Dare followed her into the room.

"You're just putting on a show because you have a problem with them knowing we had sex."

No filter between brain and mouth, but it was working for her right then.

Dare didn't move. He slowly shook his head. "My team is my family, Jenna. They know who I sleep with." He closed the space between them. "In my world, bed partners can be your worst enemy. No one is on this team who doesn't understand there is no privacy."

"Then why did you follow me in here?" she asked. "You wanted me out of sight. Mission accomplished."

His lips thinned. "I need to make sure we have a clear understanding."

"I think you're making it clear you didn't care for the attraction between us."

His lips twitched, curving up and giving her a glance at just how handsome he was when she wasn't facing his professional mask.

"It's there, baby and trust me, you don't want to encourage me."

There was a warning in his tone. The problem was, Jenna was in the perfect mood to jump at the challenge. She propped her hand on her hip. "What evidence do you have to support the fact that I'm a little frightened rabbit who is somehow scared of your big-bad-wolfness?"

There was a strange little thrill twisting through her insides again. This time, it lit her passion up faster because her body recalled precisely how much she'd enjoyed the way they connected.

"You're playing with fire, Jenna."

She snorted at him and flicked her hair. "Won't be the first time I've lit up my own hair. Does save on haircuts though."

His eyes narrowed for a moment. "You actually set your hair on fire?"

"I'm hands on," she offered with a shrug before she reached out and gently tapped the new scrape on his chin. "I sort of expect you to get it. Maybe I'm wrong. Door is behind you."

He was torn. She watched the way he contemplated her, half his rigidness gone while he stubbornly clung to his desire to press her into the position he'd decided served his team best.

"I . . . get . . . it . . . Special Agent Servant." She jabbed him in the center of his chest with her index finger. "I'm just a thing. A piece of supporting evidence. Well I'm neatly stored away so you can get back to your case now."

He caught her hand.

Not her wrist, but her hand.

The touch shocked her because it was so tender. Innocent and sweet. He dropped his professional mask while he stroked her fingers

"Alright, I feel like I should have had more restraint," he admitted. "You're new to the situation, I'm experienced."

A stab of jealously took her by surprise, and knowing that she logically didn't have a hold on him failed to shelter her from the impact.

"No, I haven't had a relationship with a witness before."

"Ahh . . ." She was stepping away from him.

You mean recoiling . . .

"It's kicking my ass," he admitted, holding onto her hand and following her. "I know better. You don't."

He lifted her hand to his lips, kissing the back of it. Remorse was in his eyes, undermining the hold she had on her fear. All of her doubts about her future came rushing toward her.

"Don't pity me." She pulled her hand free and held it against her chest. "I can't take that."

His expression tightened with some sort of decision. "We need some space."

Dare caught her hand again, wrapping his fingers firmly around hers as he turned and led her out of the room. His team members looked up as they emerged but he only took her through the living room and out the open sliding-glass door.

The sun was almost gone, but there was still plenty of warmth in the air. He took her toward the barn, moving around to a set of stairs she hadn't realized ran up the far side of it.

They creaked ominously as he started to climb them.

"They're sound," he advised as he kept climbing up to a door.

She was free for a moment while he dug out a set of keys and opened the door. She followed him through, curious to see where he was taking her.

It was a loft. A railing ran along one side, and there were several large bins stored along another side. Dare moved toward one and pulled the lid off. He lifted something out and turned around to send it unrolling across the floor.

"A sleeping bag? How did you know that was there?"

He raised an eyebrow at her question as he yanked the zipper open and laid it flat.

"I wouldn't let my team move you anywhere I hadn't scouted out first, Jenna."

There was a hard edge in his tone, one that struck her as protective. "I trust you."

And she did.

His lips twitched in response. "Maybe you shouldn't, Jenna." He unclipped his chest harness and held his badge up for her to get a solid look at it. "This is my life."

And he was warning her that he wasn't going to choose her over it.

"But nothing seems to change the fact that I can't stop thinking about getting you alone. I know the logic, and it just won't sink in this time."

He dropped the chest harness beside the make-shift bed, watching her to see her reaction. His hands were curled into fists as he waited.

Waited for her . . .

Jenna moved toward him, laying her hand on his chest and rising onto her toes so she could kiss him. He let her lead for a long moment, standing still while she teased his lips with soft motions of her own.

And then he was framing her face with his hands, his fingers threading into her hair as he took command of the kiss.

She let out a little sound of bliss, the need to kiss him back growing into a hungry impulse that defied any sort of thought process. There was only the way he tasted and the rush of sensation it unleashed and the way she craved more.

"We're going to do this right this time, baby . . ."

He's pulled away from her, maintaining his hold on her head. His midnight eyes glittered with determination, making her insides twist with anticipation.

"I'm not going to rush," he promised.

There was a solid warning in his voice, one that made her shudder. He leaned over, sweeping her hair aside so he could press his lips against the delicate skin of her neck.

"Ohhh . . ."

"Like that," he whispered next to her ear before he was kissing her neck again.

It was slow. So slow she felt like she was caught between the moments of when he was in contact with her and the time that she waited for the next connection to happen.

"I didn't bare you last time . . ."

She shivered, suddenly feeling like her clothing was too hot. But Dare kissed her neck again, this time lingering over her skin and nipping her.

She jumped; earning a soft chuckle from him.

"Two can play this game," she muttered as she turned and slid her hand up his chest. He was hard beneath his shirt, the cotton fabric frustrating her because it was keeping her from the contact she craved.

"I hope so."

There was longing in his tone. It poured fuel on her confidence as she worked the buttons loose on his shirt and moved down to his waistband. His breath was raspy as she popped open his fly, dipping her hand inside to stroke the bulge of his cock.

"God, you drive me insane," he rasped.

It was a rough compliment, the tone of his voice telling how much he wanted to be in control.

But neither of them were. He stepped back and shucked his clothing. Peeling it away as he locked gazes with her, watching her reaction.

Jenna stepped back, enjoying the sight of his skin coming into sight. They'd had sex, and yet she'd never gotten a look at him. Now she watched as he revealed a dark mat of hair on his chest that tapered down into a V around his cock.

He was already hard and swollen, his cock jutting up, thick and ridged.

She reached forward, curling her fingers around it and drawing her hand up to the head.

"Christ . . ."

He leaned his head back, the muscles along his throat tight as she reached down and clasped him at the base.

She caught his scent, inhaling it deeply as she drew her hand up his cock. His breathing was raspy, and her heart accelerated. Honestly, she'd never been so aroused in her life. She could feel her folds growing wet, her clit throbbing softly with need.

It was blunt.

So very physical and yet the most erotic experience she'd ever had.

What had been awkward before felt perfectly right tonight. She slipped to her knees, pumping her hand up and down his shaft. He caught her hair, and, once more, it fit the moment. She opened her mouth and licked him.

"Jenna . . ."

Her name was just an expression, coming from him in a guttural tone of voice that told her how much he was her companion in the moment. Both of them slaves to their cravings.

Junkies of a sort.

She was high on the scent of his skin and the taste, too. She opened her mouth and sucked him, licking through the slit on the head of his cock as she worked her tongue on the underside of it.

His hand tightened in her hair.

His hips thrust toward her as his cock hardened even more.

All of it combined into an intoxicating moment when she was driving him over the same edge that he seemed to be able to push her toward with just his presence.

Well, she was taking him with her.

"Enough . . ."

He was trying to pull her head back but she resisted, taking more of him inside her mouth and working her hand up and down the part of his cock that she couldn't take.

She heard him gasp and shudder and then he was losing the battle, his control slipping as she felt his hips thrusting toward her. His release was hard, his cock spurting its load a moment later.

He ended up pressing a hand onto the wall once it was over, his chest working at a frantic pace as he tried to draw in enough breath.

"Minx . . ."

It was sort of an outdated word, yet the way it rolled out of Dare's mouth made her smile. Jenna stood up as he opened his eyes and gave her a glimpse at the satisfaction glittering in those dark orbs.

"Payback . . . is going to be my pleasure . . . my extreme pleasure . . ." he informed her.

Jenna lifted one finger into the air. "My turn."

Dare straightened, determination glittering in his eyes. "Oh no, baby, it's definably my turn."

He came toward her.

Stalking her really.

It stole her breath, hitting her with more arousal than she'd ever felt. She fell back, the single step making his eyes narrow.

Dare surged toward her, lifting her high as she squealed and kicked. He spun her around before lowering her to the sleeping bag.

"How's your back?"

He'd laid her out like a kill.

Or a feast . . .

Jenna stretched out in answer. It earned her a flash of a grin before he was popping open the waistband of her jeans and dragging them down her body.

"Better . . ." he muttered before he went back for her underwear. They ended up tossed aside before he was grabbing the hem of her shirt and baring her torso.

Jenna was sitting up, her bra the only thing left on. She was suddenly so aware of how much bigger he was than herself. Every inch of his body was sculpted and packed with muscle. From his jaw to his feet, he was a force to be reckoned with.

He noticed the shift in her mood.

Of course he did. The guy was too sharp to miss it.

"Show yourself to me baby . . ."

He was waiting for her to. His dark eyes focused on her as he waited for her to unfreeze.

"I've kicked myself over not taking the time to undress last time. You're stunning."

He reached out and cupped her hip. Pleasure washed over his features, the kind that couldn't be faked. It melted through the paralysis that had settled on her. She unhooked her bra and let it slip down her arms.

"Perfect . . . just perfect."

He was cooing and moving over her. Joining her on the soft flannel of the sleeping bag as the outer weatherproof layer crinkled slightly against the floor of the loft. He pressed her down, smoothing her hair back as he kissed her. He surrounded her, their limbs tangling as they tasted one another in a hungry jumble.

She wanted him inside her, shifting her thighs apart so that he'd be cradled between them.

"Not . . . a . . . chance . . . baby . . ."

There was a hard warning in his tone. He pulled her

head back, controlling her with his greater strength. Promise was dancing in his eyes.

"I told you Jenna . . . it's my turn . . ."

He was slipping down her body, pushing her thighs apart with his hands, hovering over her sex.

"Maybe . . ."

She really wasn't sure what she'd intended to say. Her brain was shutting down, refusing to make sense of anything except touching him.

Dare looked up her body. "Why do you think I brought you out here?" The hard warning was back in his tone. He was looking up her body, freezing the breath in her lungs with the look in his eyes. "I want to hear you scream, baby."

She was a hair's breadth from it already. The first touch of his breath on her folds made her squirm, but Dare held her, lowering his head and teasing the delicate skin along the outside of her sex.

She let out a little sound of bliss.

He chuckled.

And then there was only the storm of him driving her insane. He licked and sucked, moving around her clit while she withered in need of just a little more pressure to send her over the edge. He denied her that, keeping her poised on the edge of the climax.

"Dare . . ." she growled. "Stop teasing me."

He lifted his head, looking up her body. "You want me to make you cum?"

She'd never vocalized such a thing before. Jenna bit her lip as she shied away from saying such a thing. Dare slowly rubbed her clit with his thumb.

"Don't hide from me baby . . . tell me what you want . . ."

So simple and yet more exposing than she'd ever

dared to be. There was a demand for control in his eyes, one she was used to seeing, only this time is was much, much more personal.

"I want you inside me."

His eyes narrowed, and then he was rising above her. The sight stole her breath. He fumbled for a moment with a condom before covering her again.

She let out a groan. Maybe it wasn't a polite sound but it was so very honest.

"That's right baby, this time we don't have to be quiet . . ."

And they weren't. Sound went bouncing off the walls of the barn, his, hers, Jenna could no longer distinguish where he ended and she began.

And she didn't want to either.

They moved together, caught in a quest for a common goal. The instinct went deeper than any need she'd ever encountered before. Dare was right there as well, trying to get closer, straining deeper as she lifted her hips to take everything he offered. There was more pleasure in the motion, something that made her want to resist the final explosion.

She wanted to be trapped in the moment forever, but her body would not be denied. Climax swept through her, snapping like a board under too much pressure. It was harsh and yet a release and then there was only the pleasure.

A blinding amount of bliss spun her around while Dare shuddered and lost his own battle to fend off losing control.

CHAPTER FIVE

"Kids still in the barn?" Zane asked.

"If they were kids, they wouldn't be in the barn," Thais replied.

Zane sent her a cocky grin. "Don't bet on it."

Thais looked over her workstation, sending Zane a scathing look.

"Now don't make promises you aren't going to keep, lady." Zane laid a hand over his chest. "I have a delicate heart."

Thais slowly stood. She fell into a soft swaying pace as she moved toward the new agent. Zane lost his playful smile as she approached him and trailed a fingertip along his back while circling him.

"You're one of those . . . I see," she said in a husky drawl. She smiled, leaning closer to the agent while tapping him in the middle of his chest and pushing him back in his chair.

"One of what?"

Thais was leaning over him, captivating him with a playful expression. A moment later she'd pulled his gun and leapt back out of his reach.

"One of the men who thinks I didn't earn my badge and that I'm only here for when the work entails slipping between someone's sheets."

Zane had gone deadly serious. "You seem a little touchy on the subject."

Thais laid his gun down on the table near her. "And you're the new guy. Don't judge my team lead."

Zane picked up his gun and slid it back into his chest-harness holster. "Or the fact that he's nailing his witness?"

"The situation is unique," Greer added.

Zane wasn't intimidated. He crossed his arms over his chest. "Sorry, my mistake. I thought Shadow Ops meant we were dealing with the unusual but still performing our duties with professionalism."

"Go ahead, keep shooting me daggers lady." He looked up, catching Thais. "I enjoy knowing I have your attention."

Thais's lips pressed into a moue before she returned her attention to her work.

"Have something to add?" Zane turned to return the look Greer was sending him. "Because I'll tell the lot of you what I think of hanky-panky on a case."

"By all means, enlighten us," Greer said.

"It gets people killed." Zane spoke in a tone that expressed just how intimate he was with the reality of what he said. "Good agents who are stuck with a lead who is distracted. Yeah, I'm the new guy because I survived. So don't expect me to keep my mouth shut when I know how something like that—" he used his thumb to gesture toward the barn—"can translate into all of us getting whacked."

No one argued with him. Silence stretched out because

there was a hard foundation of logic supporting his statement.

"Like you said," Greer said at last, "we deal with the unusual. Just consider this one of those times when the lines are blurred."

Zane didn't care for the comment, but Greer sent him a stern look that made it clear the Scot wasn't all too worried about the fact that they were in disagreement. Thais returned her focus to her equipment, letting the two men take each other's measure.

She was alone.

Jenna opened her eyes, feeling the chill of night.

"Don't move."

Dare was moving around, his voice coming out of the darkness.

"What's wrong?"

She sat up as she heard a zipper opening.

"You're cold," he said.

Dare came close enough for her to see him again. He brought a second sleeping bag with him, pulling her back down and tucking her against his side as he settled the second sleeping bag over them. She shivered because the fabric was cold.

"Give it a moment," he muttered as he smoothed a hand down her side.

He'd put her on his left, with her head on his shoulder. The moon was rising, offering enough light for her to see his gun lying next to his right hand.

"Should we go back inside?" she asked.

He tensed, the hand on her side gripping her hip. "If you want to."

She didn't . . .

Silence surrounded them for a long moment before Dare let out a snort.

"Going to just leave me hanging?" She decided not to let the issue go unanswered.

"Maybe I'm worried I'll spook you if I tell you I want to stay right here," Dare answered her.

There it was again, lack of filter between brain and mouth. Only this time, she giggled at her own expense. Dare shifted, cupping her chin and lifting her face so he could see it.

"What's funny?" he demanded.

She bit her lip.

One of his eyebrows rose. "Want me to make you talk?" His lips rose into a menacing grin.

Jenna gasped but too late. He flipped her onto her back and dug his fingers into her belly.

"No . . . Don't . . ." she gasped as he tickled her, keeping her in place and tormenting her until she was ready to pass out from lack of oxygen.

"Spill . . ." he demanded with his hand poised in the air above her.

Jenna shook her head, her lips parting in a smile as she closed her hands around his cock. "Checkmate."

"Not even close." He rolled onto his back to evade her.

Jenna followed, clamping her thighs around his hips. She was sitting on top of him, his length pressed into her folds as the second sleeping bag fell off them.

"Hmmm," he mumbled as he reached up to cup her breasts. "There might be merit to letting you think you've won."

She leaned down, allowing his cock to rise up. "Trust me, Dare Servant, I can kick your ass."

He slid his hands down to her bottom, gripping it and

keeping her poised above him. "I know you can, baby. Why do you think I was such an ass today?"

It was an admission, one that warmed her heart.

What did it mean? She wasn't really sure, only very certain she didn't want to waste the time they'd stolen on things like contemplation.

The moment was theirs, and she had every intention of savoring it to the fullest.

The sun would rise right on time. Until then, Dare Servant was hers.

A phone buzzed sometime before dawn.

Jenna shifted, waking up completely due to how much sleep she'd had in the last week.

"My boss."

Dare swept the screen and held it up to his ear. "Stand by."

Their make-shift bed was kicked aside as Dare stood and stepped into his pants. He surged into his shirt and grabbed his gun, shoving it into the waistband of his pants before he was lifting the phone to his ear again and striding toward the door.

Damn, he was a force of nature.

Jenna focused on just how much of a thrill she got from watching the way he moved. That was what she wanted to take away from her time with him, not a bucket full of pity for something that just wasn't going to happen.

Because he's decided his job is more important.

She snorted at herself.

Don't get pissy . . . you made a choice.

Yeah, and the flip side of the coin of living in the moment was shouldering the choice she'd made.

She refused to regret reaching for Dare when she'd had the chance.

She was going to treasure that moment and it looked like her reminiscing was going to start really soon.

"I'm here." Dare kept his voice low as he went down the steps.

"Don't be too sure," Kagan replied.

Dare felt his brain shift into a different mode. He knew Kagan, and the tone his section leader was using wasn't a good one.

Shit had just hit the fan somewhere.

"Ji Su is dead," Kagan stated flatly.

"How?" Dare demanded.

"Inside interrogation. And they didn't even bother to try and make it look like suicide. Someone sent us a message."

"Fuck," Dare snarled.

Kagan grunted. "Scrub your operation. There aren't a whole lot of men who could pull something like this off, and my short list has Carl Davis at the top of it."

"And if he knew about Ji Su, he can find my team," Dare finished.

"I'm sending you a drop point," Kagan continued. "Witness protection can't be trusted. Give the girl your scrub kit and send her to the pick-up. Scuttle everything and regroup. I will handle her pick-up." Kagan cut the line to avoid having the call scanned and picked up.

Dare didn't want someone else to handle Jenna. Yet it was the logical thing to do. One Dare shouldn't have taken any issue with.

It wasn't the first time he turned a witness over blindly either.

But he found his temper rising. He'd been up against Carl Davis in the past. Backed Saxon Hale and Vitus up on missions where Carl was a major player. It had been tense, involving betrayal and honorless men.

Today, he was dangerously close to losing his temper with the man. But Kagan was right on the money. Carl had a reach that was impressive. Keeping Jenna near would be a death sentence for her.

Dare punched a code into his phone. His team would respond inside three minutes to it. They'd begin a very precise and quickly executed departure, one he'd participated in numerous times before.

Only today he didn't see dropping off his witness as a closure.

Well, at least one that he was looking forward to.

His temper was red-hot now. Carl Davis needed to die, but the odds were stacked against Dare and his team instead.

That fact got him moving. If Carl had gotten someone in an interrogation center wacked, digging up Dare's location wouldn't pose much of a problem. They had to move before it happened.

Jenna's life hung in the balance.

Jenna found her clothing and dressed. The night was giving way to first light, the first bird song filling the air. She was wrestling with the top sleeping bag when she heard Dare return.

A chill touched her neck.

It didn't make a whole lot of sense until she turned and got a good look at his face. He was locked up, his body tight as he contemplated her.

"I'm getting the feeling this is the last time I'm going to see you." Jenna didn't bother to lament the lack of filter between her brain and mouth. She pretty much knew without a doubt that even if she'd been the queen of tact, there was no way she'd have managed to hold in her thoughts.

His lips thinned as he clenched his jaw.

Right. She'd known the way it was going to go.

It was time to prove she could deal with it.

Jenna lowered her eyes, her gaze landing on Dare's chest harness. The breaking dawn was illuminating the badge.

His badge . . .

She reached down and snagged the harness, straightened up, and offering it to him. "You were clear about how you felt."

She expected him to take the harness, maybe give her a quick glimpse of him looking somewhat regretful that they were parting.

But in the end, he'd put the harness on.

Just as he'd promised her he would.

"Jesus Christ," Dare growled before he framed her face with his large hands.

She gasped, the contact the last thing she'd expected. It shattered her composure, baring her emotions.

Which was why she recoiled. Pulling away from him in a desperate attempt to keep her wits when all she wanted to do was have a meltdown.

Dare drew up tight.

"I can't think when you touch me." She shouldn't have said it. "Fuck. Sorry, that was emotional. You made it clear . . . last night . . . the way you feel."

He caught her around the waist, pulling her against his body and pinning her to his hard length as he threaded one hand through her hair and pulled the strands tight enough to make her his prisoner.

"I'm a hard ass . . ." he growled before he kissed her.

It was a hard kiss.

A desperate one.

He was moving so fast, she struggled to keep up. His lips parting hers, frantic to make sure he was kissing her deeply and completely. Jenna soaked it up, reaching for him, melting into his embrace as she kissed him back with all the hunger she had inside her.

Dare pulled away, the sound of their panting filling the loft. "I have to get you away from me."

He was suddenly turning around and grabbing his shoes and socks.

"Why?"

He sent her a look that chilled her blood.

"I can't tell you, but I've got to get you some place safe."

He finished up by buckling his chest harness and checking his gun. He reached back and grabbed her wrist.

"Which means you're not in a safe place," she said.

Dare turned on her. She bumped into him and he cupped the side of her face with his hand.

"This is my life, Jenna." His eyes glittered with hard purpose. "I choose it and I can't tell you why, but I need it to keep my demons on a leash." He rubbed the side of her face. "Believe me when I say, this is the first time, you're the first time, I've wanted to second-think things."

His face hardened, locking her outside his emotions.

"But circumstances are not going to allow me that luxury. I've got to get you moving."

He was fast on action, turning away from her and tugging her toward the door by the hold he had on her wrist.

It was all happening too fast.

She didn't have a chance to think.

Greer was coming across the yard toward the barn,

the agent looking like he was expecting a battle to erupt at any second. He fell into step behind her, his eyes moving along the roof line and behind them.

She'd never felt so at risk.

The reason was plain enough. Dare and his team had always been relaxed and in control except for those few moments she recalled from the docks when they had been in action.

It was a stark difference, one that alarmed her and sent a shiver down her spine.

They were moving her quickly. The kitchen passed in a blur as they went right into the living room of the house. There was a frantic packing party in progress—Zane, Thais, all pulling cords and shoving laptops into cases with a speed that flatly horrified her.

They expected trouble.

As in the deadly sort.

"Here." Zane tossed something at Dare.

"Put this on Jenna."

He didn't wait for her to comply. Dare opened the black ski mask and stretched it wide so he could pull it over her head.

"Vest," he muttered while she was still adjusting to the knit fabric clinging to her face. Greer actually opened the vest behind her while Dare pulled it up her arms and buckled it around her chest.

He gave a node of satisfaction when it was done and the rest of the team finished.

"Zane . . ."

The agent pulled his gun and went through the front door first.

"Clear."

Thais went next, weighted down by luggage.

"If something happens . . . keep moving," Dare said before they were following his team.

Her damned heart was pounding so hard it felt like it might just bust through her sternum. Dare pulled her across the driveway and was pushing her up and into the SUV before she got a chance to even look around.

She half fell across the seat as Dare came up behind her and pushed her into the center. "Keep your head down, Jenna."

Doors slammed shut and the SUV was pulling back as Dare pushed her head down. She bounced around in the seat as Zane took them down the road and around a corner. She caught just a glimpse of trees and street lamps as they went down the road. The SUV slowed down for a traffic signal and then she listened to the engine revving as they accelerated up a ramp leading to the freeway.

Dare rubbed her back. The soothing motion of his hands sent tears into her eyes. At least having her face on her knees allowed her to keep them secret. They jolted down the road for another twenty minutes before she heard the engine slowing.

"You're doing fine, Jenna." Dare was stoking her again. "We're going to do this quick and clean."

The SUV was turning, accelerating, and then slowing as it turned again.

"Mask and vest off."

Greer pulled her up by the back of the vest. She let out a sigh of relief as the mask was removed, lifting her hands to brush her hair out of her face. Dare was unbuckling the vest as Jenna caught Thais looking at her in the little vanity mirror on the inside of the sun shade in the passenger seat.

"Hair and make-up." Thais was turning around, offing a brush. "You have bed head."

"No time," Zane announced as he slowed down for another turn. "Drop point."

Thais shoved the brush toward Jenna as the SUV glided to a stop. Dare was pushing the door open in the same moment. He pulled her through the open door as Greer tossed a windbreaker and backpack at him.

A second later, the SUV was pulling away and Dare tugged her into a storm drain.

It was a huge cement pipe. A dark trail of algae marked the bottom of it but the water was long gone.

"Fix your hair."

Dare was shrugging into the windbreaker, covering his chest harness and badge. Jenna tugged the brush through her hair a few times before Dare was gesturing her down the drainage pipe.

"I wouldn't do this if I didn't have a choice."

It wasn't that she questioned whether or not he'd spoken, it was what he said that gave Jenna pause.

He sounded like he cared.

Don't go there . . .

Dare pulled her deeper into the tunnel. It wasn't really dark because sunlight was streaming in from the opposite end where Jenna could see the dry river bed. Above her head, traffic was flowing down the interstate they were walking beneath. Dare pulled her to a stop before they made it to that opening.

"This is why I can't get involved," Dare continued.

He was looking at her, showing her something Jenna had never seen in his eyes before.

Regret.

He caught her by the upper arms. "What I do is dangerous."

—"I just left a house wearing a ski mask and body armor," she muttered. "I'm pretty clear on the dangerous part."

He shook his head. "Someone killed my other witness while she was in interrogation lock up."

Jenna felt her eyes widen.

More like bug out . . .

"That sounds mega bad," she said.

Dare nodded. "It means we have a leak. One with a lot of resources. My team is being scuttled to protect them."

He offered her the backpack.

"Supplies including cash and untraceable wealth. Keep it hidden, use only what you need, you're going to be traveling for a while."

He pressed it against her chest. Jenna clasped it, trying to get her brain to keep up.

"But . . . Where . . ."

"Walk out there, head north . . ." Dare pointed. "Walk under as much cover as you can, stay on the rocks to avoid leaving tracks. Keep going until someone shows up to get you."

"What?" She looked at the dry river bed. "I'm just going to know what stranger to trust?"

Dare cupped the side her face, bringing her gaze back to his.

"Trust me, Jenna, you'll know." He jerked his head behind them. At the far end of the tunnel, Thais was waiting, the black body armor and ski mask on. "The kind of people who I'm investigating know me. I'm marked, anyone on my team is marked. You have to disappear without me."

"You're going to put yourself out as bait . . ."

Dare nodded.

Jenna fought the urge to retch.

"Don't," he warned her softly. "Don't think about me. I knew what I was getting into."

"So I shouldn't realize how much danger you're putting yourself into on my account?" she demanded.

His lips twitched, flashing her that grin that made him far too handsome. "You were spot-on to tell me it was my fault you were here. I can't even say I'm sorry because I'm not." His fingers tightened on her cheek before he was moving back.

"I'm too selfish to truly regret knowing you baby," he said.

She felt like he was ripping himself away from her. *He was . . .*

There was a hardness to his expression, one she'd seen the first time he'd interrogated her. He was going to do whatever he felt was needed, no matter the cost.

He pointed behind her, ordering her to go.

Jenna slowly smiled and crossed her arms over her chest as she stood in place. He grinned in response, shaking his head.

Turning around took more effort than it should have. *You knew he wasn't the sticking-around kind . . .*

Yeah, but tears still stung her eyes. Walking into the morning light made the water droplets sparkle where they were hanging off the ends of her eyelashes. She shrugged the backpack onto her shoulder and ventured out into the dry riverbed.

It was time to begin a new chapter of her life.

Her scent was still clinging to his skin.

Dare watched as Thais was handed off to a set of agents who had no idea who she was. They were handling her like a civilian, and his very capable Shadow Ops agent was bristling. Not that Thais allowed it to show on her face. No, the only real tip-off was the fact that if anyone took a close look, they'd notice the rather bored look in her eyes that betrayed how much she wasn't afraid of anything. She'd played bait before. In body armor and wearing a ski mask, anyone tailing them would follow her.

Dare turned and walked down a length of sidewalk. He ducked inside a pharmacy and headed for the pre-paid phones. He tossed cash down on the counter and made his way outside before punching in the number the two agents had handed him on a slip of paper.

"Glad to hear you're alive," Kagan answered.

"Jenna?"

"She's being handled," his section leader replied. "I'll have your ride find you."

The call ended. That was Kagan's style. Short and to the point. Normally Dare thrived on it. Today, he realized he would have liked to know more about Jenna's circumstances.

You can't ever know anything about her again . . .

It was exactly what he'd thought he'd wanted out of life. The path he'd chosen and worked his ass off to put his feet on.

So why the doubts now?

Dare wasn't too comfortable with knowing he was asking himself that question. Ji Su's death proved he was in far too deep to ever contemplate something like having a relationship.

And yet, he was thinking about Jenna. Recalling the details of her scent, the way her pixie haircut swished around her face and made her look playful. She stuck her chin out when she was getting ready to stand up to him, and he loved her curvy butt.

A Jeep slid up to the curb in front of him. Dare opened the door, frowning as he recognized Greer.

"You don't need to remind me of the definition of scuttle." Greer had a military-grade desert hat pulled down over his head. The brown-and-tan fatigue fabric went well with the dented-up Jeep.

"I disagree," Dare informed his teammate. "Because you're here and you should be gone."

"Not leaving you," Greer responded, his attention on the traffic in front of them. "Not now or ever."

"This shit with Carl is going to get nasty."

Greer headed for the freeway. "The moment Tyler Martin sold us out, there was going to be no way it was going to be settled without blood."

Dare nodded. "Too bad killing Tyler Martin didn't teach Carl Davis to leave us alone."

"We're messing with his money supply," Greer replied. "Kirkland keeps Carl in front of every voter. The media empire his father built is too complex for Carl to not want at his disposal. Why do you think Kirkland is a mega-music sensation? His songs are given priority on the airwaves and in television and movie productions."

"It's going to be a fight to the death, Carl Davis or Shadow Ops," Dare said.

Which was why he had to stop thinking about Jenna.

"You're thinking about the girl."

"When are you going to tell me what the deal is with your sister?" Dare countered.

Greer surprised him by bristling.

"Now I really need to know," Dare said after a few miles.

"Because it gets under my skin?" Greer's Scottish accent was bleeding through, proving the subject was a sensitive one.

"Because I can't back you up if I don't know what to look for," Dare answered. "You were tearing into Caxton's men pretty deep."

Greer changed lanes to go around slower traffic, his knuckles white because he was gripping the steering wheel so hard. "Sorcha is an operative."

Dare made a motion with his hand suggesting Greer should continue.

Greer snorted. "Those bastards want me to forget she exists. Won't even give me a fucking phone number to reach her with. The truth is, I got this badge to make sure I had enough security clearance to talk to me own blood." He snarled softly and cut Dare a warning glance. "Put any of that in my file, and I'll rip your balls off."

Dare sent Greer an equally hard glance back. "I survived my family's slaughter. My Dad took on big drug pushers and they killed my Mom and siblings in front of him. She shoved me in a cabinet, promised me a slice of cake if I stayed quiet. I walked past her body on the way out the door. This badge is how I deal with it."

Greer sent him a surprised look. "Guess that explains why you turned the girl loose."

"It was for her protection."

Greer scoffed at him. "Ye could have sent her to the nest and you know it. Saxon would have let you join his happy team of married agents."

He could have.

Dare wanted to move past that idea, but it clung to his mind as the sun set.

He'd known her less than two weeks. There was no reason to be hung up on her. Logic dictated he scuttle her and stick to his life plan. There would be other women he'd enjoy sex with before returning to the job he'd pledged his life to.

So why did he feel like such a fool this time?

"You'll know . . ."

Jenna heard Dare's voice in her head as the sun was setting. Her feet were killing her, she was starving, and she'd sweat so much, she felt like a glazed donut.

But she knew him when she spotted the guy.

He was built like a linebacker. As in a really effective linebacker. His head was shaved and he had a look in his eyes that reminded her of professional mix martial-arts fighters. A love of the action that would override anything like pain. He fought because he was addicted to the thrill of flesh-on-flesh contact. Pain was just proof of his own invincibility.

He was hunkered down beside a huge boulder. Even on his haunches, the guy's head was level with the middle of her chest. Jenna stopped and felt every one of her aches as she stared at the guy, but she faced him with a steady look because there was no way she was going to shirk.

"Guess you're 'the guy,'" she said.

He pushed to his feet and contemplated her. "Name's Kagan."

Vitus Hale knew Washington D. C.

But not in the same way other people did. He was an ex-SEAL, which only meant he was retired from active duty. He pressed his thumb into a fingerprint scanner and waited for it to identify him.

Retirement had once been a profane word.

Now? It represented a happiness he'd been too young and stupid to understand. The door in front of him slid

open, allowing him inside what looked like a very ne-
glected hallway. There were cobwebs along the edges
of the ceiling and tracks in the middle of the floor where
people had walked. Vitus moved down its dingy length,
making two turns before he stopped and pressed his face
against another scanner that would use his retina for
identification.

This time, the door that slid open was double sealed
and reinforced. There was a marine on duty, armed with
a high-powered rifle. He was encased in a bullet proof
case that had a narrow slit for the muzzle of his rifle to
poke out of. He watched as Vitus stopped at a third identification station and waited for a thermal scan of his
face.

When the system cleared him, he offered the soldier
a salute before moving down the hallway. He'd made it
almost all the way to his wife's quarters when Damascus
came around a corner and threw herself at him.

"Princess . . ."

She let out a sigh before he smothered it in a kiss. Vitus
pulled her as close as her distended belly would allow.
Even so, their daughter kicked him before he released
his pregnant wife.

"She's your baby completely." Damascus smoothed
a hand across her belly. "I don't get a moment's respite."

Vitus grinned, placing his hand over where their un-
born baby was wiggling. "I seem to recall you being more
than spunky a few times."

"Spunky and obnoxious are two vastly different
things," Damascus informed him with a twitch of her
lips. "This kid has got to be a boy. I don't care what the
sonogram suggested."

Vitus followed his wife into her underground living
space. The top-secret labs she worked in were sealed to

prevent leaks of the highly contagious pathogens being researched there. Diseases that could so easily be applied as weapons of mass destruction if they made it into the hands of some fanatical nutcase who believed he was serving some higher being by wiping out a section of the population.

"Now tell me why you're here, Vitus Hale." Damascus turned on her husband.

"To see your mother."

Damascus had propped her hands onto her hips. Her belly stuck out, pleasing him in a way he'd never suspected it might.

"Why?" she demanded.

"I don't know," he answered truthfully. "That's why I came to see you first. I might not have a chance afterwards. Since it's the last stretch of the election vote gathering, I imagine she called me for something important."

His wife knew what he was. Knew he worked with the Shadow Ops teams. But it shocked him to see her eyes fill with tears.

"Princess . . ."

Damascus sucked in a hard breath and muttered a word he didn't often hear cross her lips. "Hormones . . ." she groused as she wiped her eyes. "I cry over the stupidest things these days."

"Nice to know it isn't concern for me."

Her eyes flooded again, this time spilling over onto her cheeks. Vitus had started to grin, but his enjoyment of teasing his wife died in horror as her cheeks became streaked by salt-water drops.

"I should let you feel guilty," Damascus muttered before she was hugging him and pulling him down for a kiss. "But I'm just so happy to see you."

"Likewise, Princess," Vitus muttered before he buried his head in her hair. "I've got to go. Promise me you'll stay in the labs until I give you an all clear?"

"Wait a second." Vitus had set her back, shooting her a very serious look that she recognized from when he'd had to rescue her. "You didn't come by to see me?"

"I did," he insisted in a guarded tone.

Damascus shook her head. "You"—she pointed at him—"came down here to rat on me to Colonel Magnus and make sure he keeps me inside while you're dealing with whatever my mother needs you for."

"That doesn't mean I didn't come to see you as well, Princess," Vitus defended himself.

"Glad you filled her in."

Damascus gasped and spun around. Colonel Bryan Magnus was sitting in a chair on the far side of the room. The commanding officer of the labs sent her husband a cocky grin. "Because I sure didn't want to be the man on the front line." The colonel stood up. "Pregnant women get away with everything. Half my staff will put salt in my coffee if they think I caused her tears."

"It would serve you right if I cry during tomorrow's staff briefing," Damascus muttered.

The Colonel shot Vitus a hard look. "I can't begin to tell you how much I hope you call me before tomorrow."

Vitus nodded and looked back at his wife. "Be good, Princess."

Damascus narrowed her eyes.

"Your mother called me. Let me give her my full attention."

His wife stiffened and nodded. She was back in his arms, kissing him good-bye.

Kagan was watching her. Jenna contemplated the house he'd driven them to.

It's got character, she decided.

The little house was half hidden in an overgrown orange grove. The trees were growing wild now, some of them dead where drought had taken its toll but there were still several that were huge, their limbs weighed down by fruit-laden limbs. The lack of tending meant there were piles of dead branches and leaves and dead tumble weeds from the last winter.

"Tell me there is running water and I'll be ecstatic," Jenna said.

Kagan was wiggling a key in the weathered lock. There was a crunching sound before he was able to turn it and push the door in.

"Don't count on hot water," he advised as he peered inside.

"Beggars can't be choosers," Jenna said, eager to find a shower.

Kegan held up a hand, warning her to stop. "Stay here."

He was gone a moment, moving through the little house on silent feet. The sun had set, bringing with it the evening breeze. It blew across the threshold, disturbing the pile of dust and dried foxtails that had worked their way under the doorjamb. There were vintage wooden floors inside and plywood over the windows.

She heard the distinct sound of running water from beyond the living room she could see into.

"I'll take that as an invitation to enter the premises," she said loud enough for Kagan to hear her.

He reappeared in the hallway, filling the space completely. "Make yourself at home. I'm going to find some dinner."

The house was tiny. Just two bedrooms and a single bathroom.

Yeah, well there is a shower.

Jenna dug beneath the sink for a moment, grinning when she found a bar of soap among the jumble of cleaning supplies and towels that looked less than fresh. She opened up one of the towels and gave it a snap before stripping down.

She sucked in her breath at the temperature of the water. It was a cruel twist of fate that the temperatures above ground was so dammed hot but the water stayed so cool in the pipes. She worked the soap through her hair and down her body.

She shouldn't still smell Dare.

But she did as she climbed back into her clothing.

You have to move on.

She left the bathroom, going into the bedroom. There wasn't any furniture in it, just a pile of camping gear.

The sleeping bag sent a memory churning through her.

You knew it was only for the moment.

Yeah, that still didn't keep her from noticing how much she missed Dare.

Dare . . . she'd never asked if it was his real name. He might not have told her, and, honestly, it made more sense that he'd have given her no way to reach out to him.

Right. He told you he'd go on with his life.

And he had.

So she would as well.

"Vitus . . ." Miranda Delacroix gasped.

Her hotel suite was plush and polished.

"Replace your security," Vitus said from where he was leaning against a pillar.

"Dunn said the same thing." Miranda shook her head and waved her hand in the air. "Not that it matters."

"It matters because I'm in here and they don't know it," Vitus insisted.

"Yes . . ." Miranda was distracted by going across the suite to where her purse was sitting on a desk. "This is why I called you . . . the number I had for Kagan wasn't any good . . . and I think you'll want to see this . . ."

Vitus listened, watching the video. His body tightened as it played.

"Who else knows you have this?" he asked.

"No one," Miranda answered. "Carl knows too many people and even more are kissing up to him because it looks like he's going to win the election."

Vitus nodded. He took the phone and plugged it into the laptop sitting on the desk. "I'm making a couple of copies."

"Yes, that's wise," Miranda answered.

"I'm also ratting you out to Dunn," Vitus informed her.

Miranda stiffened. Vitus sent her a firm look. "I married your daughter, and your husband was an asshole. I did a background on you. You are Dunn's birth mother and gave custody to his father after you ran away with a man your family didn't approve of." His lips twitched. "Damascus is a lot like you."

Miranda turned white. Vitus cussed as he lunged up, catching her by the forearm as her knees started to buckle. He had to let her down or risk tearing her shoulder. Miranda landed on the edge of a glass coffee table. It was just a sheet of glass lying on the frame, and the thing flipped up, falling over onto the polished title floor with a crash.

The door of the suite opened a moment later. "Freeze!" Miranda's security looked down their guns at Vitus.

"It was just an accident," Miranda sputtered. "Clumsy of me."

"Oh . . . sorry, Madam Delacroix . . . I didn't realize you had family over."

"Because you didn't see me come in," Vitus informed the guy. "Leave your post again and you'll answer to me."

The guy didn't care for the reprimand, but he nodded and pulled the door shut.

Vitus helped Miranda to her feet. "No one should know . . . not even you."

"I doubt many people could find the link. He looks more like his father, which is good considering he's around you more often these days," Vitus said

"Who Dunn is in relation to me has nothing to do with why I called you, Vitus. There is no reason to bring him into my life where someone else will realize he's my son," Miranda tried to reason.

"I owe Dunn," Vitus said as he finished with the computer. "And he helped us find Damascus. Dunn is a good man, one to be proud of. He'd never forgive me if I didn't tell him you're not secure, and this"—he waved the phone at her—"this could send Carl Davis over the edge."

"If you are talking about a cliff, I certainly hope so," Miranda said. "It's far past time for him to get what he deserves."

Vitus flashed her a smile. "I'll do my best to make that a reality."

"And I will call my son myself, thank you."

Vitus crossed his arms over his chest and faced off with her.

"I have lived all of my life with men controlling every detail of my day," she insisted. "You need to allow me to help myself."

Vitus drew in a deep breath and let it out while contemplating her. "I'll be in touch."

He gave her a nod before he was striding across the tile floor. Housekeeping was just outside the door, coming in to clean up the mess.

Miranda went into the bedroom to hide her smile. They wouldn't understand how good it felt to know she had put in motion something that would help bring Carl Davis down. There had been few times in her life when she'd felt like she'd done something significant.

Tonight was one of those moments.

"It's untraceable wealth."

Jenna looked up at Kagan, her jaw still hanging open. The backpack had yielded some stunning surprises.

There was a small zip-lock bag in her fingers with several loose diamonds inside it.

Kagan didn't even blink. "Diamond values are kept inflated by crafty marketing and a monopoly on most of the mines. It makes them a good source of untraceable income. Once you're resettled, you can sell those to establish another residence. We can't liquidate your condo and send the money to you. It would leave a trail. Those are a trade-out for what you're losing to secure your identity."

"Right." She tried to sound like she had it together but the truth was that composure was just a whisper on the wind. The little shiny diamonds should have represented the power to establish a life that was hers but all she saw was the permanent separation from Dare.

"There's a decent selection of canned goods in the pantry. I turned the gas on so you can use the range," Kagan continued. He wasn't really at ease.

Well, he doesn't look like the sort of man who ends up on babysitting duty.

No, he didn't, but he was making an effort for her sake.

"Great." Jenna stood up, trying to at least look like she had a grip on herself.

Kagan's expression didn't give his thoughts away, but he definitely struck her as the type of guy who wasn't impressed by bullshit.

"Know how to use this?" Kagan held up a gun.

"I've got the basic idea," she answered as she took it from him.

"Good." He watched her for a second. "No one knows you're here. Everything you need is laid out on the kitchen counter. Follow the instructions and you'll be fine."

He was leaving her.

Jenna bit her lip to keep from saying anything.

"Thanks." Seemed lame.

So she watched him leave, standing in the doorway as he got in the truck they'd driven to the house in and backed up the driveway.

In the distance, there were lights where a housing tract was. They'd passed lines of construction equipment on their way into the orange grove. The house was scheduled for leveling so a new community could be built.

New chapter.

Right . . .

Moving into the kitchen, she looked at the items he'd left her. A hat with a note that said to wear it when she was in the city to shield her face. A set of keys and another note telling her a car was in the garage. Jenna didn't go and look. Instead she stared at the passport on the counter. It was open to where her picture was.

Katie Sherlock.

And according to the passport, she lived in Florida.

There was a job and a history but she found herself left cold. A new chapter would include excitement. Only she was still dealing with the death of the last part of her life.

You'll be fine . . .

Maybe.

Just like the house, she was being wiped off the face of the earth, no one left to remember her.

Dare would.

Come on . . . he'll move on to the next case . . .

It was a bitter truth, one she'd thought herself prepared for.

Well, she wasn't but at least she was alone.

No one would know how many tears she cried.

Or how many of them fell for the loss of Dare Servant.

"I took care of Ji Su."

Carl Davis enjoyed delivering his information to Kirkland. "She will never tell anyone anything at all."

"Now that is what I'm talking about," Kirkland muttered. "You know how to man up when the times call for action."

"You're an arrogant little puss bag," Carl said. "If you hadn't been born into the right family line, you'd be nothing more than another struggling artist who turned to street crime to make ends meet. Your daddy's empire makes sure your songs get heard by the masses."

"Big words from a man born with a silver spoon in his mouth," Kirkland snorted. "I earn everything I have.

My daddy didn't leave it to me. I was just smart enough not to get my brains blown out when he did."

"I earn my way, too," Carl Davis shot back. "No one else could have gotten to Ji Su before she started spilling her guts about you and the entire operation you have going on down there. The spa girls, the pornography you force them to make, all of it makes you rich because you don't have to pay them anything. I worked to keep the heat off your daddy so he could grow that empire so you're going to share some of the feast."

"Alright," Kirkland relented. "I hear you."

"Good," Carl grunted. "I better see a spike in the polls from all your media blasts, and don't forget the cash."

"The girls haven't been working since Servant and his team have been sitting on us."

"You think I'm stupid?" Carl asked. "You don't have the money you do with shit for brains. You might have had to shut down your porn production but you would have those bitches working somewhere. Don't get greedy on me."

Carl killed the call. Eric Geyer held out a hand for the burner phone. "The prick doesn't realize how simple it would be for me to let him fry."

"It is an option to consider," Eric advised.

Carl sat down and began to lean back. He froze and fixed his security chief with a hard look. "Explain."

"Shadow Ops teams are effective. As president, they'd be a resource," Eric said.

"They're too devoted to justice," Carl groused.

Eric offered his boss a tilt of his head. "That has purpose. It motivates them to perform above and beyond the call of duty."

"They won't perform for me," Carl Davis said. "Tyler

Martin was one of their number. I bought him and he sold them out. That's the sort of thing they don't forget, and, as you noted, they're devoted to justice. To their way of thinking, I've crossed too many lines. I have to wipe them or they will take me out. I need the revenue and media coverage Kirkland brings to the table. It's about survival now. Mine and yours."

Eric nodded. "They scuttled the other witness. I'm working on locating her."

"Good. I don't need her deciding to pump up the volume of her life in a couple of years when she's sick of hiding by popping her head up and making accusations and writing tell-all books. Make sure I never hear from her again."

Carl waved a hand in the air. The girl was insignificant. He had Eric to deal with annoyances like the one she presented. In another era, she'd have been a peasant, and it wouldn't have shocked anyone to hear him say he was her better.

But he was.

She was the working class and he was a ruler. It was the destiny he'd been born to pursue and Kagan and his teams weren't going to stand in the way.

Carl wouldn't be the first ruler to take the crown through spilt blood.

In fact, it rather felt like a rite of passage.

Florida was muggy.

Used to the dry heat of Southern California, Jenna let out a little huff as she picked up a map and squinted at it before deciding which way to turn at the next intersection.

An honest to goodness paper map.

The car she'd found in the garage was a small pickup truck with a shell on the back. Maybe she was reduced to using a paper map to stay off the grid but the truck had been filled with Rubbermaid bins containing all sorts of lovely essentials.

Sam would have cackled over her delight at finding clean underwear.

But she'd been a little more intimidated by how all the clothing were the same brand and style as what she'd had in her dresser drawers.

Crap . . . Dare was still giving her a buzz.

In that sharp-as-hell way he operated.

The truck itself was a decade old. It ran smooth as a whisper though and didn't have a single on-board computer. She'd found a little bin of CD's on the passenger seat floor to keep her company as she drove across the country.

"Now for the big moment . . ." she muttered as she made a few more turns and double-checked the address. It was a newer tract home. Jenna pulled up into the driveway and happily climbed out of the driver's seat. The exterior of the place was a tan stucco, and one of the keys on her ring fit into the front door. The plants were immature along the whole block giving the place a very new-to-the-world feel.

Inside there was the delightful feeling of air-conditioning. She closed the door behind her and noted the empty space. It was a three-room house and the only furniture was a bed and a dresser with a television sitting on top of it along with a washer, dryer, and refrigerator. Everything was brand new, the warranty information laid out for her, the sheets still in the package and sitting on the mattress just waiting for her to make the bed.

"Clean slate . . ." she muttered as she took another turn around the house, noting her own footprints in the carpet that had been vacuumed before she arrived.

It was interesting to see how good Dare's associates were. Everything she needed was there, and the empty space was left for her to build her new life.

Well, she had the funds for that as well and a job. Jenna pulled the little history page from her backpack and looked at the job title again.

Crime-lab specialist.

She was going to be testing evidence samples. It had been an option as a career choice back when she'd been in college, one that hadn't snared her interest once she'd taken a tour of the Jet Propulsion Laboratories. Blasting things into space was fun. Testing evidence samples was going to be mundane. Important, yes. Boring, you betcha.

You mean life without Dare is mundane.

Well that wasn't a newsflash.

And she was done crying over it.

Keep telling yourself that . . .

She snorted and opened the garage door so she could start unloading.

It looked like she was home.

And the damned tears stung her eyes anyway because she'd never felt so utterly alone in her life.

"Collect your team, I want you back on Kirkland's tail. Remember, I want him on human trafficking. Don't haul him in for the small stuff. He's got too much money for those charges to hold him very long."

Dare was accustomed to Kagan's way of launching into business. His section leader did it to reduce the time the call was active and visible to tracking.

"Except Sinclair, I need her on another assignment," Kagan continued.

The call ended. Dare dropped the phone in his pocket as Greer came into the room and leaned on the door-jamb.

"We're back on Kirkland," Dare informed his fellow agent.

Greer grinned. "Good. I didn't want that bastard to get off the hook."

"We're going to need something more concrete to hold him," Dare muttered. "Let's hope he's not smart enough to shut down so we can't nail him."

Dare sat down at the chair he'd been using at the table serving as his desk.

"You didn't ask about her."

Greer could always be counted on to have his back, which meant his fellow agent knew him well enough to gauge his reactions.

It also meant Greer knew how to read him.

Too well.

"No, I didn't," Dare confirmed.

Greer didn't take the hint to leave well enough alone. "You're stuck on her."

"It will pass." Dare concentrated on finding Zane.

"In your dreams, boy-o . . . I don't have a choice when it comes to seeing Sorcha. So don't expect me to turn a blind eye to what I see when you look at Jenna."

Dare turned a hard look on his teammate, but Greer had already started back toward his computer.

Which left him alone with Jenna's ghost.

It pissed him off how much she was on his mind.

"Did you make the fatal error, Servant?"

Dare jumped, the chair flying back as Vitus Hale

asked the question. Greer was scrambling from the other room as Dare recognized the ex-SEAL and fellow Shadow Ops agent.

"Isn't your wife going to give you a kid?" Dare asked as he shoved his gun back into his chest-harness holster. "Maybe you should lay off the jerk moves so you live to see it."

Vitus only grinned. "Kagan should have told you he was sending me down since you'll be short Sinclair."

"Sorry, mate, but you're just not what I'd call a fair exchange. Sinclair has better legs than you," Greer muttered. "And Servant did make the fatal error."

Dare sent Greer a look. The Scot only shrugged and moved off again. Dare picked up his chair and sat back down.

Vitus slowly chuckled: "Never give a shit about the package."

That was the fatal error as far as Special Ops went. From Seal to Ranger to FBI. It was a rule learned early so it would be ingrained by the time operators became seasoned agents. Men in the field learned to become desensitized to their witnesses and rescue victims because it kept them from forming attachments.

"You don't get to say shit about it," Dare muttered. "Because you married your package."

Dare knew Vitus was grinning behind him. It took a lot to not turn around, but he wasn't having a conversation about Jenna.

No, she was too personal a topic and admitting it just ticked him off again because he was face-to-face with how obsessed he was with her.

Fatal mistake?

Yeah and yet he realized he wouldn't trade knowing

her for anything. So he'd deal with his lapse in judgment in his own way.

"Like the new job?"

Jenna put her car keys down on the washing machine
as she came in to find Kagan in her house.

"I didn't expect to see you again," she said.

His lips twitched. Jenna wouldn't exactly call it a
smile but there was a minute curvature.

"Thought I'd take you out for some target practice."
He swept her from head to toe. "Make you feel a little
more in control of your situation."

"I'm fine, but I'm in," Jenna muttered. "As it happens,
my social calendar is a little light this weekend."

Kagan pointed at the floor just outside the laundry
room she was standing in. A military green canvas duf-
fle bag was sitting there.

"Gear up."

Kagan was a man of few words.

That didn't mean the man failed to communicate.
Jenna caught the look he sent her and adjusted her grip
on the gun.

Actually, rifle was more the word.

As in, fully automatic rifle.

Kagan had started with a hand gun and moved right
along to military-grade weapons. Since he'd also brought
her to a military base for their weekend adventure, no
one even gave them a second glance.

Although compound was really more the word to use.
There was a serious lack of buildings. Everything was
covered in dirt and nets to make it harder to see from
the sky. Men moved about in fatigues and Kagan had

included her own set in the canvas gear bag he'd brought along.

Jenna clamped her jaw shut to keep her teeth from rattling and tried again.

"Better," Kagan offered.

She looked up the field at the target she'd been using but couldn't really tell if he was humoring her or not.

"Enough work," Kagan announced. "It's Saturday of a holiday weekend. Go have some fun."

Jenna put the rifle down. "Thanks for the lesson."

He nodded. "You'll understand later why I brought you out here."

There was a soft confidence in his voice.

"Okay. Sounds like a plan."

Kagan offered her a half chuckle. "It's a pisser, being in your shoes."

Jenna kept pace with Kagan as they walked away from the firing line toward where a few vehicles were. She resisted the urge to answer him for a long moment because complaining was only going to make the wound sting.

"I only really care about Sam and Paul," Jenna admitted. "Friends like those two don't come along every day."

"Cutting ties is hard," Kagan said as he opened the driver side door of the Jeep he'd driven her out to the compound in. "Safer though."

"So I've been told."

Kagan was a man of few words. He drove back toward where they'd parked her truck. The little tract house was infinitely more welcoming after twenty-four hours out in the dirt. She went inside, grateful to be in a place she could call her own.

It was actually paid off.

A month ago, she'd been twenty-five years from being able to say she owned any piece of property free and clear.

You paid a high price for it though . . .

That was the truth. Sam's and Paul's faces floated through her mind as she took a shower, washing her hair twice to make sure she got the dirt out of it. When she finished, it was almost three in the afternoon.

So what was Kagan about? Fine, she was being paranoid but a man like him didn't strike her as the bleeding-heart guy who'd showed up because he was worried she was bored.

And gun training?

She didn't even want to think too long on just why he was making sure she knew how to handle a firearm.

The little house suddenly wasn't as safe as it'd felt when she got home. She strained to listen, realizing her senses were heightened.

Jenna wandered out of the master bathroom and froze. Sitting on her bed was a packet of papers that she knew for a fact wasn't there when she'd arrived.

It sent a prickle across her skin.

Okay, and it made her feel strangely better because her suspicions were born of paranoia.

Which was strange too but she'd rather know she could keep up with Dare and his fellow agents instead of knowing she was busy being completely oblivious to what was happening to her.

Pathetic . . .

Yeah, that was the word for it. She reached for the papers, determined to do something other than dwell on Kagan and the fact that he represented her only familiar face. There was a sticky note on the front of the envelope.

"Have some fun . . ."

Inside there was a ticket to a concert, along with a hotel reservation.

Kirkland Grog.

She wasn't a huge fan of the guy but his songs seemed to play everywhere so she knew the name. She flipped the ticket around in her fingers for a moment before dropping the towel she had wrapped around herself.

You're not sitting home moping . . .

A little slice of pain went through her as she thought of Sam. It made her move faster, dressing, putting on a light dusting of makeup. None of it took very long. Her wardrobe choices were rather limited.

Another reason you're going . . .

Maybe there would be some shopping wherever the hotel was. Jenna used the canvas bag to pack her overnight stuff and headed for her truck.

She was going to have fun.

And not think about Dare Servant.

And that . . . was . . . well . . . that.

Except she was going to keep her eyes open. Because the tingle on the back of her neck was a warning she'd be a fool to dismiss as an over-active imagination.

"There's one thing about this Kirkland Rys," Vitus Hale muttered as he studied a monitor. "He doesn't seem to have inherited his father's need to stay hidden."

"A need that only became a necessity after Marc Grog was set to go to trial for leaking Military secrets to Conrad Mosston," Zane offered from his own seat.

Dare nodded but didn't take his eyes off the monitor in front of him. The truth was, a lot of an agent's life was spent scouring video feed looking for evidence. Today, they were hacked into the security feed from the stadium where Kirkland was getting ready to perform.

"He's on tour to cover his ass," Dare growled.

"Agreed," Vitus said. "But I don't think he's smart enough to keep his nose clean."

"Let's hope not," Dare muttered. "We need to cut off the support he's giving to Carl Davis before Carl gets elected. And shuts us down."

"Nothing would make me happier than ruining Carl Davis's day," Vitus replied.

Dare suddenly stiffened. He blinked and leaned closer to the monitor. "Fuck me."

His team knew him too well. Profanity wasn't necessarily cause for concern, but his emotions were bleeding through. He tapped the screen and enlarged a woman sitting in one of the private boxes.

"Jenna Henson," he muttered.

His team was clustered around his work station.

"Another coincidence?" Greer muttered. "That's hard to swallow."

"Impossible for me." Dare pushed his chair back, unable to stay still. "She's played us."

Vitus held up a hand. "Circumstantial."

Dare faced off with him. "That's a five-thousand-dollar box seat. More if she's got backstage passes for after the show."

"Looks like cheese to me," Vitus muttered. "Laid out in a trail. It's too easy, too sloppy."

Dare tightened his hold on his temper and tried to think. Vitus was someone he respected. The man was an experienced operator in the field, his gut instinct was something Dare respected.

"Or Kirkland thinks that since we were scuttled, he doesn't have to watch his details. In any case, she shouldn't be there." Dare defended his position.

"Agreed," Vitus responded. "Too many coincidences with the same name attached."

Dare didn't care for the way his gut was burning. It was one thing to be pissed, another to be sick over the fact that Jenna might just have been playing him from the start.

"She might have been a plant at the house," Dare said. "Pull her two buddies in and see what they know."

"And the girl?" Greer asked.

"I'm going in," Dare told his team.

There were more than one pair of lowered eyebrows in response. Dare stood up to the scrutiny. "If we haul her in, we've got nothing without a confession. Kirkland thinks we're scuttled. He isn't the only one who can play the coincidence game."

"Sure you're the right man for the assignment?" Greer asked. "I think your objectivity is compromised."

Dare bristled, his temper spiking.

The problem was, he was honest enough to admit he was pissed off by the idea of another agent playing up to Jenna.

He was jealous.

"I am the logical choice. Sending in another agent will triple the timeline," Dare said. "We don't have that sort of time."

And he was going. But he realized his determination stemmed from the certainty of knowing he was going in to gather enough evidence against Jenna to put her in prison. As far as life lessons went, it was an epic one. Complete crash and burn with no survivors.

Well, he'd walk away from it. Because he was an agent. It was his life, because he'd chosen it.

So why the hell did he hate it so much today?

It wasn't the first time a beautiful woman was on the wrong side of the law. It wasn't even the first time he'd gone into an operation knowing it might entail some night maneuvers.

A box seat.

There was a private attendant to call with the press of a button and a tablet to show her menu options. She scrolled through the items, her eyebrows lifting when she encountered an "intimacy" package.

Condom and tiny tube of lube.

Jeez . . . the people at the top lived a vastly different life than she did.

Well, she was going to enjoy it. Kirkland might not be her favorite hip-hop man but the box seat was pretty neat.

Except you wish Dare was there to share it . . .

She felt heat teasing her cheeks and didn't shy away from the memory of the way he'd kiss her neck.

There had been such an intensity about their encounters. It was a little life lesson because she'd clearly been settling for substandard sex.

Sure it wasn't more than that?

Now she shied away from her thoughts.

No, she wasn't sure, but she was very certain she was never going to see Dare Servant again.

And there were going to be no more pity parties.

She'd seized the day, lived in the moment, and wasn't going to ruin it by sitting around. The light began to flicker, the band starting up. Jenna moved forward, hanging over the edge of the box and screaming out with the rest of the crowd. She let the rush of excitement from the people in the pit along the edge of the stage hit her.

After all, she was alive, and she had a very new appreciation of that state of being.

She wasn't going to waste any of it.

Eric Geyer liked his position.

Truth was, he'd never thought he'd rise above an adolescence full of stupid choices and dumb stunts. As it turned out, those marks were the ones that helped elevate him to his current position.

He owed Tyler Martin a lot.

Tyler had recruited him because of his fearless spirit. The willingness to snatch a prize, even when it wasn't yours to take a shot at.

Brass balls.

That was what Tyler had called it.

And Tyler was dead. Eric didn't spend too much time dwelling on his mentor's demise. Taking chances meant facing the risks. Better to go out in a blaze of glory than die an old feeble man.

Tyler knew it better than anyone else. Eric wasn't going to turn soft now. Especially when he was the man stepping into the vacancy Tyler Martin had left.

"Tell me personally when you get a fix on her."

Federal agencies were wonderful little ego-filled things. In this case, Homeland Security didn't think they needed to answer to anyone else. That made it so much easier for Eric to use them. They had the best face-recognition software on the planet and people who excelled in using it. From social media to traffic cameras, the millions of images captured around the country were being scanned in the interest of making it harder for terrorists to operate.

He was going to use it to snatch a prize. In this case, that reward would be a position next to the President of the United States.

Man, if his buddies could see him now.

Eric stopped outside the door of the office and grinned. If those ass-wipes could see him, at least the ones who were still alive anyway. His face was there, behind Carl Davis's. Kirkland made sure Carl was everywhere.

It was a sweet place. One that came with all sorts of perks. Like having men at his command. Eric checked in with his subordinates before heading out to the private home where Carl was a guest.

Getting inside was a chore. There were triple layers of security and no one walked around the house, not even Carl's personal man. Eric made it inside and enjoyed the exclusive look into a world very few knew about. The top floor of the house had rooms inside of rooms where any manner of tastes might be satisfied.

Dope? No problem.

Girls? There were sweet ones and others with pierced nipples.

Boys? Yeah, there was a room for that sort of thing, too.

Carl lifted his hand, flagging Eric over to him as he sat in a small meeting area while members of Congress tip-toed down the hallways to seek out their different interests.

"Did you find her?" Carl asked.

"Soon." Eric responded. "Servant scuttled her. She doesn't know enough to keep her head down. It's a matter of time until we catch sight of her."

Carl nodded but it was clear his mind was drifting to other things. Eric made sure the guy he joined in a private room never got a look at Carl's face. It was part of the job, making sure Carl's reputation stayed crisp and clean.

Jenna Henson fell into that category as well. Eric would deal with her, to make sure she'd never surface with a claim against Kirkland or Carl.

And of course there was the money. Honestly, that was what it all boiled down to. Carl wouldn't get very far without funding. They needed Kirkland because he'd inherited an empire that was cash rich. Dirty dealings paid best.

Jenna Henson wouldn't be the first person to disappear over control of a fortune.

CHAPTER SIX

Hotel room was an understatement.

Jenna followed her GPS and ended up at a resort. There were towering palm trees along the well-groomed paths that led to the reception desk. She enjoyed the balmy breeze and the way it rustled the leaves of the trees.

"Welcome Ms. Sherlock, we have a sky suite waiting for you. We already have an account open for any incidentals. Just put everything on your room."

Anything with the word suite used to describe it sounded amazing. She wasn't disappointed either. She took the elevator to the thirty-sixth floor and followed the signs down the hallway to a door. It actually had a door bell and her key card opened it.

Inside, the lights came up as she entered. Softly illuminating creamy tile flooring and a sitting area with a plush set of sofas. The small kitchen area sported a complimentary basket of treats for midnight munchies and a tablet with a menu displayed for room service.

The bedroom was separate with a bathroom that came complete with a huge Jacuzzi tub.

Even Dare would have fit in it.

Stop thinking about him.

Yeah right. She took her canvas bag into the bathroom and stripped down. Everything was polished and immaculately clean. Music was just a tap of her fingertip away, and there was even a selection of spa-quality bath essentials for her to make use of.

Boy, she could get spoiled fast.

But a ping of loneliness went through her. All the luxuries in the world didn't make up for the fact that she couldn't count on Sam calling her up and launching into a venting session over his latest brush with the out-of-touch-with-reality clientele his business dealings brought to his storefront.

And Paul wouldn't be along with a slant-eyed look at his husband while uncorking a bottle of wine to toast another event well done.

A touch on another tablet closed all the curtains and set the air-conditioner humming. Jenna crawled into bed, grateful for the training session with Kagan because she was tired enough to fall asleep.

Tomorrow, she'd get busy laying down the foundation of her new life.

There was nowhere to go but forward.

"Take backup."

Dare felt his fingers tightening around his phone. "I can handle it."

"If you're telling me you're going to make contact with a resettled witness and blow her cover to sherds, you're taking a team to document," Kagan laid out his opinion.

"She's already back in contact with Kirkland," Dare explained. "That's three coincidences. Two too many."

Kagan was quiet for a moment. "Take the team. Keep her in sight. This case is bigger than any of us realize."

Dare dropped his phone as Kagan ended the call. Greer and Zane were leaning in the doorway, watching him. Neither agent looked like he was planning on budging.

"You win," Dare grunted. "Kagan says the team goes with me."

"Like I said," Greer muttered. "You're compromised. No way I'm letting you near that girl without eyes on your back."

"I will perform my duties," Dare insisted. His tone came across a little too dangerous though. Vitus caught him by the back of the neck and steered him through a doorway into a small bedroom.

"I don't need a lecture," Dare warned him.

"I'm more of a kick to the ass sort of man," Vitus responded as he braced his feet wide and faced off with Dare. "But in this case, I've been in your shoes."

Dare shook his head. "No, you haven't. You thought your wife rejected you because you weren't good enough. Jenna is a criminal who duped me."

"You don't have that evidence yet," Vitus argued.

Dare snorted. "And you damned well know we have to act on our hunches because the cases we run don't give us the sort of openings that allow for sitting still when we come across something that hints at evidence."

Vitus nodded. "Agreed. Which is why you need the team. You're going in, and it's clear you're very distracted by the target. It's also clear that's our best advantage to use to bring her in and gather the evidence we need."

Dare knew it. He'd been on teams that backed up agents who used the same ploy.

"Don't be a dick . . ."

Jenna's words rose from his memory like ice water. They cooled his temper, but that only pissed him off for another reason.

He didn't need to go soft.

Not when the facts were stacking up against her being the innocent she portrayed. There was no way he'd buy the fact that she just happened to be at Kirkland's concert because she'd decided to get on with her life.

The connection was too strong.

In his world, things like that didn't just happen.

She wasn't innocent.

And he was going to have to get the evidence to prove it.

"You sure about this?" Thais Sinclair asked.

Kagan turned to look at her. "I'm sure Carl Davis is very good at making sure he has other people take the fall for his dealings."

Thais nodded.

"If we want something significant to stick, we're going to have to up the level of our game." Kagan delivered his plan in a soft voice. "Servant can't know I'm manipulating the situation. The girl was already collateral damage. My choice is to take advantage of the opportunity or watch Kirkland slip through the net and keep going."

Thais knew the tone. It was the one her section leader used when he was laying out his action plans. The detachment was admirable, if you could adopt the same level of insensitivity.

She'd been raised on it. People looked at her slim figure and thought she had tough mental discipline.

The truth though, was she was sick to her stomach

most of the time. Turned off by the way people applied values to one another. So very blind to what was most important in life.

"You normally don't have such tender skin, Sinclair," Kagan observed.

Thais offered Kagan a smile. A very practiced one. It didn't fool Kagan. His eyes narrowed, which was quite an extreme reaction from her cool-as-a-glacier section leader.

"I can be what you expect of me," she muttered.

Kagan studied her for a moment. "Just don't be foolish enough to forget you have a brain under all that pretty wrapping."

Thais offered him a rare look past the mask she wore so often. Kagan locked gazes with her as she let her eyes snap at his. She watched the way he absorbed it.

"Is there a reason you object to this mission beyond the fact that the suspect is a female?" Kagan asked.

"Yes." Thais didn't elaborate. She turned and moved toward a doorway.

Her life wasn't one that had much room for soft feelings. She might think it a shame to see Dare tossing aside his chance at happiness, but it was his choice to make.

And she had made hers, so she'd be the agent Kagan expected her to be. She understood Dare because she'd made the same choice. Her badge was her family.

It was strange to spend someone else's money.

Okay, it was also really surreal to not have to worry about a budget. Jenna was free-floating through her life, without things like a mortgage or monthly payments to chain her.

Part of that was majorly cool.

She woke up sometime before noon, eager to enjoy the resort. She flipped through a local-sights book that was on the coffee table and settled on a couple. Room service came through with flying colors, delivering a meal that had her licking her fingers. But the surrealness continued as the waiter refused the cash tip she tried to give him, claiming it was already included in the bill.

Well, you've paid in blood for it so . . . enjoy . . .

She grabbed her purse and set off to explore the grounds. The sun was sparkling off the palm trees again, music filtering through the landscaping from cleverly disguised speakers. There were several pools for the resort guests. A flash of her key card gained her accesses to a private suite. There were large coolers of cucumber water and waiters in blue polo shirts offering her words of welcome.

She moved toward a waterfall, pulling out her new cell phone to captures some pictures.

Making memories . . .

It was a challenge she embraced, jumping into a tour van at the last second because she'd stumbled on it. The guide happily sold her a ticket before she climbed into the backseat.

"Window of opportunity is open," Dare informed his team through a tiny microphone hanging from his earpiece. "Get the suite wired."

"Copy," Greer muttered from where he was hanging out in a housekeeping closet on the thirty-sixth floor.

They'd have it done in a smooth action that the team had performed a hundred times. Behind him, Zane was already hacked into the security feed from the hotel.

"Any sign of Kirkland?"

"You'll know when I see him," Zane replied.

"You have the van, Greer?" Dare asked.

"Please," Greer's voice came across the airwaves. "It's a tour van. I'll hand you my badge myself if I lose it."

"Don't get complacent," Dare advised. "Kirkland is a master at making sure he doesn't leave any dirt clinging to him."

"Right," Greer replied before he went silent.

Dare didn't care for the silence.

Because you've got too much time to think.

Right. And notice how much he'd enjoyed seeing Jenna again.

She was smiling . . .

The sight should have filled him with determination. Instead he caught the unmistakable sensation of dread.

Fuck. He didn't want to be the one to nail her.

That was the rock-bottom truth. His temper stirred because he had too much evidence pointing toward her. There was no way he could dismiss it.

So he'd do his job and maybe it would serve as a damn hard lesson on just why getting involved with a witness was a cardinal sin.

The resort had a casino, which meant the place was swarming with people by the time Jenna returned. There were smartly suited men with dressed-to-kill women on their arms. The bars were in full operation as the sound of the gaming machines filtered into the lobby. People were happily drunk on excitement and eager to enjoy the night.

The gaming floor was too crowded for her taste. She walked around the edges until she found an alcove where there was a Scotch and shots bar. It was brass and polished wood from floor to ceiling, the barkeep wearing cufflinks and a vintage vest. The smaller space suited her mood, making her feel less like she was drowning in the open ocean without a soul in sight.

The barkeep served up her drink in a cut crystal glass. The aroma tickled her nose before she took the first taste. The seventeen-year-old liquor burned a path down her throat and warmed her stomach. She closed her eyes while she took a second sip, savoring the experience. It was heady and sharp, and the warmth was spreading through her body by the third taste.

But she opened her eyes and blinked.

Dare Servant was leaning against the pillar facing her.

Jenna looked at the Scotch suspiciously. But then the tingle she'd felt on the back of her neck returned.

Dare Servant wasn't the sort of man who had coincidences happen in his life.

His voice touched off a memory of him that rippled all the way down her spine to her toes. He was just as devil dark as always, his gaze sharp enough to cut away everything until it felt like he was looking into her soul.

Wait . . . she'd been trying to think about something important.

He moved forward and plucked the glass from her frozen fingers. Lifting it to his lips, he took a taste of the liquor. "You like things that bite you, Jenna."

He dropped into the vintage-looking chair next to her and fixed her with his midnight black eyes. "Want me to leave?"

He was settled in place right next to her. Not across the table.

Of course not, it's Dare Servant. He's pushing on your comfort zone . . .

A tingle of awareness went across her skin. Goose-flesh rose up as she felt the unmistakable sensation of her nipples puckering.

Shit . . . she really didn't want to think . . .

"No answer?" He took another hit from the glass before offering it to her.

"Maybe I'm trying to decide if I should look the gift horse in the mouth." Maybe she was showing all her cards, but she just couldn't help it. Seeing him was like a cold drink of water after crossing a dessert.

His lips twitched, giving her a glimpse at that grin he didn't allow to break up his professional mask very often.

"That works for me. Let's not over-think the situation." A second later, he'd captured her hand, reaching up to stroke the inside of her wrist before closing his fingers around hers.

She jumped. Jerking her hand away as she stood up, unable to sit still.

He was a live wire . . .

The burly barkeep looked her way, one of his eye-brows rising up in question. She shook her head and pulled her key card out of her purse for him to swipe and add the tab to her room.

Dare was watching her.

It rattled her.

When she turned around, he was contemplating her, and there was no mistaking the anger in his eyes. He slowly stood, the measured pace only doubling just how powerful he was. He moved closer, making her tip her head back to maintain eye contact.

"So was I just a perk of the moment, Jenna?"

His tone was sharp, slicing into her. "What? No . . ." She shook her head. "But how are you here? It doesn't make sense. You're the one who said no contact . . . The word you used was scuttle . . ."

He caught her wrist and pulled her around his body, taking her right outside the little alcove bar.

"It's a surprise for me, too. I left you on the other side of the country," he muttered.

His tone was husky, and he was far too close for her to keep her wits. He pressed her right up against the same pillar. "I should have walked away before you saw me."

She hated the way that made her feel.

Like she'd do anything to keep it from happening.

But the impulse wasn't interested in how pitiful her feelings were.

Dare stroked her cheek, the motion sparking off a memory that made her heart accelerate.

"I couldn't seem to make myself do it, baby."

He was so close his breath was teasing her lips. Everything inside her was tightening, anticipation making her senses ultra-keen.

He smelled so much better than she recalled. It felt like they weren't close enough. She needed to touch him, felt like she'd go insane if he didn't kiss her. Things like reasons and conversation didn't seem to matter a bit. He was there, and she was on a fast track to melting into a puddle at his feet.

But at least she caught the flicker of need in his eyes, too. It was hard and promised her no mercy.

Which suited her perfectly.

"We've got to get out of here," he muttered.

He backed away from her. She shuddered, her cheeks flushing when she realized they were in a lobby, for Christ's sake.

"Too many cameras," he continued.

"Right," she muttered.

The word "scuttled" floated above her impulses. Casinos had a ton of cameras. Dare had her wrist again, pulling her into step beside him as he headed around the gaming floor. He pulled her into the elevator.

"What floor?"

"Thirty-six," she answered.

He punched the button and the doors slid closed. There was a jerk as the car started being pulled up.

"But how . . ." she began.

"Too far," he muttered before he pulled her against him, cutting off her question with a kiss.

His kiss.

It was hard and demanding, just the way she remembered.

Only a hundred times more intense. She melted. It was that simple. He was everything she yearned for. It truly was a need. As essential as water and food, she felt the hunger rise up from where she'd locked it away. Driving her forward, reaching for him as he pulled her mouth open with his thumb on her chin.

The kiss was raw.

He took her mouth, pushing so completely into her space, she lost track of where he began and she ended. The car jerked, the doors sliding open. He groaned and pulled her through the hallway.

Dare reached into her purse and pulled the key card out of the slot where she'd stuck it in. For just a moment, she was jerked out of the hold passion had on her by the way he intimidated the hell out of her. This guy just operated on a different level.

Which was one of the things she found so irresistible about him.

It gave her a major buzz . . .

Not because she liked being dominated.

Don't lie . . .

Dare turned her into the sky suite and pushed her up against the wall as the door was still closing. He framed the sides of her face, his big hands covering her cheeks and sending a shiver down her back.

She wasn't lying.

No, he took command and she loved knowing she kept pace.

They stripped on the way to the bedroom. Fighting to bare each other's skin. There was a frantic pace to their motions tonight, Dare stripping her like some prize he'd claimed.

Or intended to claim.

Jenna wanted more than to be taken. His presence was a gift from fate, another taste of what she craved. Even knowing how hard the fall would be when he left again didn't stop her from letting him take her up the mountain of bliss his touch evoked.

And she had every intention of making sure he was just as out of control as she was. She cupped his balls, rolling them gently as he lifted his head and let her look into his eyes.

Devil dark . . .

Like a midnight sky. They glittered with hard determination, which spiked the arousal twisting through her insides.

But he scooped her up and dropped her on the bed. She bounced for a moment, looking up as he followed her down.

The sight froze the breath in her lungs.

He was hard and determined, his eyes narrowed as

he pressed her flat, capturing her wrists and pinning them above her head to the surface of the bed.

"I'm in charge tonight . . ." he rasped.

There was a warning in his tone. One that sent a jolt through her. He drew one hand down her body, stroking her cheek, across her jaw, and along her neck. She arched up, the level of sensation nearly unbearable.

Which was what made her crave even more of it.

He was being the dick she'd accused him of being and yet there was something about the moment, the knowledge that he was taking her, that made her feel more attractive than she had ever felt before.

He cupped her breast, teasing the tender globe with his fingertips. She shifted but the hold on her hands was solid and unyielding.

He chuckled. "You're mine to do with as I please, Jenna . . ."

She forced her eyelids up, her breath catching as they locked gazes. For a moment, she was sure she was going to have blisters from how hot the flames were in his eyes. But in the next she was crying out as he pinched her nipple. He stopped just shy of pain, taking her to the edge of where enjoyment ended and keeping her there by cupping her breast.

It was a potent mixture of strength and control.

One that intoxicated her.

"I'm going to be calling the shots tonight."

He was moving his hand lower, trailing his fingertips across her ribcage and onto her lower belly. Her clit was throbbing with anticipation, but he lingered over her midsection, driving her insane with just his fingertips.

She jerked and he held her down, one of his thighs locked over one of hers.

"Let go . . ." her tone was unrecognizable. So husky. *So needy . . .*

"I've got you right where I want you . . ." he muttered against her ear.

He was teasing her curls now. The hairs ultra-sensitive like he'd engaged a circuit she hadn't known her body came equipped with.

"Right where I can have my way with you."

He proved his point by slipping his fingers into her folds. She jerked, unable to control herself at all. She was just twisting under his touch, completely controlled by the need he was building.

And he didn't grant her the mercy of fingering her clit. No, he toyed with the outer folds of her sex first.

"I can't take that," she growled.

She heard him let out a little grunt.

"But you will," he continued on with teasing her. "Because you're mine right now, mine to toy with."

She tried to pull her hand loose and heard him chuckle. A moment later he was rubbing her clit. His lazy demeanor had evaporated. Now there was hard purpose and action. She gasped and cried out.

"That's it Jenna . . ." He didn't let up, rubbing her clit hard and fast. "Mine to toy with now."

He sure knew how to handle his toys.

Climax was rushing toward her. She withered because she just couldn't get close enough to him. Every muscle she had was straining, her hips lifting toward his hand as he worked her clit until climax slammed into her.

She let out a cry that was long and thin. It bounced around the room as her passage contracted, and the plea-sure felt like it went all the way to her core. Sharp and intense, she forgot to breathe as it twisted through her and dropped her back on to the bed where blackness ended her efforts to do anything but surrender completely to the moment.

Dare wasn't a stranger to being disgusted by the details of a case.

He worked with underworld thugs and criminals who would do atrocious deeds to accomplish what they wanted.

Tonight, he was disgusted by himself.

His cock was hard, throbbing with need, and it took every ounce of self-discipline he had to roll off the bed and head for a cold shower.

He'd expected a sexual response from his body.

That was only logical.

The state of arousal he was in was something different. He flipped on the shower and walked straight into the spray. The cold water hit his skin, making him clench his jaw.

He still could see Jenna as a component of a case.

It frustrated him more than anything he'd come up against in his career. There were plenty of stories of agents who had fallen for a bad girl. There was even some stupid psychological name for it.

At the moment, he called it fucking irritating.

He went all the way under the spray, letting it blast the cold water into his face.

Wake up dumb shit . . .

He hadn't cum.

Jenna fought to wake up because something was wrong.

That dammed tingle on her nape that she'd felt when she was in her shower . . .

There was an ache in her abdomen from how hard she'd been straining. She could still feel the hold he'd had on her wrists, and her folds were wet with how hard she'd climaxed.

Something was very different.

The satisfaction was tainted somehow and she realized it was because she'd been alone in the moment.

And she still was.

The shower was running. She crawled off the bed that wasn't even turned down. She stared at the coverlet, realizing she'd have been fine if they'd been in such a hurry they just hadn't taken time to pull it down.

The path of clothing leading back into the front entryway confirmed Dare had been in a hurry, but she realized he'd been keeping her mind occupied.

He was working.

That was the reason for the gun lesson from Kagan.

Dare was still working the case, working her.

She wanted to throw up.

Nausea twisted her belly as she started to dress, fighting with her underwear because she was shaking. She succeeded and grabbed her pants.

"In some kind of hurry Jenna?"

Dare had left the shower running so she wouldn't know he was on the move. He lowered a towel from where he'd been rubbing it over his head. Water still glistened in the dark mat of his chest hair but he had his pants and shoes on.

Because he wasn't at ease . . .

Okay, maybe she didn't really know what he was like when he wasn't on a case, but there was something very off about the entire moment.

"What are you doing?" She decided to forget trying to filter her thoughts.

One dark eyebrow rose as he tossed the towel aside.

"Cut the shit, Servant," she countered as she grabbed her top and pulled it on. When her head popped out, she realized he was doing the same thing.

Christ, they were both preparing for battle . . .

"What are you worried about, Jenna?"

He was moving toward her, his expression reminding her of the first time she'd met him in that bedroom.

Right before he'd slapped a shackle on her wrist.

"Why are you here?" she demanded.

"Hooking up with you."

She let out a half sound of mocking laughter. "That"—Jenna pointed at the bed behind her—"wasn't hooking up."

His lips rose into a grin, but there was nothing nice about the expression and it didn't make it all the way to his eyes. Those black orbs continued to glitter with hard purpose. "You enjoyed it."

"But you didn't." Her tone betrayed her by coming out in a shaky whisper.

His eyes narrowed. Just a fraction. Like she'd hit him with an unexpected fact.

"You applied yourself . . ." And the realization was making her sick.

"Didn't expect you to be so critical."

He offered her a shrug.

"And now you're trying to introduce an emotional element in the hope of distracting me."

There was a flash of admiration in his eyes, but he didn't budge from his stance.

"Fine," she muttered. "Stick to your story. I'm out of here."

Her canvas bag was on the entry room table. Jenna hooked the shoulder strap and swung it up onto her back.

"You're being emotional." Dare caught her wrist and sent her stumbling past him into the living room so he was between her and the door.

"And you . . ." Jenna faced off with him. "You weren't even involved."

"Is this because I didn't fuck you?" He moved closer. "I can fix that."

There was distaste in his eyes. He'd gotten close enough to touch her, reaching out to close his fingers around her wrist.

It was such an impersonal touch.

And it gutted her.

Pain slashed through her. She gasped at the sheer intensity of it, feeling the burn of tears flooding her eyes. Dare went still, their gazes locked. His mask broke for a moment, as he grimaced with distaste.

And she knew she was right.

She reached up and smacked him. Hard and sharp against the side of his face. The sound popped around the little sitting area as he turned with the blow.

She ducked under his arm while he was distracted but that was as far as she got before he turned on her.

"Do you have this room bugged?" A second wave of horror was looming over her. "Did your team . . . *watch*?"

She was nearly gagging.

And Dare was wearing a mask of stone. His body nearly rigid as he closed the distance between them. "I never . . . will never apologize for doing what I have to for a case, Jenna."

He'd pulled his phone from his pocket and tapped something. A moment later he'd dropped the thing back into the pocket and hooked her around her bicep.

"You're under arrest."

Cold and impersonal.

Exactly what she'd suspected.

Only it hurt a thousand times worse than she'd warned herself it might.

Kirkland was watching her.

Thais fingered the steam of her martini glass, slow and unhurried before she gave the beverage a bored look and turned around.

Kirkland lifted his hand and beckoned her toward him.

Thais contemplated him for a long moment before she walked off in a different direction. The beaded trim on her skirt was hitting the top of her thighs and barely covered her bottom. More than one man looked up as she passed, proving they were exactly what she thought they were.

Creatures of impulse.

Oh, there were expectations. She'd earned a Shadow Ops badge because it allowed her to work with men who had souls.

Her counterpart moved into a doorway so she could see him. He shot her a raised eyebrow look. Thais didn't bother to educate him. She knew what she was doing, crossing the elusive nightclub floor and lowering herself onto a plush sofa. The place was a members-only establishment. A privilege that came with a thirty-thousand-dollar price tag. Among those with too much money, the stench of entitlement was enough to make her retch.

And people wondered how she kept her figure.

"You playing with me, girl?" Kirkland dropped down beside her, slouching down until his butt was on the end of the seat cushion in some attempt to impress her with his nonchalance.

"You have plenty of toys to play with," Thais replied as she flicked her newly manicured fingernails through her hair. "I have different tastes."

"You might like being my toy," was Kirkland's arrogant reply.

Thais turned and caught him in her stare. She stood up, giving him her back.

"Hold on a moment, girl . . ." He caught her wrist and pulled her back.

Thais turned and went down onto her knee. She heard Kirkland draw in a stiff breath as she stopped just shy of being in his lap.

"Sex," she muttered huskily, "is boring."

"Not with me it's not baby."

She let her gaze drop to his lips. Lowering her head, she hovered over him for a long moment before abruptly pushing back.

"Maybe . . ." she offered with a delicate shrug. "Like I said, you have plenty of toys waiting for you."

Thais looked across the club to where Kirkland's companions were shooting her killing looks.

"What's it going to take?" Kirkland was on his feet and doing his best to crowd her with his larger body.

"Danger . . ." Thais let her eyes flash. "Something to make me feel alive."

Kirkland was surprised. She watched it flash in his eyes a moment before he was chuckling under his breath. "Who's your daddy?"

Thais laid a hand on her chest. "My daddy is . . . rich . . ."

"No kidding," Kirkland answered. "That's why you're bored."

Thais shrugged again. "Have fun with your toys . . . they look like they miss you."

Kirkland looked back at his entourage but turned around and caught Thais close. She allowed him to turn her with his body, pressing her close as he caught her hand and pressed it over the gun he had tucked into his belt under the suit jacket he had on.

"I can spice up your night . . ."

Thais ran her finger along the opening in his shirt front. "I'm intrigued."

Kirkland smiled, flashing his teeth at her as he made the fatal mistake of thinking he'd won her over. She twisted her fingers in his chest hair and yanked. He let out a yelp as she slipped away from him.

"Just don't think all it takes is a quick little feel." She let disgust show on her face. "Men always think that's all it takes . . ."

Kirkland caught her hand. His face had gone serious, his playboy image abandoned. "I got you covered. Truth is, I've been bored, too."

He turned and tugged her along with him, giving his party a signal to leave them alone.

Sex was boring.

Thais didn't dwell on that aspect of her job. It wasn't that she believed Kirkland might be cock led. No, it was more a matter of him being so arrogant as to forget she had a brain in her head. When he was finished with what he wanted, she wouldn't matter.

Not that it would be simple to get the jump on him. Kirkland was his father's son all the way. He covered his tracks or had people in his inner circle who made sure he had clean hands.

She'd see.

"I can sit here all day, Jenna," Dare informed her when she kept her lips sealed.

The corners of her mouth twitched up as she lifted her bound hands from the table she was shackled to. They clinked just a bit. "So can I."

It was an honest-to-goodness interrogation room. The table had what looked like a section of a crowbar welded in place for handcuffs to be secured through. The room itself had a cracked concrete floor, and one wall was composed of dark glass mirrors.

Two-way glass . . . Just like on television.

Her sarcasm amused her even as Dare Servant flattened his hands on the table in front of her in an effort to make sure she felt intimidated.

"Start at the beginning, Jenna." His tone was clipped. "Do it now."

She flipped him a double bird instead.

His fingers drew back into fists, delighting her.

Oh sure, she should have been buckling under the pressure.

"You don't get it, Servant. Thanks to you, I just don't have anything left to lose. My dignity was the last of it," she said.

His knuckles turned white. "You can lose your freedom." There was a touch of compassion in his tone.

And she hated the way it made her feel. Like he cared and that she liked knowing he did.

Fuck . . . that . . . shit.

She jerked on the handcuffs so the sound of the metal against metal bounced around the dismal room. "I feel so free . . . it's just overwhelming."

"You were resettled," he cut back. "Financially better off than you were before."

"And you showed up to rain on my parade," she growled.

"So take me through what you've been doing and help me get you back to your life."

Jenna shook her head. "Know something? You contradict your own statements. What happened to scuttling and relocation and no contact because you're marked? Did you send me up that riverbed just to enjoy knowing I was sweating to death in the blazing heat? And what the hell was that performance in my bedroom? You could have arrested me before humiliating me but I guess it's all part of breaking me down."

"I can help you get out of this Jenna, if you just come clean." Dare wasn't willing to be distracted.

His tone had lowered and his gaze shifted away from hers.

"Liar."

His attention returned to her instantly.

"Jenna . . ."

"Fuck . . . off." She enunciated each word precisely.

He contemplated her for a long moment. Jenna stared straight back, unwavering in her choice. He let out a grunt before shaking his head and leaving.

The sound of the door closing was harsh. Like a nail being hammering into the lid of a coffin she was lying in.

Well, at least she wasn't going down whimpering.

Betrayal left a bitter taste in her mouth. The humiliation of knowing his entire team had listened in on their last round of sex was nothing compared to the knowledge that Dare had applied himself to her in such a way.

You just want him to value you more . . .

She sure did and knowing he didn't was a knife straight into the heart of all the feelings she'd developed for him.

Okay, she'd been a fool. He'd never misrepresented who he was.

So maybe it was better.

Yeah, keep telling yourself that . . .

Unshed tears were stinging her eyes again. It pissed her off, making her more determined than ever to make her feelings bend to the will of her mind.

She would tell herself . . . over and over . . . and over.

She would push Dare Servant into the same category he'd put her in.

She would.

"I told you," Thais said, pushing away from Kirkland. "Sex is boring."

He was sitting in the middle of the back seat of his limousine, his pants open as he tried to get her to suck him off.

"Don't play the bitch," Kirkland said.

Thais offered him a flutter of her eyelashes. The limo was stopping at a traffic light. "I told you, my daddy is rich. I don't have to be your pet."

She opened the door and stepped out. There was a word of profanity from Kirkland, but it was drowned out by the whistles from other drivers. Thais made it to the sidewalk in spite of the Jimmy Choo stilettos on her feet.

Her mother had made her practice often enough.

The personal memory was unwelcome. Thais banished it as she made her way in the opposite direction. Even if Kirkland told his driver to turn around, they wouldn't make it around the corner in time to see her slipping into the back of the van her back-up was driving.

"The car is bugged," she said. "But I didn't risk putting one in his clothing where he might find it."

The agent driving offered her a nod of approval. It was grudging, which made her enjoy it all that much more. Ploys were ploys. Thais rather enjoyed knowing hers were put to use some place where it truly mattered.

Of course, in her old life, there were plenty of friends and family who would have argued that making sure they were secure in a rich man's bed was something that mattered.

It had left her so empty, she'd realized she preferred death.

So she'd learned to use her talents for Kagan.

And she was happy with the arrangement.

There would be no looking back.

Jenna's newest accommodations came complete with cells. As in a whole cell block of old-style jails. Bars ran floor to ceiling, the doors swung out and there were only little windows along the upper edges of the cells to let in sunlight. There was a chill in the air that never quite diminished, and the air was beyond stale. Dust clung to the floor like paste.

Concrete and more concrete. The cell she was in had a cot that someone had tossed a pile of bedding onto. Just rough, army issue wool blankets and a pillow. Meals were just as dreary. A dry sandwich was sitting on the cot across the cell from her with a bottle of water. Even after sitting in the cell all day long, Jenna still wasn't inclined to sample it.

Maybe that was because the toilet was sitting between the cots, open to view.

At least the concrete was good for something. She heard anyone coming into the cell block. A creepy sort of crunching sound as the dirt on the floor was smashed beneath their shoes.

Creepy is the word alright . . .

Jenna looked around, pretty sure she could hear the whispers of the inmates who had been locked away and forgotten by the world. Maybe some of them deserved it but that didn't keep her from feeling sorry for the waste of life the cells represented.

Crunch . . . crunch . . .

Jenna stiffened as she heard someone coming.

Not someone, Dare.

It really pissed her off that she still felt a buzz when the guy came close.

"Remember her?" Dare tossed an 8×10 glossy print down on the end of the cot Jenna was sitting on.

Jenna didn't really need to take more than a quick look because the face of the dead girl from the container on the dock was still branded into her mind.

"She has friends," Dare continued as he dropped a few more photos. "That's what motivates me Jenna. This guy treats them like slaves, disposable humans."

Jenna jerked her attention away from the photos. "I went back into that container to help you take him out and I don't know everything you do." Jenna looked at the girl she remembered. "Seeing her was enough for me."

Dare hadn't unlocked the door of the cell. Just tossed the pictures through the bars. "I do what I have to in order to catch the sort of men who do things you can't imagine."

Jenna stood and faced him. "If that was some sort of apology, it fell really short of the mark."

He slowly shook his head. "I don't apologize for working a case." He stepped close enough so he could point at her through the bars. "Not ever, Jenna."

"What you did," she cut back at him, "wasn't working a case. I would have told you whatever you wanted to know. But you didn't ask. You wanted to break me down, and you used the trust that had been established between us to do it."

"I am working a case, Jenna." He pointed at the pictures. "Their case. I told you, my life will go on after anything that happens between us. You were warned not to ask for anything."

"The only thing I asked from you was for you not to be a dick," she replied. "And you're so far into dick territory, you've earned the title of flaming dick."

She turned around, so full of rioting emotions, facing him was impossible. But it afforded her a view of the photos.

Damn it!

He was a good guy at heart.

But a real dick.

Yeah, a flaming dick. Jenna heard him walking away as she started walking in circles.

"She might be on the level."

Dare didn't care for Vitus's comment. The cell room was linked to their command center with black-and-white video. The old facility was in the midst of a remodel. Above their heads, the five stories of the vintage court house were being stripped and readied for new plaster board and top-of-the-line internet.

For the moment, the formal holding cells were a prime location for their team while the construction crews took the holiday weekend off.

"The evidence chain is there," Dare replied.

"So is the fact that she has a solid background of being a law-abiding citizen." Greer turned away from his workstation to look at Dare. "Someone working with Kirkland would have a thicker skin when it comes to intimacy."

He knew it.

"Let's hope Thais brings in a case cracker," Dare said.

They needed a solid link. Just one. Dare had seen other cases succeed with just the right piece of information. Kirkland's wouldn't be any different.

The only difference was how personally involved he was with the case. Vitus was right, he'd made the fatal error of getting involved with his witness. There was a reason Special Ops called their civilians "packages."

It was to desensitize them from the human element involved.

He'd failed and it was ripping him up because being uncertain about any aspect of his life wasn't something he enjoyed.

"I was a dick," Dare admitted.

Greer grunted approval, and Vitus offered him a thumbs-up. Zane, on the other hand, sent him another one of the agent's judgmental looks.

"But I meant what I said to Jenna, I've still got three dead girls and I will do anything to bring Kirkland in. If any of you think that's going to happen without a fight, you need to have Kagan reassign you."

His teammates shifted. They nodded in the way only men who went up against the darker elements could. It was an imperfect solution but the only one they had at their disposal.

Dick?

He was.

And yet, part of him hoped Jenna would understand the necessity of it. Not that he was planning on ever sharing his feelings with her. Nothing had changed about that part.

Bull shit.

He was lying to himself. A habit that seemed to have appeared along with Jenna. Hopefully it would vanish with her departure as well.

She deserved that from him.

Eric Geyer picked up his phone. "Yes?"

"We have a hit on Dare Servant and Jenna Henson."

Eric grinned. "Send it to me."

He killed the call and waited. The current era with its lightning fast internet didn't disappoint him. An email hit his in-box almost instantly. A quick tap and he was looking at surveillance photos that had been fished out of a secure network with the help of face-recognition software and the Patriot Act laws that allowed Homeland Security to browse freely.

Got you . . .

Eric printed off some copies before going to look for Carl Davis. In the home stretch of the campaign, the plane they were on had several members of the press aboard. Eric made sure he smiled as he passed them on his way to Carl's office.

"We've got Servant and the girl."

Carl looked at the photos for a long moment. One of the pictures showed them in the elevator, kissing passionately.

"Getting rid of her will be a bigger problem than I thought," Carl said gravely. "Servant won't let anything go if it touches his girlfriend. I've had this problem with Kagan's teams before. My advice is drop anything to do with her."

Carl was drumming his fingers on the desk top. "I need Kirkland's money."

Eric kept his face expressionless.

"Use the slush fund. Hire someone to get the job done. Completely this time. Get a fucking team," Carl insisted.

Eric hesitated. "A professional hit will draw the Hale brothers into action."

"I'll be president by the time they can prove it's linked back to me." Carl's face was flushed. "I'm so fucking sick of these ass wipes. It's going to be a pleasure to sign an executive order to disband them."

Carl slapped the table top.

"Get it done or I'll find someone with the balls to deal with business."

It wasn't the first time he'd been threatened. Eric still didn't care for it but there were more important matters. Like being given free access to a slush fund.

Sure, he'd perform the duty Carl asked of him.

And Eric was going to make sure he got paid handsomely for his services. The money would be his nest egg. A fall back plan in case he needed to disappear.

So long as doing business with Carl Davis was lucrative, Eric would be his dog. Carl was just stupid enough to forget that dogs could kill their masters from time to time.

CHAPTER SEVEN

Dare woke to a phone buzzing.

But it wasn't his.

It kept buzzing as Greer woke up and dug into the pocket on his shirt that was beneath his chest harness. They were bunked down together in close quarters. Something Dare expected his team to roll with when circumstances demanded comfort and personal privacy be cut in favor of security.

"Sorcha, slow down . . ."

Dare had rolled over but he sat up, swinging his legs over the side of the cot as he caught the sound of Greer's voice.

"I do believe you. I'm your brother, I've seen you work before," Greer said.

Greer was pushing his feet into his boots as he spoke. It was enough action to have Dare and Vitus doing the same.

"I'll do my best to convince them." Greer was on his feet. "I can't leave my team, Sorcha. I won't."

Greer killed the call and faced off with them. "Sorcha

says we have a problem heading our way. A really big one."

Vitus pulled a military-grade rifle off the floor.

"What's her source?" Dare demanded as he checked the monitors giving them a feed from outside the building.

"Herself," Greer stated flatly. "My sister is a precognitive psychic."

Dare turned on him, but Greer was dead serious.

"You saw it yourself, Dare. Why would a woman like Sorcha be so important to a unit of Rangers? I've seen her work. If she says someone is heading out here to kill us, you'd better listen."

"She's an Unperson?"

Vitus asked the question. Dare turned and sent a questioning look at his fellow agent.

Greer nodded. "You've heard of them?"

"Crossed paths with one, once," Vitus said as he looked at Dare. "Did she give you details?"

"More than one coming after us. We've got minutes," Greer answered.

Vitus looked at Dare, waiting for him to make a decision.

"You and Reid out the front," Dare instructed. "Vitus, with me."

He didn't have time to ponder the validity of the warning. If there was even a sliver of a possibility of it being valid, he needed to act.

He was left with regrets over what he hadn't said to Jenna.

Dare pushed the thought aside as he put his back to the concrete wall, another rifle in his hands as he waited for Vitus to make the first entrance into the hallway that connected with the cell block. His senses were heightened, adrenaline surging through his bloodstream, making time slow down.

Jenna opened her eyes.

Crunch . . . *crunch* . . .

She heard it, knew what it was, and yet she blinked as she tried to clear her brain and decide what it was that seemed different.

Crunch . . .

And then a different-sounding crunch.

There was a full moon. The yellow light was coming through the thin windows above her head making a weird sort of ceiling lighting.

She caught motion in the shadows.

But from the wrong direction.

Crunch.

She rolled over the side of the cot, landing in a push-up position and rolling right across her cell until she was under the metal cot attached to the wall.

Maybe she was over-reacting. Dare could certainly enter the cell block from a different door.

Please let her be wrong . . .

The darkness was split by a flash and pop. The cot she'd been sleeping on shredded as bullets tore through it.

She jerked and shoved her hand into her mouth to stay silent.

And answering shot came from the direction Dare usually came from.

"Federal Agents!"

Gunfire flew through the area. Suddenly the concrete she'd found so dull and lifeless was keeping her alive by giving her a shield to hide behind.

There was a gasp and a dull sound as someone hit the

floor. Whoever he was, he'd died right next to the door of her cell, a shiny fluid flowing out from his body.

He'd come closer to make sure she was dead.

It was a sickening thought, but it sent her forward across the dusty concrete floor, reaching out for the rifle that had fallen from his grip.

There was more gunfire. Dare and his team were still thirty feet away, and she watched the approach of whoever was coming from the opposite side.

Jenna rolled onto her back, pulling the rifle through the bars and turning its muzzle toward the oncoming threat.

She loved Kagan at that moment.

Her lesson yielded enough confidence for her to lift the rifle into position and fire. There was a grunt and a word of profanity as one of the assailants was hit. He was a dark form in the semi-darkness, dropping heavily to his knees before he pitched forward and lay sprawled next to his companion.

"Jenna . . ." Dare was suddenly there, pushing a key into the lock and turning it.

She rolled onto her feet, clutching the rifle in a death grip as she stepped over the two bodies.

She didn't have time to think about the fact that she'd just killed someone.

It was him or you . . .

Dare pulled her toward a door, his fellow agent going through first, the muzzle of his rifle pointed forward. Vitus raised his fist and Dare was pushing her forward with a hard grip on her shoulder. The outside of the building was cast in eerie moonlight and darkness. Vitus hugged the wall, only peeking around the corner with one eye before rounding it.

Gunfire erupted behind them.

Both agents turned but they fell back, taking her into the underbrush and over-grown trees.

"Run Jenna . . ."

Dare grabbed her hand and tugged her as they started over rough ground. Branches and tree limbs slapped into her, leaving cuts and welts all over her arms and face. She ducked her chin to protect herself but never flinched.

The need to escape was far stronger than some stinging cuts.

She was breathing hard, but the instinct to put distance between her and the men trying to kill her was more important.

It was the only thought in her head.

Dare suddenly pulled her to a stop, dragging her down behind a berm of some sort. Just on the other side there was a set of railroad tracks. In the distance, she could hear the rumble of a train making its way toward them. She slid the safety on to the rifle as she panted softly.

"Where did you train, Jenna?" Dare demanded.

Dare was recovering his breath faster than she was.

"Don't give me shit either," he warned her. "That's a military-grade weapon, and you knew how to work it."

Vitus had his head turned so one ear was aimed at her but his sight was on the direction they'd come. "Kagan taught me," she said.

Her answer gained an immediate reaction from both men. Vitus turned to stare at her as Dare's eyebrows rose.

"What did you say?" Dare asked incredulously.

Jenna wiped her forehead with her arm, suddenly feeling every ache and pain. "Kagan," she said as she realized both men were glaring at her. "The guy you sent me up a riverbed to . . . know him when I saw him. He said his name was Kagan and he showed up a couple of nights ago and took me out to some military base thing and showed me how to use one of these . . ." She lifted the rifle. "Or one like it. I'm no expert."

"Describe him," Dare demanded.

"Big, impossible to read, but even so, he's the kind of guy I wouldn't get his martini order wrong if I was serving him."

"He just showed up and took you shooting?" Vitus asked.

"He was in my house when I got home. Even packed me a bag," Jenna answered. "He took me shooting and sent me to a concert and that's how I ended up at the casino. Know something? I got the feeling he was there because things weren't as finished as things appeared. Kagan didn't look like the sort to waste his time making sure I had some buddy time."

Vitus and Dare shared a look. The tension was thick enough to cut with a knife. The train was getting closer, filling the night with the sound of its metal wheels moving over the rails.

"The game is bigger than we thought," Dare said to Vitus.

"Who is Kagan?" Jenna asked.

"I've got to get Miranda out of the line of fire," Vitus said without answering her question.

Dare nodded. "I'm going off grid with Jenna."

"No contact through the nest," Vitus continued. "Too risky."

"Agreed."

Vitus reached out and hit Dare in the shoulder with a closed fist. It was a gentle touch but one that made Jenna's eyes round with alarm. The guy was gone a moment later, slipping into the darkness like he'd never been there.

"Who is Kagan?" she repeated. The ground was starting to vibrate as the train came into sight. It was moving at a crawl.

Dare looked at the train before looking back at her. "My boss."

He suddenly cupped the side of her face. "If he's placing you in play, the stakes are high."

Whatever else he'd wanted to say, the train cut off the opportunity for conversation. But he rubbed her cheek like she was somehow precious to him.

You're seeing what you want to see again . . .

Maybe. But there was no time to ponder her thoughts. Dare was pointing at the boxcars passing them. He shrugged the shoulder strap of his rifle over his head.

Jenna felt her eyes widen as she caught on to exactly what he was planning. She struggled to get the shoulder strap of her rifle over her head before Dare spotted an open door on one of the approaching boxcars. He reached down and gripped her wrist, tugging her after him as he went toward the open door.

"I don't know what an 'Unperson' is"—Zane wiped his forehead before continuing—"but I love your sister."

Greer grunted. He had a lot of mixed feelings when it came to his sister Sorcha. More than half of them could have neatly fit under the term "resentment."

"We've got to alert Kagan," Zane said. "Make sure he puts the other teams on alert."

Greer nodded and flashed his badge at the security man standing in front of the doors of a DMV. There was a line of people stretching around the building. They let out several unflattering comments as he and

Zane made it through the doors without the security officer raising an objection. Inside there were scores of people holding their waiting numbers as the different stations worked through the scores of people needing services.

Greer flashed his badge again as he came through the opening to the back-office area.

"Excuse me?" a clerk declared as she turned around from where a woman was arguing about having to take a written exam for the renewal of her driver's license.

"Federal Agents." Zane flipped his badge open.

"Um . . . hmmm . . ." she grumbled. "That doesn't tell me what you're doing in my office."

"We need a phone," Greer said on his way to the back room.

"A private one." Zane stepped into the path of the woman as she stood up, intent on taking issue with Greer. "We'll be gone before you notice."

Greer picked up the phone and dialed.

"We were hit," he informed Kagan.

"How bad?"

"Zane and I dropped one on our way out," Greer explained. "Vitus and Dare went for the witness. Four hours ago. We left everything behind."

"Right," Kagan replied. "I'll get a team on it."

"We survived because my sister called me and gave me a head start," Greer said.

There was a long pause on the other end of the line.

"I didn't realize you had a means of contact with Sorcha," Kagan admitted.

Greer felt his patience wearing thin. "You can be sure it was her idea and no one liked hearing it. We'd be dead if she hadn't called. It was a full tactical team. They knew location and came in from both sides."

"Stay off grid," Kagan ordered. "Check in schedule Charlie."

Greer hung up the phone. He understood Kagan's orders and he hoped his section leader had heard him when it came to his sister.

Zane was guarding the door to the back room. His huge frame meant the rest of the staff of the DMV was cutting him a wide path even if more than one of them was shooting Zane a scathing glance.

"Are we done here at the hen house?" Zane asked when Greer reappeared.

"Charlie."

Zane nodded as he sat down at a terminal and punched in a clearance code. The computers all flickered before he finished typing in another line of commands that had more than one employee muttering an expletive.

Greer held up his badge as the supervisor faced off with him. Zane's typing finished and he was up and out of the chair as every system in the placed crashed to begin a reboot.

"Give it ten minutes," Zane informed the supervisor with a wink.

"I think she flipped you off," Greer muttered as they cleared the building.

"Don't blame her, but still I'm not sorry." He pointed down the road. "Civilian police. Let's grab a lift."

The police officer was a little more welcoming. A gleam flickered in the guy's eyes as he disconnected his body camera and killed the on-board surveillance system.

"I'll admit," the guy said as he pulled into traffic with Greer and Zane in the back of his squad car, "it's kind of nice to have something to do that might make the world a better place." He started to look in the rearview mirror, but Greer cleared his throat and the guy corrected his angle of vision. "You get what I mean."

"It's not all fun," Greer replied.

But he did admit to enjoying the fact that they were still alive. After all, someone had gone to a lot of trouble to make sure they weren't.

Now that part was fun and it was going to be a blast when he got the chance to bust in the door of whoever had sent a team after them.

A real party and a half.

Kagan turned a pen over in his fingers. He stopped for a moment and rotated it a few more times.

A full tactical team didn't come cheap.

And on American soil, it was likely they were ex-military.

He stood up and left, moving through the office building as work continued like he wasn't there. No one looked up and that was the way he liked it. Washington D.C. was bristling. The approaching election meant a slew of posters were attached to every available surface.

Carl Davis's name was everywhere.

Kagan turned down a few streets before he entered a bagel shop. He took off his hat and put it on a hook hanging from the wall. The guy serving behind the counter did his part by keeping the customers in front of the case distracted as Kagan slipped through a hidden door in the back. Inside a hallway, there were several agents working at terminals. One of them that was the same build as he was took his jacket and went up to sit in the bagel shop with his back to the street.

Kagan continued on down to where Colonel Bryan Magnus was running his secret research facility beneath the city streets.

"I need assistance," Kagan began.

The colonel punched in a code on his keyboard. The door behind them locked with a soft click.

"A full tactical team went after one of my teams four hours ago." Kagan sat down in front of the colonel's desk. "They knew when and where to find them. I want to know who ran the trace."

"There are only two agencies that come to mind," Bryan offered as he typed. "Did Vitus Hale make it out?"

"Yes."

Colonel Magnus was reading the information coming across the screen. His face tightened as he slapped a command into the printer.

"Homeland." He said as the printer started spitting out pages. "I'll give you one guess who requested it."

"The office of Congressman Carl Davis," Kagan answered.

The colonel nodded. He grabbed the sheets from the printer tray and pushed them across the desk to Kagan. "Be aware, Homeland tried to erase the record of the search but we have a catch basin for all federal agents who are identified through the system. It's a backdoor only those with enough clearance know about."

Kagan studied the log ins and looked at the picture of Dare Servant kissing Jenna Henson.

"Do me a favor and keep a tight leash on Dr. Damascus Hale. Her husband is working a case for me," Kagan said.

"Can I assist?" Bryan asked with menace in his tone. "There's nothing I'd like better than helping bring that prick down."

Kagan looked up and locked stares with the colonel. "As a matter of fact, yes you can do something. I'm going to rattle Carl's chain. Make sure he knows he's not the only one who can use the system."

Bryan cracked his knuckles. "How can I help?"

"It's a dangerous game," Kagan advised him seriously. "He's threatening to shut down my Shadow Ops teams with an executive order."

The colonel slowly grinned. "He's dumb enough to do it, which means we have to keep him out of the White House." Bryan's face became serious. "I'm still in."

The box car was drafty.

As the train gained speed, it felt like they were in a wind storm. Jenna drew her knees up and tucked her hands between her calves and thighs, but her cotton sweatshirt was little protection against the high-speed gusts of wind.

"Come here . . ." Dare came close. Gathering her against his body.

She pushed away from him.

He cupped her chin, raising her face so their gazes met. Determination glittered there. It frustrated her because it was too damned noisy to demand an explanation from him. All she was left with was the way he cupped her chin with a tenderness she'd nearly died from having him discard.

Was she being overly emotional?

Fuck that.

There was a stark difference and she felt it nearly bone deep.

She really shouldn't.

As in. . . . really . . . really . . . shouldn't trust the guy. Not in the personal sense anyway.

Except he'd just saved her life. At least, she thought

he had. Maybe they were just kicking fate's ass to-gether.

He smelled good.

Jenna! She scolded herself. Remember? Dick? She did and yet, at the moment, he was her rock. The rifle slung across her back made her feel pretty darn cool for being able to keep up with him, too.

Sorcha McRae let out a sigh of relief when her brother answered the phone.

"I'm good, Sorcha," Greer informed her. "You saved us. I'm going off-grid."

"I'll call again," she promised.

The called ended, leaving her clutching the phone to her chest as the vision that had sent her scrambling to warn her brother played across her mind again. It was weaker now, the part where she'd seen Greer laying in a widening pool of blood fading like it had never happened.

It hadn't.

She drew in a deep breath and felt her mind shifting focus. Her grasp on reality increased as her sixth sense stopped broadcasting at top volume.

"Are you in the present?" Major Caxton asked.

Sorcha was very used to the way her commanding officer shadowed her. He was light-footed and too damned keen for her own sense of self at times. He knew her, studied her. All in the interest of being more effective in keeping her alive, but still.

Sometimes she felt caged.

"Yes," she answered as she turned her attention on him. Her grip on the phone tightened.

"I'm not going to ask for it." Caxton's gaze dropped

for a moment to the phone. "Just advise you to keep it off so you can't be tracked."

"They were going to kill my brother," she defended her actions.

Caxton offered her a tilt of his head. He had his mirrored sunglasses on, making it impossible to read his emotions.

"I'd be pretty heartless if I denied you the chance to help your own blood when all I do is take you on mission after mission," Caxton answered.

Sorcha discovered herself uncertain about Caxton. They'd only been together for half a year.

"The look on your face says your last C.O. wasn't as accommodating."

She shook her head.

"In that case," Caxton looked around before pulling his shades off, "make your calls inside the hangar from now on. I don't need someone reporting it." He sent her a hard look. "It's none of their business."

Sorcha slowly smiled. She took off toward the hangar where she'd been assigned to a bunkhouse. They didn't keep her with the other members of the military. An "Unperson" wasn't supposed to be seen, and the powers that be made sure she lived in the shadows.

But Caxton was an interesting surprise.

Oh, he was still as rigid as the last few C.O.'s she'd suffered. Men devoted to their duty and the greater good, and, in many respects, she was on board with it all.

Sometimes though, she wanted to be Sorcha. She wanted to be more than an operative.

Not that she got much of a chance.

More and more she felt stifled. Like she was slowly being pulled off the ground by a noose. There wouldn't be any quick death from a broken neck. No, she was going to suffer through fighting for every breath until she just couldn't draw another one.

But you have your phone . . .

Her next breath came a little easier.

And that was really nice.

Really, really nice.

"We need to jump."

The train was slowing down.

"Before we hit the yard." Dare raised his voice enough for her to hear him. "To avoid the security cameras."

The boxcar was still jolting along but as the speed decreased, it became more of a lumbering roll that was much easier to walk through. Dare was braced by the open door, looking ahead of them. She came up beside him, and he pointed.

"Ready?"

Jenna didn't think it through. She nodded and tightened her resolve.

She was keeping pace with him.

Yeah . . . right . . . and you're about to jump out of a moving train!

It terrified her and left her thrilled, too.

She needed to call it the "Dare" effect.

He looked back at her as the spot came close. She aimed her best ready-to-take-on-the-world look back at him. The corners of his lips curved up in approval. A moment later, he was pulling her though the open doorway by a hard grip on her upper arm.

They were weightless for seconds that felt like hours and then they hit the ground with a hard jolt. Dare pulled her into a ball, rolling over and over with her in a tangle of limbs until they stopped in a gully.

Jenna landed on her back, looking up at the sky. She blinked, feeling bruised, and tasting dirt in her mouth.

But she chuckled.

"Fun?" Dare asked as he rolled up and onto his haunches.

Seeing him poised and ready deflated a little of her confidence. "Traveling with you is never normal."

At least her tone didn't unmask her. Her voice sounded slightly husky and partially amused. She gained her feet as Dare started off in the direction of a riverbed.

"The guns will draw too much attention." He stopped beside a tree and contemplated their options. "But I don't want to leave them where some kids might find them."

"Here." Jenna handed her rifle over as she pulled her sweatshirt off. She reached back for the rifle and pulled the garment over it. Dare watched her for a moment before handing his to her. With the hood up and hooked over the butts of the weapons, she could put them against her shoulder like a baby.

Dare nodded. "Guess you'll have to look like you like me since we have a kid."

Jenna narrowed her eyes in response. "You would have done better not to bring up—"

"How much of a dick I was," he cut her off. "Problem is, we've got a fair bit of ground to cover before I can feel secure in taking the time to talk the matter though."

"There is nothing to talk about," Jenna informed him.

He cupped her cheek, but she recoiled. "I can't think when you do that."

It was a confession.

A very deep and personal one.

A weakness . . .

"I know the problem, baby," he reached down and hooked her upper arm, pulling her onto the road as he started walking. "Which is why we're going to have that talk."

"No need to bother," she informed him. "You've made your position clear enough. I'm just a case."

He reversed course and hooked her around the waist. She was suddenly up against him, rifle baby and all.

"You're more."

He smothered her retort beneath a kiss. She sputtered, but he caught her nape and refused to release her.

But it wasn't a hard kiss. No, he worked his mouth over hers like it was some sort of reunion. Teasing and coaxing her mouth to open for him.

She melted.

Principles didn't hold up against the way he tasted. Her insides twisted, and her nipples tightened. Cold logical lectures were no defense against the way his kiss made her feel.

But he was suddenly pulling away from her, turning around to face a truck that was coming down the road. It was a huge big rig and hadn't really gained any speed. The air breaks hissed, and the cab jerked and rocked as the driver stopped.

"You kids need a lift?"

Dare nodded as Jenna realized he'd stuck his thumb out.

"Ready to get out of here?"

Ricky Sullivan didn't want to be eager, but his fucking mouth started watering. Kagan wasn't carrying the black backpack he always arrived with. Ricky wasn't stupid.

"Since you don't have the backpack with you, I can't really say no," Ricky said.

Kagan only offered him a bland expression. "Timer is ticking. Are you coming with me or staying here?"

"I'm coming," Ricky said.

Kagan backed up, leaving the doorway clear. Ricky did enjoy walking through it. He'd stared at the stupid thing too many hours to count. But he wasn't going to count his chickens before they hatched. Kagan had only kept him alive so the section leader might use him.

All in all, Ricky sort of liked the guy. Or maybe it was better to say, Kagan was the sort of man Ricky could do business with.

The building he'd been imprisoned in was a dark, crumbling mess on the outside. Located in a suburb of Washington D.C. in what had once been a bustling manufacturing plant. Now it was being reclaimed by nature on the outside.

"What do you want?" Ricky asked. "Or have you come to escort me to my execution?"

Kagan tilted his head to one side. "Bram Magnus would like me to do that. Run and I'll let him know where you are."

Kagan climbed behind the wheel of a Jeep. Ricky opened the passenger side and got in.

"I need you to reconnect with Carl Davis," Kagan said.

Ricky scoffed. "I killed his boy Tyler Martin. What makes you think Carl wants anything to do with me?"

"He'll want to tie off the loose end you represent," Kagan answered.

Ricky grunted. "So you're feeding me to him?" He looked out the window, but they were going too fast for him to dive out of the Jeep.

"I want him rattled," Kagan stated clearly. "Knocked out of his stride. Seeing you will make him realize he's not as confident in his position as he believes."

Ricky enjoyed the idea enough to grin. "He is an arrogant puss bag alright. What's the deal you're offering?"

"I'm offering you a chance to earn a passport from me. Your accounts are still where you left them, all you need is the freedom to exit the United States and enter Ireland legally." Kagan kept his eyes on the road. "Leaving the U.S. won't be much of a challenge for a man like you."

"Setting up a legal life in Ireland will," Ricky answered. "Why are you willing to work with me? I tried to take out one of your precious Shadow Ops teams."

"You work with scum," Kagan replied. "The kind of scum I need you to rattle so I can do my job. I sort of thought you'd enjoy getting a chance to mess with Carl Davis. He left you to rot in Mexico."

"You left me to rot in that apartment," Ricky growled.

"I put you on ice for a bit. My teams weren't the only ones trying to kill you," Kagan corrected him. "If you can't see the difference, you're not smart enough to see the value in my offer."

Kagan abruptly pulled off the highway. The tires spewed dirt and gravel, the Jeep rocking because of how fast Kagan stopped.

"Enjoy your freedom," Kagan said.

Ricky was tempted.

He looked out the window of the Jeep at the thick trees and bushes growing along the side of the highway.

He'd be gone in a flash.

Yeah, but gone to where, boy-o?

The life he'd played so hard to get, the money that

would allow him to open a fight club, have a big house
and live like a king wouldn't be his. Sure, the money was
waiting but without a passport, he'd spend the rest of his
days avoiding any place with security cameras and face-
recognition software.

"I'll enjoy it more with that passport you were talking about," Ricky admitted.

Kagan nodded. "Kill any of my team members and
the deal is off."

Ricky slowly grinned. "Noticed you didn't include
Carl Davis in that warning."

Kagan slowly grinned. "I'm not hiring you to kill
him. That isn't how I work."

Ricky laughed. "You're not too bad." Kagan was pulling back onto the highway as Ricky contemplated
him. "I'm not saying I like you but you're not too bad at
all."

"Hope you don't cross the lines I lay down," Kagan
replied. "Because I can make you look like a nun and
that place in Mexico a spa."

"I'm going to try and kick your ass someday, just for
the fun of it."

Ricky caught the hint of a chuckle from Kagan.

"So give me the details of the job," Ricky said.

"Sure you want off here?"

Dare nodded. "Appreciate it."

The truck driver shook his head but shifted gears and
pulled his big rig to a stop. "That's the quietest baby I
ever met."

He winked as Jenna climbed down, doing her best to
look like she was cradling a child.

"Thanks for the company!" The driver called as he
started back down the road.

He hadn't stopped talking the whole way.

"He knows it's not a baby," Dare told her. "He had a revolver stashed beneath his seat."

"You could have told me," she groused as he started off the side of the highway. "My shoulder is stiff from holding it."

"I'll rub it out for you."

Dare was cutting under an overpass that allowed for river water to flow under the road. The water level was low because of the season, leaving a tangled mess of dead tree limbs mixed in with garbage.

People really needed to learn to use trash cans, she decided.

Dare fought his way alongside the concrete embankment that supported the highway. He was pushing at limbs of trees, baring the wall hidden behind the foliage.

Whatever he'd been looking for, he found. There was a groan, like metal grinding, and then he was pulling a door open.

"Stay here."

He pulled his gun and ducked inside with the weapon leading the way.

Her curiosity was impossible to ignore and she moved closer, peeking inside the door. All she saw were stairs leading down. There was a flicker of lights from a room below.

"Come on down, Jenna," Dare said. "Pull the door shut behind you."

She eased through the doorway, angling the rifles so she could get them inside in spite of the branches. When she tugged on the door to close it, she heard the limbs scraping across the surface of it on the other side.

The air was stale, but the stairs were surprisingly

clean of dust and cobwebs. It was a narrow set of stairs with a low roof. When she reached the bottom, she stared at a control room.

"Whoa . . ." she muttered as she put the rifle baby down.

"Cold War–era communications bunker," Dare explained. "It was cutting-edge technology in its day."

Now the control panels looked ridiculous because of how big they were. Two padded chairs faced an entire wall of screens and buttons. Five separate key locks were installed in the dashboards of the systems.

Dare was across the room, punching a large button. There was a groan and then fresh air was suddenly blowing in the vents above their heads.

"That will make it better in here," he muttered. "Living quarters will be back here."

"As in . . . there might be a shower?"

Dare turned and winked at her. "I think we've earned a little reward."

She followed him through a doorway. Above their heads, she heard a distant rumble and realized the bunker was built directly under the highway.

"We're in the middle of nowhere," she said.

Dare had moved into a small kitchen. He reached out and turned the faucet. A little groaning and suddenly water came out of it.

"But we're in the middle of nowhere in Florida." Dare shut the water off. "Which was somewhere back when listening to Cuba was essential to defense. One of the reasons the theme parks were able to pick up such a large chunk of undeveloped land. The government had kept it tied up."

"Right," Jenna replied.

Dare was opening cupboards and pulling out a few

packages to read the labels. "The food is less than fresh but soap doesn't really have a spoilage issue. Try the bathroom. See what there is."

Jenna moved through a doorway and ran her hand along the side of the wall looking for a switch. The light flickered on to show her a bunk house. Two bunks on either side of a concrete walled room. A door was at the far side of the room, and it opened up into a bathroom.

The shower didn't have a door. It was just one side of the room, tiled from floor to ceiling with a shower head and shelf for a soap bar.

She turned the control and smiled with delight as clear water started flowing from the head. Turning it off, she rummaged through the small cabinet until she found a tin with soap bars. They were a little dry but she pulled one out and headed for the shower.

She shied away from thinking about what was going to happen next.

One emergency at a time.

Being clean would help her recharge.

At least that was the plan she was going with.

Being free was better than he'd remembered.

Ricky Sullivan tipped his face back and let the sun bake his face.

Oh yeah . . . the darkest hour was always before the dawn.

His mother had taken solace in faith when his father ended up in prison, leaving her to fend for herself. There had been a few pictures in the dump he'd grown up in to show what a beauty she'd been before time and poverty had taken their toll on her.

He'd learned to fight to bring home scraps for them to share.

He'd been good at it, too. And smart. He'd learned to find the fat cats who he could milk. Men like Carl Davis thought they were entitled to more than other men and that the rules didn't apply because they had money. They happily let men like Ricky's father take the fall for their grand ideas. His father had gone to prison for making a bomb in the interest of freeing Ireland and Carl Davis's man Tyler Martin had tried to use Ricky to make sure there was no one left alive to incriminate Carl while he ran for President.

Like father, like son . . .

Money turned brother against brother and made good men turn their principles over in favor of being successful. A man such as Carl would smile and swear he was honest but that was just another lie.

"Remember," Kagan advised him softly, "stick to the plan. It's simple enough."

"It's also likely to get me shot," Ricky replied.

"You can leave anytime," Kagan reminded him.

Ricky shrugged. "I want the passport. You know it, old man. No need to bust my chops."

Kagan didn't give him so much as a raised eyebrow. Ricky lifted two fingers to his temple and offered a mocking salute before he was off. With money in his pocket and an identification card, he had places to go.

And be seen.

That was the deal.

Ricky snickered as he climbed into a taxi and headed for the airport. Carl Davis was going to shit himself. At least, Ricky sure hoped the man was startled by Ricky's reappearance.

Kagan was a smart son of a bitch.

A crafty one, too.

After so much time on ice, Ricky was going to enjoy being in the ring again.

"Yes, sir," Vitus Hale growled the expected response.

"I know you're not happy," Kagan said. "If you weren't there, I wouldn't trust him near the congresswoman. It's a chance we have to take."

"Understood," Vitus replied.

"Shoot him if he crosses the line," Kagan said.

Vitus grinned and killed the call. Miranda was waiting for him to fill her in. "Kagan is sending in a resource. One he feels will knock Carl Davis for a loop."

Miranda softly smiled. "I'm in favor of that."

"It's Rick Sullivan."

Miranda's eyes widened. "Excuse me but I don't believe I heard you correctly."

Vitus nodded. "You did. The man who tried to kill all of us during Bram Magnus's wedding. Kagan's had him on ice but feels it's time to put him into play."

Miranda surprised him by thinking the situation through for a long moment. "Carl really will not be very happy about seeing the man."

"Carl needs to feel vulnerable," Vitus explained.

"Yes," Miranda answered. "I can see the wisdom of the plan."

Vitus watched his mother-in-law for a moment.

"I will be right here," he said.

Miranda sent him a smile. "You should be with Damascus."

Vitus slowly grinned. "She'd send me straight back to your side after tearing a strip off my hide for leaving you."

"I believe you are correct."

* * *

Dare Servant was a magnificent specimen.

Jenna froze with her fork in her mouth when he came out of the bathroom wearing only his pants.

But she was suddenly recalling the moment in the sky suite when he'd looked the same.

Water glistened in his dark chest hair, but a look of solid determination was on his face.

She dropped the fork and stood up.

"I was a dick," Dare stated clearly and firmly.

She'd started to turn toward the sink under the guise of cleaning up her dish.

"Guilty as charged," he continued as he closed the distance between them. "We spotted you in the box seat and that was too much coincidence."

She wanted to be pissed. Her pride sort of demanded it, and yet there he was talking to her, not just telling her the way it was going to be. She turned to face him.

"I don't make the connection," she said.

But she wanted to. Or at least she was trying to listen to him when all she really wanted was to hit him. Somehow inflict the same amount of pain he'd given her.

Jenna made a get-going motion with her hand. "I think we might actually be having a conversation here but I'm confused as to the coincidence you mention."

"Kirkland," Dare said. "He owned the house we first met in."

"What?" Her brain was having trouble. It was too crazy an answer to the entire mess.

"I am investigating Kirkland Grog for human trafficking," Dare clarified. "You were resettled and showed up in a box seat at his concert. Something you didn't have the money for."

Oh fuck . . .

"Kagan gave me the tickets . . ." she muttered.

"Seemed stupid to sit at home doing nothing . . . Damn I knew he took me shooting for some reason."

Dare grunted. "I don't know why he put you in play, but I can guess it's because Kirkland is very good at making clean get-aways." Dare perched on the edge of the table. "Kagan knows you wanted to help gather evidence against Kirkland on the docks. Looks like he gave you a shot."

Jenna was in too tight a space. She wanted to pace but only had a few feet on either side of her.

"That's insane," she said.

"It's logical." Dare's voice was smooth and soft. "I should have seen it."

"Don't put on the kid gloves now, Servant," she muttered. "Anyway, I told you not to pity me."

"It's not pity to feel bad about . . . treating you like a case," he argued.

"No," she agreed. "I'm pretty sure you deserve to feel like crap except . . ."

Dare lifted an eyebrow. "We're having a conversation . . . remember?"

Jenna locked gazes with him. "Except those pictures of the dead girls sort of justify your motivation."

Which just returned the shine to his good-guy image.

Oh, she was happy about that end of the deal.

"So what now?" She opened her hands. "What is the plan to deal with the people trying to kill you and your men?"

Dare straightened up. "We're not changing topics, Jenna."

"You were doing your job . . . I get it. Understand it . . . sort of agree."

His lips twitched. "You're still pissed."

She sent him a raised eyebrow back. "Wouldn't you be a little worried if I weren't?"

Which earned her a chuckle that turned into full laughter. "You're a minx."

"Because I don't go for having your team listening in while we're in the bedroom?" she asked.

Dare shook his head. "Because you don't take my shit and push me over lines I would have bet my last dollar against me never crossing."

"You're losing me."

His face tightened. "I'm trying to gain you back, Jenna. Let me break this down for you. I have all the authority backing me up to do everything I did and worse. Shadow Ops means we take the cases from the gutter and there's only one way to win a street fight, baby . . ." He came closer, pinning her against the range. "Fight dirty."

He was looming over her. She witnessed the battle in his eyes and it struck something deep inside her. Moving past all the bruised emotions to touch her heart. "I saw her, the girl. I get it."

Dare reached up and stroked her cheek. "My dad used to do this to my mother, before he went to work." His tone had lowered. "I never got it until I met you." His eyes glistened with emotion, freezing her in place with the level of intensity. "He loved her."

Dare was suddenly pushing away from the range, the tiny concrete room too small to contain all the rage coming off him.

"He was a cop . . ." Dare turned and pegged her with a hard look. "His work followed him home and they killed everyone except for me. While he watched and they made sure he lived long enough to know the pain of losing his family."

Jenna wanted to retch. Her belly was rolling with the need but she wanted to soothe him more.

Dare recoiled from her. "I can't love you."

It wasn't a rejection. No, what she heard in his tone was far more intense. It was the need to shelter her, protect her, and it was by far more of a declaration than any muttered "I love you."

His face was a mask of determination as he shook his head and took another step away from her. "The sort of criminals I deal with don't just come after me. Letting you go is how I protect you, Jenna."

Something snapped inside her.

"Sounds great," Jenna replied. "Except for one detail."

He raised an eyebrow in question.

"The moment I met you, fate grabbed hold of me and doesn't seem to give a fig for what I logically think or decide."

She moved toward him, feeling like she was actually in control of the moment as he stood and watched her approach.

Damn, sometimes she forgot how big he was . . .

She had to tip her head back to maintain eye contact. "So don't . . ." She laid her hands on his chest, feeling the connection between their flesh like a live wire. "Don't whine about dealing with the exact same thing happening to you . . ." she threaded her fingers through his chest hair. "This is happening . . . to both of us."

He cupped her hips, sending a little jolt of awareness through her. It was deeply erotic, traveling into her core.

"Fair is fair?" he inquired as his eyes narrowed and she rubbed her hands over the hard bulges of his pectorals.

"Exactly," she muttered, stretching up to kiss his jaw.

So simple, and yet she realized she craved the lightest of contacts with him just as much as the harder ones. There was an intimacy in kissing his chin, a spark of excitement rising from the way she felt him shudder in response.

"You make me understand intimacy," she muttered in a whisper.

He scooped her off her feet, cradling her against his chest as he carried her into the bunk house. He laid her down, smoothing her hair back from her face as he stared at her for a long moment.

"I half expect to wake up and find this nothing but a dream," he said.

Jenna reached up, curling her hand around his nape. "Let's let the dream continue . . . All we have to do is refuse to doubt it."

"Works for me," he said in a husky tone.

He was all man-animal. At the moment, he was hard and warm. There was a slight scent of soap clinging to his skin as he claimed her mouth in a kiss. She pushed her hand into his hair, finding droplets of water still clinging to his scalp.

There was something raw about knowing he was fresh from the shower.

Just as there was something about his kiss that made her crave more of his skin.

What started out as a moment of soft enjoyment was rapidly giving way to urgency. Part of her just didn't want to risk the dream bubble popping and dropping her back into a cold reality where Dare was someone she couldn't reach.

She reached for him, sliding her hands along his chest as she sat up and purred when he tugged her shirt up and over her head. The little hooks on her bra lasted only a moment before Dare was stripping the undergarment down her arms and tossing it aside.

"Pretty sure this bunk hasn't seen this type of action before," he muttered as he cupped her breasts.

"Not in the flesh anyway," she countered as she stood up and stripped out of her jeans.

"I love your ass . . ."

Jenna turned away, but he caught her up against his body, reaching down to cup her bottom.

"I . . . love"—his lips were so close to hers, she felt his breath—"this . . . butt . . . don't ever lose it."

The proof of his words was pressing against her. His cock was hard behind his fly.

And it was too tempting for her to ignore.

"I have some favorite parts of you . . ."

He chuckled softly, allowing her to open his waistband and reach inside to free his cock.

"I hope to God that's one of your favorite parts . . ."

It was a wholly male thing to say. As in, locker-room vocabulary.

She liked it though because they were alone and the only person he was bragging to was her. "I have to admit . . ."

She drew her hand along his length to the head, where she worried the underside of it with her thumb.

He drew in a harsh breath. "Admit . . . what?"

Jenna pumped her hand down to the base of his length and then pulled upward as she let her fingers milk him.

"Oh . . . would you prefer we . . . talk?" She aimed wide eyes at him, pumping her hand up and down his cock a few more times.

His lips thinned, arousal flickering in his eyes. "Talk . . . no . . . scream . . ." There was a flash of warning in his eyes. "Let's not waste all this concrete."

His complacency evaporated in a second. She watched the way his expression changed, sending a thrill of anticipation through her insides as he scooped her up and cradled her on her way back onto the bunk.

"Dare . . ."

Was she warning him?

Or encouraging him?

Truthfully, it felt like a mixture sure to intoxicate her with the combination. The hint of being pushed out of control was the spice that added a little burn to the experience.

Hell, sex with Dare was an epic experience.

"Now . . . let's see if I can't do this right . . ."

He'd pulled her knees over the edge of the bunk and pushed her legs wide. It left her sex exposed to his gaze. He reached out and teased her folds, slipping his fingers along the outer edges where the skin was so sensitive that she tried to roll away.

"Easy, baby . . ."

There was a note of coaxing in his tone but what thrilled her was the flash of determination in his eyes.

Like she was the sole purpose of his existence.

He leaned forward, allowing her to feel his breath against her spread sex before she let out a cry as he lapped her. She was in a state of heightened arousal with his mouth hot against her. He licked her from opening to clit, closing his lips around the little throbbing bundle of nerves and sucking.

"Christ!" She gripped the blanket, curling up, but at the same time, her hips were lifting toward his mouth, seeking more pressure. Her insides were churning, the need to climax building incredibly fast. She was being fast-tracked, her self-control left behind by the frantic pace. He moved down and rimmed her with the tip of his tongue, awakening a whole new set of cravings inside her passage.

She wanted him inside her.

Wanted to fuck.

It was blunt, just like all of her impulses were when it came to Dare.

"I didn't use my mouth before . . ." He was standing up, enjoying the way she was laid out in front of him. There was a purely male glow of satisfaction on his face.

"That would have been too personal."

He shucked his pants, his cock jutting out from his body. "I want to be very personal with you, Jenna."

She curled up, clasping his length and taking it inside her mouth. It seemed the most natural thing to do, like a completion of the moment. Just being in contact with him was what was important. His hand was in her hair, fisting in the strands as he growled. She coaxed the first few drops of his cum from his cock before he was pulling her back, denying her a victory.

"I need more, Jenna . . ." He was gathering her up against him, turning and pressing her back to the wall. "I have to have *more* . . ."

His eyes glowed as he lifted her up and impaled her. She gasped, her head rolling back as she locked her legs around his body and held tight to his shoulders.

"Give it to me . . ." She rasped. "Give me . . . *More* . . ."

He didn't hesitate. Flexing his hips to work his cock back and forth, thrusting hard into her as she cried out. There was too much to contain, so she just let go and went with the moment.

His cries . . .

Her cries . . .

It was all a jumbled mess that bounced around inside the walls as they strained towards each other. Control had long since vanished, leaving them both at the mercy of the intensity of the moment.

Cravings . . .

Hunger . . .

Those were the only things left in her world and the man feeding those urges. She strained toward him, absorbing each thrust as the wall behind her supported them both.

Climax was hard.

It felt like it ripped through her, sending her spiraling out of control. She screamed, needing a release as she heard him growl.

Not a low sound of amusement, this was savage and full bodied. He enunciated it with a hard thrust that buried his length in her to the base. His balls slapped against her while she felt the spurt of his release.

God, that was the final thing.

The feeling of his hot cum flooding her. She came again; this time it felt like her womb was tightening.

"Too . . . damned . . . fast . . ." Dare was panting, leaning against her as he quivered.

But he didn't let her down, he carried her into the shower, where the cold water was refreshing and the perfect ending to the moment. He washed her. Running the soap along her limbs as she turned and let the water ease the ache from how hard she'd been straining. He cupped her breasts, teasing her nipples as he lathered them up before turning her to face the spray.

"Too fast . . ." He muttered against her shoulder.

"Let's do something about it . . ."

Jenna took him by the hand, leaving wet footprints through the doorway on the way back to the bunk.

Yeah, live in the moment.

No matter what.

Campaigns involved lots of people.

Carl soaked up the cheers, even enjoying the protest signs present. His path to and from speaking engagements was always well secured. His supporters were pressing up against the barricades, trying to shake his hand. He dove from one side to the other, making contact with people.

And then his blood froze.

His poise faltered as he stared at a ghost.

Rick Sullivan.

Eric was quick to notice, easing Carl forward. Shock held him tight though and he looked over his shoulder expecting the guy to be gone.

Just a trick of stress.

But he was there, leaning past people to smile and wave at Carl.

"Let's let the dream continue . . . all we have to do is refuse to doubt it."

Jenna was asleep, but her words rose from his memory. Dare smoothed a hand along her hip, enjoying the way she was curled against his side.

"What are you thinking about?" She lifted her head and locked gazes with him.

He offered her a grin. "Not bad, I thought you were sleeping."

She shifted her thigh against his. "And waste this moment?"

She was suddenly moving, rising up and straddling

him. Her breasts were in perfect position for him to cup as she rocked back and forth against his cock where it was lying between the folds of her sex.

She was still wet.

From him.

It was erotic and tender and everything he'd decided didn't have a place in his life.

Maybe she was right. They should let the dream continue.

"You'd better listen to me . . ." Carl hissed at Kirkland. "I've got a fucking picture of him and it's Ricky Sullivan for sure. He knows too much about both of us."

"I thought you said he was killed by Shadow Ops." Kirkland's voice was full of doubt.

"It's him," Carl insisted.

"Then get off the fucking phone," Kirkland replied. "Someone is messing with you, don't lead them to me."

The line died, leaving Carl looking at the tumbler of whiskey on his desk. The liquor held no appeal for a change.

He was so close.

Mere weeks separated him from the election.

But Sullivan knew a hell of a lot. Carl paced around the office for a moment before his assistant chimed in on the intercom.

"Ten minutes, sir."

Below him, there were people paying two thousand dollars a plate to hear him speak. It would all go to charity. Just the right touch for the final days of the election.

Fuck.

He grunted and collected himself before letting his security detail escort him to the ballroom. The sea of faces was a happy one, applause bouncing around the

room while he made his way to the podium. It took a
long time for the crowd to settle down enough for him
to speak.

That fueled his confidence.

He was leading in the polls and the time was running
down. Even Rick Sullivan wouldn't be able to stop him
soon. His passion rose as he finished his speech, the
crowd rising up to give him a standing ovation. The
smile he flashed them was genuine.

It was too late in the game.

He moved around the room greeting movers in the
state of Florida, pausing for pictures until it was time to
leave. His exit was rehearsed. Both options. Eric was by
his side as they took to the stairs and stepped out the
back entrance of the hotel.

Carl settled back into the plush seat of his armored limousine, reaching for a whisky, his earlier upset forgotten.

But he never tasted the liquor. His hand was frozen
half-way to his lips as he looked through the tinted
window and found Kagan looking back at him.

Half concealed by a loading dock, the Shadow Ops
section leader was in a perfect place to be seen as Carl's
driver followed the instruction laid down for him.

It was no coincidence.

Kagan sent him a solid stare before melting back into
the darkness.

Carl wanted to be pissed.

Instead, he ended up reaching for a napkin to mop
away the cold sweat from his forehead.

*"I can't kill you, because that would make me no
better than Tyler Martin. And I believe that no matter
how unfair life can be, there is still a good helping of
karma out there."*

Kagan's words rose from Carl's memory. No, Kagan

wouldn't have to kill him, Ricky Sullivan had more than enough reason and motivation. And now he had Kagan's resources behind him. Carl felt his belly heaving with the need to vomit.

The fact that he'd done the same to others without blinking or losing a wink of sleep didn't cross Carl's mind. What he was consumed with was just how vulnerable he felt.

He picked up the phone and dialed Eric.

"Get the fuck out."

Kirkland threw the towel he'd used to wipe away his cum at the girl who had been shucking his cock.

She didn't duck, just lowered her eyes and took the insult as though she believed she'd earned it.

Right. She was his bitch and knew it. One of the lucky ones he'd picked out of the lineup and kept as his own instead of sending her to work in the massage spas he owned.

Beyond the cinder-block wall, his fans were still buzzing. The media empire he managed made sure the stadiums were full when he performed.

He was a king.

The girl? Just a pet.

Carl Davis? A fucking thorn in his side.

Mack knocked before entering.

"Did you find the asshole?"

Mack nodded. "As far as I can tell, it's Ricky Sullivan. I've got a net laid out to find him before he comes looking for you."

Kirkland grunted, pacing around the performers' room for a minute. He stopped though, something catching his eye on the security cameras.

He flattened his hands on the makeup station and

touched the screen, scrolling back through the last few images.

"So the ice princess is here," he muttered as he stared at a picture of Thais in one of the prime box seats. "Who is she?"

Eric swiped his finger across the screen of his smart pad and looked at the financial records.

"It's coming up as private."

Kirkland turned and looked at Mack.

"The box was paid for in cash."

Kirkland watched as she drained her shot glass and started to get up. "Invite her back here."

Mack pressed down on a tiny button on his ear phone. Kirkland enjoyed knowing she'd come to him.

Yeah, because he was the master, and she was just another bitch for him to school.

"She declined."

"What?" Kirkland demanded.

"She said backstage was boring."

Kirkland felt his temper stir back to life. Whoever the hell she was, she was exactly what he needed to work off the stress of seeing Ricky Sullivan surface from the grave.

"Think I'll go meet her. Don't lose her."

He was off a moment later.

Thais moved across a sky bridge toward a high-end hotel. Miami catered to the rich, and they liked their air-conditioning.

She moved slowly, making a display of herself while also appearing like she had nothing important to do at all. Men like Kirkland adored breaking the will of those around them. He'd see her as a pet to be tamed. Her spirit to be broken. He was watching, she knew it.

As far as doing her job, she was getting it done. Kagan wanted Kirkland watched, and she would be the perfect person to do it. Only she'd bring Kirkland to her. Make him do the work. It was really a brilliant method of surveillance.

What surprised her was when she found herself facing Dunn Bateson.

He wasn't a man anyone easily forgot. Not with his height and muscular frame that made it clear he was a very hands-on sort of man.

He also had green eyes. They were a rare combination with his dark hair and gave him a slightly unearthly appearance.

Her poise tried to waver.

Thais drew in a deep breath and forced herself to look straight into Dunn Bateson's green eyes. She'd seen good-looking men before.

But this one reached out and snagged her by the upper arm, pulling her neatly around a pillar and into an alcove where they were strangely alone.

"You shouldn't handle me," she advised him.

Dunn wasn't impressed with her narrow-eyed set down.

Most men were.

If truth were told, it was rather intriguing to find a man who stood up to her.

If you're brutally honest, you'll admit you like it . . .

"You shouldn't be pimped out by your team leader," Dunn countered.

He placed himself between her and the escape route. They weren't the only couple using the load bearing structure supports for a little privacy. Which was why it took her by surprise to feel a burn on her cheeks.

Her poise faltered.

"Don't involve yourself. We are not connected," she informed him.

Thais turned and left, ducking into the ladies' room to ensure she had the time needed to collect herself and get her mind back on Kirkland and the case.

She never blushed.

And yet, the spotless mirrors above the vanities showed her a reflection that included glowing cheeks. She actually reached up and stroked one side of her face.

How long had it been?

Not long enough was the correct answer. She had a case, one her team was counting on her to remain focused on.

And Dunn Bateson wasn't part of it.

Neither was blushing over him.

"Kirkland is taking the bait." Zane's voice came over the tiny microphone Thais had in her ear.

She dropped her lipstick into her purse and left the ladies' room.

"Something wrong with backstage?"

Thais turned and swept Kirkland from head to toe. He had on oversized clothing and a hat tipped down over his forehead while diamonds winked at her from the rings on his fingers.

"I'm not the sort of girl who gets summoned," she told him softly.

Kirkland tilted his head to one side. "Bet you come running when your rich daddy calls."

Thais smiled brightly, but added a sultry look. "I love my daddy. He is never boring." She started to move past him. "That's why I answer his invitations."

Kirkland reached out and gripped her upper arm.

He wasn't anywhere near as impressive as Dunn . . .

Thais chided herself. She knew better than to be distracted.

"Oh my," she purred. "Strong-arm tactics. How very . . . predictable."

She snapped her fingers, and Zane stepped into sight. His suit was impeccable, the little clear plastic pig tail wire in his ear adding to his look.

"Is Dunn Bateson more to your liking?" Kirkland asked as he took his hand off her.

Thais offered him a delicate shrug. "Dunn is delightfully rough around the edges. And before you think I mean spanking and flogging, I don't play games anymore."

"You might like to play those games with me." Kirkland was taking shelter in his bad-boy persona. "Come on, girl, what's it going to take?"

Thais offered him a smile of encouragement. She moved close, pressing against him as she flattened her hand over the gun he had tucked into his drawers.

"Hmmm . . . you might have potential."

She was pulling away before he really got the chance to touch her. Thais dipped her fingers into the front of her low-cut dress and withdrew a business card. There was only a number on it.

"Text me if you have something interesting to do," she said.

She slipped away, feeling him watching her.

There.

That was how a mission should go. Focused and precise.

There was no room for emotional bleed-through.

Period.

CHAPTER EIGHT

Being underground meant Jenna had no sense of time. The temperature stayed chilly and constant. The days of inactivity meant she'd slept too much.

But Dare was suffering from having been on duty.

She eased out of the bunk, grabbing handfuls of clothing on her way to the door and out into the other part of the shelter where she could sort through it with the help of a light. Easing the door of the bedroom closed, she enjoyed a little spark of satisfaction when she succeeded and didn't hear Dare moving.

There was an undeniable ache in her passage.

It made her grin as she dressed.

Sam would approve.

She ended up smiling wryly as she remembered her compatriot. There was a really big hole in her life where Sam fit perfectly. He'd been the buddy she could commiserate with and expect to kick her in the ass when she was being a wimp.

"Is that coffee?"

Dare was eyeing the little pot she had on the range.

"Depends," she answered, "on your standards for what you apply the label of coffee to."

"I was a squid, so, pretty low." He went around her and poured a mug full before leaning back on the counter and contemplating her.

Her belly did a little flip as she realized it was their first, true, morning after.

"So, is there a plan?" she asked. "I mean, not that I'm not enjoying the unique experience of staying in a Cold War–era location.

Dare offered her a half grin. "Vintage coffee, too."

"The word is 'aged,' " Jenna muttered. "And I'm pretty sure that's only a good thing when applied to wine."

"Beats camping in the riverbed," he offered as he tipped his mug up and emptied it.

Jenna suddenly choked as her mind offered up an image of them in the sand. Dare raised an eyebrow as she felt her cheeks turning red. It didn't take him very long to follow her thinking.

"Agreed," he muttered as he placed the mug in the sink. "The sand would have been an issue."

He offered her a wink before disappearing into the bedroom.

A wink.

Jenna sipped at her coffee for a moment while she savored the experience.

You are so never getting over him . . .

She wasn't, and honestly it didn't bother her a bit.

"I never got it until I met you."

His words rose from her memory. So tender and so completely putting the last nail in . . . well, whatever it was they were doing.

Was it a relationship? What type? Lovers? Fellow addicts?

All Jenna really knew was that for her, it was everything.

So there was no point in thinking too long and hard about it.

Live in the moment, girl. Sam would have agreed.

"Kirkland has his network looking for you."

Ricky grinned in spite of the fact that Kagan was calling the shots. At least the section leader knew how to toss in some fun with the work.

Kagan tossed him a phone. "It's clean."

"Even from you?"

Kagan nodded. "Just remember, you don't need Kirkland left free if you want to get on with setting up a life for yourself."

Ricky shrugged. "I know how to survive."

Kagan offered him a slip of paper. "That's one of Kirkland's phones. He's got some of the area fight-club owners looking for you. Even offered a bounty."

"How much?"

"Ten grand," Kagan replied.

Ricky punched in the number. It rang a few times before Kirkland picked up.

"Who the fuck is calling me so early?"

"Heard you were looking for me," Ricky let his Irish brogue out. "But if you'd rather I hang up . . ."

"No . . . Fuck . . . Give me a second."

Ricky swallowed his snickers, hearing the sounds of women muttering as Kirkland got out of his bed. He hoped the guy was buck-assed naked, too. There was nothing better than catching a guy with his shorts down.

"I was looking for you alright" Kirkland was trying to sound congenial. "Who gave you my number?"

"Since you only offered ten grand for him to call you,

I gave him fifteen and told him to forget he saw me," Ricky said. "I did a lot of business with your daddy. Good business. What the fuck are you doing putting a bounty out on me?"

"I heard you were top notch," Kirkland came back. "Even heard you were dead."

Ricky chuckled. "Not even close. Sullivans don't die easy. Tyler Martin found that out."

"He was a prick."

"So get on with telling me what sort of business you have in mind." Ricky shot Kagan a solid stare. "I've plenty to do now that Tyler isn't in my way with his fucking FBI network."

"I need help with a Shadow Ops team that's crawling up my ass," Kirkland elaborated. "You'll remember Dare Servant."

"I know him," Ricky answered. "Guess you are your daddy's boy all the way. No way you'd have a Shadow Ops team looking at you if you didn't have something stinky buried. What are you dealing?"

There was a pause. "Meet me and I'll show you. In fact, you might be just the sort of man I could use as a partner."

"Don't kiss my ass," Ricky grunted. "I prefer pussy."

Kirkland chuckled on the other end of the line. "It will be worth your time. And there will be plenty of pussy."

Ricky let Kirkland sweat for a couple of seconds. "Alright. It's a deal."

He listened to the details before killing the call. Kagan was contemplating him with an expression that was almost pleased.

"So." Ricky looked at Kagan. "What's the deal with Kirkland? Forewarned is forearmed."

Kagan's eyebrow lifted. "Don't forget who I am, Sullivan. I won't work over like most of the people you encounter. However, in this case, I want you to know what we're looking for."

Dare used a towel to wipe their fingerprints off every surface in the bunker before they left. Once outside, he sealed the door, leaving the bunker in darkness just like they'd found it.

"I've got to check in," he offered. "See what has happened while we've been off-grid."

"Lead on."

He caught her up against him instead. "I have to finish this case, Jenna. What I said, when I dropped those pictures on the bunk next to you, I meant it."

"Kirkland needs to die," she agreed.

"I'm going to do my best to make sure he gets locked far away from his lavish lifestyle, in a box, just as he does to those girls. No quick death for him."

He was brushing the hair back from her face. His eyes shimmering with emotion. It touched her so very deeply. "I understand," she offered sincerely.

He bit back a word of profanity as he backed up. He was fighting with something, struggling to deal with the same surge of unexpected emotions she was.

"You don't have to say anything."

"I sure as hell do." Dare caught her up against him again. "The truth is, I've spent so much time telling myself I wouldn't go and let myself fall in love with anyone, now, I haven't the first idea how to start."

Jenna reached up and placed her hand against the side of his face. He went still, their gazes locking. In that moment, she honestly didn't know where he stopped and she began. It was like they were one entity. Separating

would mean death because they simply couldn't survive
without each other.

"You know how to start . . ." she whispered. "You
learned how, from your father."

He closed his eyes, savoring the feeling of her hand
on his face. When he lifted his eyelids, his eyes were
shimmering with unshed tears.

"Let's live in the moment, Dare Servant."

His lips curved. "I'll do my best to stay out of the
'dick' zone."

She laughed as he pulled away and started around the
embankment for the river water. The sand was hard to
walk through, the bugs rising up from where they'd been
laying in the shallow water to try and feast on her unprotected arms and neck, and, honestly, she didn't think
she'd ever been happier in her life.

Ricky let out a whistle. "Now I am impressed."

Kirkland was smirking, enjoying being the recipient
of praise. "Anything you want . . ." Kirkland spread his
arms out wide to indicate the girls standing in the shadows of the warehouse. "They'll do it."

"You're a fucking slave trader . . ." Ricky contemplated the girls watching him.

It made him sick.

And he'd done a fair share of messed up shit in his life.

Murder.

Extortion.

Prostitution.

But fuck. This was different. He knew the look on
the girls faces because his mother had ended up with a
similar soulless glow in her eyes when she'd been forced
to trade her body for enough food to feed him.

"What's the business deal?" Ricky looked back at

Kirkland. "Nothing personal, but I'm a fighter, not a pimp."

"I need Dare Servant off my ass." Kirkland offered Ricky a stack of pictures. "They bugged my Malibu house and have stuck to me since. It's costing me a shit load of money every day I can't have the girls working. There's a firefighter, too. He's the one who can't keep his mouth shut. I need him gone. Permanently."

"That's more my style," Ricky muttered as he flipped through the pictures. "Who's the girl?"

"She was supposed to be catering my party. Ran into Servant's team but here's the fun part." Kirkland pulled out one of the pictures from farther down in the pile. "Seems Servant's sheets aren't as clean as he'd like me to believe."

"That's how you get him," Ricky looked at the picture of Dare kissing Jenna. "She's his soft spot."

"I heard you tried that with Bram Magnus and failed."

Ricky looked up at Kirkland. "You don't know shit. I was after Tyler Martin. That ass left me to rot in a Mexican prison. You think I can't throw a grenade and kill at least one member of Saxon Hale's team? I wasn't after them. No one fucks over a Sullivan. It was a lesson Tyler needed to learn and as you've learned, making sure that Shadow ops team doesn't have a burning need to find me is a win-win for me."

Kirkland slowly nodded.

"Half a million upfront." Ricky wrote down an account number and offered it to Kirkland.

"That's steep," Kirkland complained as he took the paper and handed it to Mack.

"So is bribing federal agents," Ricky argued. "But

hell, if you think you can find her"—he held up the picture of Jenna facing the cameras during her press conference—"show me how it's done."

"Can you find her?" Mack demanded.

Ricky spread his arms wide. "I can. But it will cost you a full million up front because I don't like having to waste my time begging for a job. My reputation gets me plenty of offers. I killed Tyler Martin, head of security to Carl Davis." Ricky let out a low whistle as he started toward the door. "Take the offer or leave it."

He stopped though, near the door, looking at a girl crouched in the corner. There were still tears in her eyes, telling him she was newly arrived, her dreams of a wonderful life freshly smashed by reality.

"And I want her . . ." Ricky reached down and grabbed her hand. He turned and looked back at Kirkland. "Any problem with my terms?"

He had the pictures in his left hand. The girl stood up, trembling as she looked at her shoes.

"You do the job, I don't give a shit what it costs," Kirkland answered. "Just don't leave her alive to run her mouth."

"I've got plans for her mouth," Ricky answered with a smirk. "She looks new to the game. I'll break her in for you."

Kirkland grunted as Ricky whistled on his way out the door. The girl didn't take much coaxing. She was happy to go, clearly understanding that one man was better than what the other girls faced nightly on the docks as Kirkland ran an underground brothel.

He'd done a good deed.

His mother would have been proud of him.

And his father . . . well . . . Ricky heard his phone ding with an incoming message as he drove away, proving Kirkland had sent the money. All in all, he'd done the Sullivan name proud for the day.

"Want me to kill him?" Mack asked.

Kirkland was pissed.

But that didn't mean he was going to be reckless.

No, that was the real difference between success and failure. He turned to look at Mack. "We need him to find the girl and draw Servant out. Send the money. It will be worth it if we can get back to normal operations."

Kirkland paced a few spaces, looking at the girls. A couple of them smiled, offering him a warm welcome because they wanted an escape.

He didn't want another man's leavings.

It brought Thais to mind.

Now there was a bitch worth breaking. He enjoyed the mental distraction of getting her exactly where he wanted her.

Hell, she wanted danger? He might just bring her along as a little entertainment when Sullivan delivered Jenna.

It would certainly be a night to remember.

"Going in" seemed to mean traveling in four different directions, under overpasses and across marshy land.

Dare looked back at her at one point, grinning at the look on her face.

"Come on, baby, you can do it."

The enthusiasm in his voice made her want to strangle him. She opted for a shrug instead. "Thought you told me not to work my backside off."

He pulled her past him and gave her a soft smack on her rump in reply. "We'll have ice cream later."

The sun was starting to sink. Dare caught her looking at the sky.

"Not much further," he offered.

They'd hitched a ride at some point, but Dare had been taking her over land for the better part of the afternoon. Florida had lots of marshland with trees. They stayed out of the deeper water as they skirted the Everglades.

"Ready to go in?" he asked at last.

Jenna nodded, following him toward a boarded-up gas station. The length of road was crumbling along the edges, the moist ground shifting and undermining it.

Inside, it wasn't much better. There was an inch of dust on everything, and she stayed near the center of the floor because the spiderwebs along the walls made her skin crawl. Dare made it around what had once been a counter and reached down.

"This way."

Jenna peeked around and looked at the staircase he'd exposed. There was pipe railing on either side because it was a steep one with lighting at the bottom.

"The full special agent experience I see," she said.

Below them there was a complex. Dare secured the door before following her.

"Nice to see you again, Ms. Henson."

Kagan was leaning against a wall watching the entrance into the area. "You know the rest of the team."

Greer, Zane, and Vitus were all present. They were clustered around a table that had pictures and maps spread out on it.

"What the hell?" Dare growled.

She was suddenly being shoved behind Dare as he noticed a man against the far wall.

"Told you he wouldn't like it any better than I did," Vitus remarked.

"I'm heartbroken," the man against the far wall informed Dare.

"Not heartbroken enough," Dare responded. "Because it's still beating."

"By my choice," Kagan informed Dare. "We need him. And before you tell me why we don't, listen in. He's got a connection with Kirkland and even brought us a witness. A live one."

Dare was still rigid. The guy in the corner was enjoying it, too. He had a devilish charm to him and a mop of blond hair. His square jaw had a few scars on it to prove the guy lived rough, and the way he was leaning against the wall, enjoying the way Dare was glaring at him, told Jenna the guy enjoyed his lifestyle.

"Ricky Sullivan," he supplied as he shifted his gaze from Dare to her. "Kirkland hired me to kill you."

"Among others," Vitus cut in. "Your name was on the top of the list," he said as he looked at Dare.

"I'm consumed with worry," Dare said.

"What matters is that Carl Davis is worried now for a change." Kagan spoke in the soft tone of voice Jenna knew meant business. The men in the room didn't miss it either. There was a grudging acceptance from Dare while Jenna bit her lip to keep from exclaiming out loud.

Shit, Carl Davis. The guy was about to become president.

"I've had Sullivan on ice," Kagan continued. "Now, he's in position to help us catch Kirkland with a load of his human cargo."

The dead girl came to mind. But Jenna still fought back a gag over the term "human cargo." Sure she'd known they were dealing with scum, she just didn't really grasp how scummy it would seem.

"Sullivan has the ability to set a meeting with Kirkland." Kagan sent Dare a hard look. "We need Jenna to make sure Kirkland shows."

"You had to say that in front of her," Dare growled.

Jenna recognized the tone Dare was using. It was razor sharp and all business. Greer and Zane shifted, clearly worried about the way Dare was taking issue with their boss.

Section leader. Keep up, girl.

"Why not?" she pointed at the chest harness he had on. "You're going out there."

"I am trained," he stressed.

"And I told you I am no coward."

"That won't make a bit of difference," Dare argued. "It's one thing to escape, another to step out into the line of fire. I'm not standing by while you do it."

"But you expect me to do the same?" she asked.

He retreated behind a hard mask.

"Not a chance," Jenna informed him. "It's my life that got shredded by this guy. I'm going to go kick him in the nuts."

"You're not going anywhere Jenna," Dare warned her.

"Without her, Kirkland won't show," Ricky interrupted. "He hired me to get her."

"And me," Dare insisted.

"He wants you off his ass but needs the girl to plug a leak," Ricky insisted. "I bring him her . . . and he'll think you'll be along fast."

Vitus looked like he was itching to reach out and snap the guys neck, but he held his position. "As much as I hate to agree with this scum, it makes sense."

"I doubt Saxon would agree," Dare grunted.

"Kirkland isn't his case." Kagan took control of the conversation. "He's yours."

Dare was silent for a long moment. Jenna felt him bending.

She realized she needed him to.

Needed to be seen as more than a victim.

She needed to be his partner.

"Call him up and see what he says," Dare spoke at last. "I want to hear Kirkland agree to some sort of exchange."

Ricky didn't budge, clearly taking exception to being told to prove it.

"Good plan," Kagan said pointedly. He turned toward Jenna and tossed her a cell phone. "Go and call that friend Sam of yours. He's threatening to go on a talk show to expose government cover-up of your abduction."

"Sam?" Jenna asked as she clutched the phone.

Kagan nodded. "Trust me, he isn't intimidated by my agents telling him how dire the circumstances will be."

"Ah . . . yeah, Sam will spit in your eye," she said.

And she missed him so much. Jenna turned and hurried down the hallway toward a door. She opened it, looking inside before she crossed the threshold. It was only after she close the door that she realized Kagan had neatly distracted her and gotten her out of the room while the main business went down.

Or at least while Dare was going to argue against her involvement.

He'd argue anyway.

Right. She admitted she'd be a tad disappointed if he didn't and besides, she was going to call Sam.

"I've got her," Sullivan declared when Kirkland answered the phone. "The chick from your house. Want me to kill her?"

"How'd you find her?" Kirkland demanded.

Ricky snickered. "It's what I do. Stupid Feds think their witness protection program is so air tight. It's not. But Servant is nowhere in sight. Bet he's back on your tail. So maybe I shouldn't kill her just yet."

"Right," Kirkland muttered. "I need Servant dead."

Dare grinned as the call was broadcast over the room.

"Can I fuck her while we're using her to bring Servant out in the open?" Ricky asked.

Dare sent Ricky a deadly glare. The contract killer enjoyed it.

"That chick I took with me was skinny. I like a little ass on my pony when I ride." Ricky explained. "Hope you don't want the other one back. I broke her."

Kirkland grunted. "I've got plenty more."

"Lucky you," Ricky sneered. "Premium ass like that, isn't all that easy to find."

"Which is why I get paid a lot of money to provide it," Kirkland said.

"Alright, fine," Ricky offered. "Don't get defensive. I found what you paid me to. Let's finish up our deal. I have jobs waiting."

"Bring the girl to me," Kirkland instructed. "Tomorrow night I'm doing a show at Universal. I'll take her out into the brush and leave her and Servant to the gators."

Kagan shook his head.

"Universal?" Ricky asked. "Too many cameras."

"Not where I'm telling you to meet me," Kirkland responded. "I have a load of honey coming in from the Caribbean. Being at Universal and on camera will cover my ass when Servant's team find his remains. I've got a couple body doubles who will take my place in the hotel while I attend to business."

Ricky let out a low whistle as he watched Kagan. The section leader nodded a single time in agreement.

"She'll cost you another million." Ricky informed Kirkland. "And some honey. Fresh honey. I don't like my treat full of other men's leavings."

"Done."

"Alright!" Sam declared dramatically. "You're fine, and I will be quiet because it's for your good. Now if it was the dirt clods who came over here and flashed their badges, well, they can eat hour-old fast food."

"Thanks, Sam." Jenna was holding the phone so tight, her fingers ached. "The only thing I hate is that I can't see you again."

Sam snorted on the other end of the line. "Better tell that hunk of yours to find a way to see me or I won't be held responsible for my actions."

Jenna grinned.

"I love you, Sam."

She did, too. Tears were streaming down her face as she finished the call.

"I'm sorry."

She gasped and turned to find Dare behind her.

"I'm good," she muttered as she wiped at her tears. "Just need a shower."

She turned and moved toward what she hoped was a bathroom. Dare wrapped his arms around her before she made it two paces.

"You're fantastic, baby," he cooed next to her ear. "Braver than you should have to be."

He placed a kiss against her neck. It was sweet, but she realized it was too sweet.

"Don't," she warned as she turned around and locked

gazes with him. "Don't judge me too fragile to keep up with you."

He caught her hand when she started to push away from him, locking his fingers around her wrists as he pushed her back and pinned her against the wall.

"I want to protect you, Jenna." His eyes shimmered with need. "Don't deny me that."

"Because of your mother?"

He flinched, the grip on her wrists tightening. *"Yes."*

"That is exactly why I have to be as strong as she was." Jenna wiggled her hands, easing from his grasp as he flattened his hands on the wall beside her face. "I have to be like the woman who gave life to you and made you fearless."

She stroked his face and then the bulge of his cock. He drew in a stiff breath. "Make love with me, Dare."

Her voice was a husky whisper. She ducked under his arm and pulled her top off as she backed toward the shower.

"Live in the moment?" he asked as he started to unbuckle his chest harness.

She nodded, suddenly feeling like conversation was beyond her ability. She was fighting with her shoes and then shoving her jeans down her legs. Dare laid his harness aside, concentrating on working the buttons on his shirt.

"Turn the water on, baby . . ."

There was a dark promise in his voice. Her skin was heating, making the idea of water inviting.

Necessary actually.

His cock was hard and jutted out the moment he opened his fly. She licked her lips as she peeled her panties off and stood for a moment, waiting while he finished undressing.

"I love your breasts." He came to her slowly, taking the moment to sear her with his dark gaze.

Up . . .

Down . . .

And finally settling on her chest.

"Those little rose-bud nipples." He was close enough to cup the mounds he spoke of and thumb her nipples. "I love the way they pucker . . ."

She felt the unmistakable sensation of her nipples doing exactly what he said. The sensitive points tingled while they tightened.

"And I love the way they taste."

She gasped as he leaned down to capture one between his lips.

So hot.

The heat was snaking down from where he nursed on her to where her clit was throbbing between the folds of her sex.

"Perfect little . . . sweets."

He moved to the opposite side, licking and sucking while she gripped his hair. The midnight black strands were caught between her fingers as she lost the ability to control herself. All that mattered was getting him closer.

Dare chuckled, pushing her back into the shower. The water hit them both, drawing a cry from her lips as it collided with how hot her skin was.

"That's it," he muttered. "I need to cool you off, just a bit baby. We're always in too big a rush."

"The key word in that sentence is 'we,'" Jenna muttered.

She reached down, teasing his length with her fingertips. "I'm not the only one . . . *ready* . . ."

"Except, you're not nearly ready enough, Jenna."

There was a warning in his tone, one that awaked a

surge of anticipation. He was gripping her hip, sending a jolt of sexual awareness through her belly. He smoothed his hand along her thigh, lifting her knee up to hook around his waist. The head of his cock nudged her folds, easing between them as he moved closer.

But he stopped. Standing still with the head of his cock between her folds and slid his hand along the side of her face.

"I want to do more than fuck."

She trembled. *"Yes."*

She tightened her leg, pulling him closer, bringing his cock into contact with her hot center.

He groaned, his eyes closing for a moment as he shuddered before opening again to send her a look full of need. "Minx."

"That's right," she whispered. "Don't shelter me."

He slid his hand into her hair, tightening his fingers so that she was his prisoner. "I will always shelter you, Jenna. *Always.*"

She trembled, absorbing his thrust. He was hard and determined, yet slow and tender. He was moving into her, each thrust controlled and driving her insane.

Yet also pleasing her immensely.

There was give and take. Need and satisfaction. Each thrust building on the last, nudging her in an even pace toward climax.

"Always, Jenna . . . You will always be sheltered."

He pulled free, his eyes flashing with determination before he turned her and pushed back into her. It was a hard moment, one that made her growl with hunger. What had been a gentle simmer of need, suddenly burst into flames as she flattened her hands against the tile of the shower and felt him grip her hips.

"Always . . ."

His voice was raspy and edged with warning. It awakened something in her, a need to prove she could challenge him.

"And I swear I will *always* argue . . ."

She was lifting her bottom, pushing back onto his cock, purring when he stretched her and she felt the sack of his balls slapping against her.

It was raw and she needed more.

Craved it.

Climax was looming and she resisted it. Needing to stay in the moment, unwilling to return to the reality of uncertainly. His cock was hardening, telling her he was close to losing his load.

She wanted to push him over the edge. Claim the victory of being the one to outlast the other.

"Not a chance . . . minx . . ." He growled as she felt him jerking with the first pulse of his climax. His seed was hitting her insides as he reached around and rubbed her clit.

She gasped and lost control, her body spasming with pleasure. It tore through her. Leaving her leaning on the arm Dare had locked around her waist. His heart was thumping against her back, sending fresh tears into her eyes as she realized just how deadly his life was. Jenna turned her face into the spray to hide them.

She loved him.

And she would never try to change him.

Because that wasn't love. No, love was complete acceptance, rough edges and all.

And she loved Dare Servant.

Normally a show put Kirkland in a good mood.

Today, he was pissed when he came off stage. His walk warned his crew away, and the look on his face

as he left gave the paparazzi fresh photos for their end-
less gossip blogs. It took a few minutes for him to
change clothing and let his body double stroll through
the lobby as bait for the cameras.

One thing his father had taught him, was do the dirty
work yourself. Be hands on. The truth was, he enjoyed
it. And there was the added benefit of knowing if his
people were cheating him because they never knew just
when he'd show up.

Only that he would most definitely put in an appearance.

Two million fucking bucks was a lot.

He was going to enjoy feeding Dare Servant to the
gators.

At least a trip down toward the docks made him
happy. There was a cargo container full of new girls for
him to use to help generate revenue. The hip hop thing
wasn't very profitable. They spent a ton on advertise-
ment to keep the stadiums full.

He drove past the docks and out toward the end of the
roads, where the street lights were farther apart and the
city further in the distance. It was three in the morning
but he'd always been a night creature.

He saw the truck in the distance. The big rig was
pulled off the road, its brown shipping container blend-
ing with the night. The driver had parked behind two old
houses, looking like he'd just pulled over to catch some
sleep. They were far enough inland to keep the DEA
off their asses and close enough to civilization for him
to split the girls up and send them to different locations
where they could be put to work.

First they had to be broken.

Kirkland went inside, the sound of sniffling letting
him know his madam was doing her job. Two of his

men were standing in the living room, their pants open as girls took turns sucking their cocks.

He flopped down on the sofa, listening as the madam yelled in Russian at the girls. Telling them that their bodies belonged to her, that their lives belonged to the men with them.

Some of the girls rebelled. They were the ones tied up and lying on the floor. The process of breaking them was something his people knew how to do well.

And Dare Servant would be no different.

"I'll be fine," Jenna tried to assure Dare.

He gripped her upper arm and sent her a hard look. "I don't like this, Jenna. Nothing you say is going to change my mind about how much I would rather handcuff you to the control panel instead of let you come along."

In the wee hours of the night, the team was as bright-eyed as though it was ten in the morning. All around them gear was being double-checked. Guns, ammunition, communications. It was all in play as Kegan oversaw the set-up of surveillance.

"Then understand why I can't be a wimp," she said.

His lips were a thin, hard line. "Why do you think you aren't handcuffed?"

"Your section leader would have something to say about that."

Dare slowly smiled. It was a menacing expression, one that sent a shiver down her back. Jenna lifted her hands into the air.

"Okay. Forget I made that comment."

Vitus gave a soft whistle. It called the team together. Jenna fell into step with them, caught in a crazy mixture of fear and anticipation. The intensity of the moment all focused on her memory of the girl lying dead next to her.

And she was going to do something about it.

Kirkland picked up his phone on the first ring. "Where the fuck are you?"

"Were you expecting me?" Thais purred. "Perhaps you should have issued an invitation if that was the case."

Kirkland slowly grinned. "How'd you get my number?"

"My daddy is rich."

"Knows people, too," Kirkland muttered.

"I'm getting tired of waiting on you."

He needed an outlet for his temper. None of the bitches in front of him offered him the challenge Thais did. "You want some excitement, baby? Come join me if you're not scared of the dark."

Thais purred. "I'm made of darkness, was weaned on moonlight."

He was grinning as he punched in a text message to her.

"Are you crazy?" Mack asked. "Her daddy might make waves."

"Don't even know who the bastard is." Kirkland shrugged and tossed the phone aside. The sex party went on. His men were enjoying the perks of their positions. It was one of the reasons he didn't have a problem with loyalty.

Sex and money.

The two things men would sell their own souls to possess.

His dogs were gorging in the free-for-all.

Kirkland realized he had an appetite, as well. But he needed more challenge in the moment.

"Come on, rich girl . . . can't wait to make you my whore."

"Thais is a go." Vitus turned and relayed the information to the other team members.

There was a shifting among them but still an acceptance of their female member's ability to take on the task in front of them.

Dare followed close on her heels as they loaded into a helicopter. Greer was in the pilot seat, starting up the rotors. The chest harness made it all very real as Dare reached over and gave it a tug to make sure Jenna had secured the shoulder straps correctly. She offered him a thumbs-up before the helicopter was lifting away from the ground.

Unlike on the site-seeing tours she'd splurged on during her vacations, Jenna's belly twisted like she was on a roller coaster when Greer took them into the air at a sharp angle. Dare patted her thigh as they leveled out, and she laughed.

Live in the moment?

She sure as hell was going to. And if she lived, she was going to make Kagan let her call Sam again.

That thought sobered her but not because she was afraid she might die.

No, what she couldn't live with was the fact that Dare would give up his life to protect her.

She'd never survive that.

But what sickened her was how real a possibility it was.

She was there to distract.

Thais knew her job, even understood the premise, and the success rate for operations that utilized female agents in such fashions.

But she hated reality and had for a long time.

It had never been a friend of hers.

"You're going to be my bitch now."

Kirkland was sitting on the sofa, like some king watching the debauchery being unleashed around him for his amusement. Except he was spoiled by the excess, desensitized to the point where he needed more and more perversion to achieve satisfaction.

She fluttered her eyelashes at him.

He frowned. "Maybe I'll let my men gangbang you first."

There was a girl laying across a dinner table suffering that fate. Stripped bare, she was being used as an example to two other women who were holding out.

"Kings don't take sloppy seconds," Thais said.

Kirkland licked his lower lip. "That's right, I am the king."

"Not my king."

He reached forward and slapped her. Pain went through her face, the impact spot throbbing as she smiled at him.

"Only Daddy is my king."

Kirkland sat back, trying to look nonchalant. "You're never going to see him again." Kirkland opened his fly, exposing his cock. "No, you're going to be my cock-sucking slave."

"If you plan to kill me, there is no reason for me to please you." Thais didn't fight against the handcuffs binding her wrists. She had a part to play. "Too bad really." She glanced around the room. "This had the makings of a good start to something that wasn't going to be boring."

Kirkland's brows lowered.

"But you should have saved some of them." Thais looked around the room. "There are men who pay a lot for exclusivity." She let out a little sigh. "Private pet parties are very lucrative. I know men who pay a lot for cherries and a pony they can ride bare back without fear of getting dirty."

Kirkland sat forward, his cock forgotten. "Who the fuck is your father?"

"Are we doing this or not?" Ricky demanded.

Dare shot him a deadly glance. Vitus stepped between them, forcing Ricky back a few paces.

"Fine," he muttered. "I'll just cool my heels and wait for you to kiss each other bye-bye."

Jenna caught the gleam of enjoyment in Dare's eyes. "I'm guessing there is a history between you two."

Dare nodded and his face tightened, but he snapped back to the current mission in the space of a heartbeat.

"Agent Thais Sinclair is in there."

"Got it," Jenna muttered.

"It won't be pretty, Jenna."

She reached out and placed her hand on his forearm. "I was in that shipping container with this guy."

Dare nodded. She watched him fight to maintain his professionalism but lost, reaching out to stroke the side of her face.

"I will be right behind you," Dare promised.

He looked straight at her as he spoke, but a moment later he lifted his attention and shot Ricky a look full of warning.

Her belly tightened as she felt the danger increasing. It didn't take very long to kill someone. Just a squeeze of a trigger. Somehow, that seemed so very wrong.

Ricky got into a car as Vitus pulled the trunk open.

Dare locked her hands in cuffs while she heard Greer pulling a length of duct tape from a roll.

An innocent sound.

At least she used to think it was.

Now her belly heaved as Dare smoothed her hair back and Greer fitted the tape across her mouth. Zane tipped her chin back before dropping fluid in her eyes. It burned and sent tears down her cheeks. The final touch was some mud from the road. Dare scooped it up and smeared it in her hair and down her clothing.

Someone had tossed a thick blanket into the trunk. Dare laid her on it before closing the trunk and sealing her inside. It wasn't as pitch black as she thought it might be. As the engine started and Ricky pulled onto the road, she could detect when they drove under a street lamp.

Was she afraid?

She wasn't sure. There was a heightened sense of anxiety in her belly but it wasn't really fear and she realized why.

She was doing the right thing. Standing up for someone who was helpless.

It felt damned good.

"Who is your daddy?"

Thais was on the ground. The blood in her mouth just made her more determined to survive.

Oh, and deny Kirkland what he wanted.

Someone hauled her back up to her knees. Kirkland was flustered.

"I'm going to start cutting your toes off." He warned her.

"Daddy wouldn't like that," she warned. "Uncuff me now and I'll think of this as just a little role-playing game."

"You've seen too much."

Thais laughed. "This?" She looked around the room. "You're a small-time player. Haven't even branched out into pet services. Besides, when it comes to Russians, you can motivate them with promises. It's only the Koreans you have to break. Anyone," she stressed, "who is experienced knows that."

Two of Kirkland's men had ventured closer to listen. She watched as they contemplated what she'd said.

"My daddy is Conrad Mosston." Thais delivered a well know name in the underworld population of men who bought and sold other men. Conrad was a spy, among other things, one who had done business with Kirkland's father. Kagan kept Conrad around, to use as bait against men like Kirkland. Conrad belonged to the Shadow Ops teams though. Kirkland could do all the checking he wanted.

Kirkland swallowed. "Unlock her."

His men hesitated. Kirkland snapped his fingers to get them moving.

"You should have told me who you were," Kirkland said dryly.

Thais rubbed her wrists. "Why? You wouldn't have invited me out here if you'd known who I was."

She climbed right up on his lap. Surprise took command of his features. "So far, it's been a very interesting evening. Don't start boring me now by being afraid of my daddy."

Thais heard the car pull up, but Kirkland was focused on her. She rubbed against his cock to make sure she had him captivated as his men moved away to give them privacy.

"Hmmm . . ." She purred as she stroked him up and down his body, finding his gun and his back up one.

Thais tugged his shirt up, pulling one of the guns in the process.

"You won't need that sort of weapon right now . . ." Thais whispered.

He flashed a grin at her, eating up the moment.

God, there were times she loved her job . . .

"Told you I got her." Ricky smirked.

Mack looked at Jenna and pulled his gun.

"Hold up there," Ricky pushed the gun away from her chest. "Your boss wants to draw Servant out with her."

Mack grunted, but put the gun away. "Boss is inside."

He grabbed Jenna by the arm and pulled her through the door of the house. The curtains were drawn tight and the moment she made it inside she realized why. Her face burned scarlet as she walked into a pornography movie.

There was actually a camera being used to film one of the gangbangs going on in the dining room.

"What the fuck!"

Jenna just had enough time to recognize Thais as she was pushed off a man who came up off the sofa. He was shoving his cock back into his pants as he glared at Mack.

"Don't bring her in here," Kirkland yelled. "Take her into the garage and put her in one of the cages."

The word 'cage' drew Jenna's attention back to Kirkland. He snickered, thinking she'd been mesmerized by the sexcapades taking place.

No, she'd noticed Thais was taking the bullets out of two hand guns and stuffing the bullets between the cushions of the couch.

"You leave the note for Servant?" Mack asked Ricky.

"Sure did."

"Good. He'll come looking for her," Kirkland answered. "And when he does, I'm going to feed the two of them to the gators."

Mack snickered and grabbed Jenna by the bicep.

"Come on," Kirkland said to Thais. "Time to go."

Kirkland reached down and picked up his guns. He stuffed them into his waistband before letting out a whistle.

His men were quick to answer his commands. They pulled up their pants and started herding the girls toward the door.

"Party over?" Thais asked.

"This one is," Kirkland answered before pushing her toward some of his men. "Put her in the truck."

"What the hell?" Thais exclaimed.

Kirkland offered her a smirk. "You're a prime dish. Just don't go thinking you're enough to distract me from checking details. I'm going to see what Conrad has to say. If you check out, you live. If not, you can decide how many toes I take off before you tell me who you really are."

"You're going to regret this . . ." Thais grumbled as she was taken along with the girls to the metal shipping container which was loaded on the back of a semi.

But once the door was shut, and she heard the engine starting up, she pulled the handcuff key out of the pocket it was sewn into on her bra strap and used it to start freeing the girls.

"Federal agent," she muttered. "You're going to be free, soon."

It would be a bitter sweet victory but better than the plans Kirkland had for them.

Yes, she was well acquainted with reality's sharp

edges. The best she could hope for was to dull them from time to time.

Today, she would count as a victory.

Tomorrow, she'd be at the mercy of fate again.

But the victories made it worth the risk.

He'd said a cage.

Somehow, Jenna hadn't really envisioned a true cage.

You should have . . .

Yeah, with everything else going on in the house, the sight of the steel bars really should have been anticipated. Mack pulled her toward it and shoved her in. It looked like some kind of shark cage, used to keep divers safe.

"Don't go anywhere." Mack smirked at her after locking the door and tucking the key inside his suit jacket.

Ass.

He'd left her in handcuffs and with the tape across her mouth.

Of course he had. She was no different from the girls he was helping his boss to turn into prostitutes. Just a commodity to generate income.

Well, she was going to be more.

She was going to make a difference in the world by helping to put them out of business.

And she would not be scared.

Absolutely not.

Dare Servant wouldn't fail to rescue her.

"Big rig is moving," Vitus reported.

"Good," Dare replied.

And it was good that there were fewer civilians in the line of fire but Jenna was still inside.

Nothing was going to feel right until she was safe. "Move in."

Dare had to dig deep for his control. He was pissed at himself for the need because a case had never mattered so much.

Tonight, it was personal.

Ricky waited for the semi truck to make it down the road so he could be heard without shouting. Standing outside the house, he wiped his nose across his arm as dust kicked up from the tires settled on them.

"I'm out of here," Ricky declared. "Servant is going to come in here with the cavalry."

"The note told him to come alone," Kirkland argued.

Ricky snickered. "Right. Know something? If you believe that, you deserve to rot in a cell. As for me," he pulled the door of his car open. "I'm not sticking around for your gator feeding."

"Not going to feed him to the gators," Kirkland sneered. "Got a better plan."

"Hands up! Federal Agents!"

Kirkland pulled his gun, attempting to fire off a round.

"What the fuck?" he growled when the gun didn't fire. He was looking at the weapon when Greer took him to the ground.

The team was fast.

Efficient.

"You wanted to see me?" Dare asked Kirkland.

"Told you to come alone."

Dare felt a chill go down his spine. There was a glitter in Kirkland's eyes, a warning of something they'd all missed. Kirkland shifted and a moment later a blast knocked them all to the ground. Dare rolled, feeling the heat as he turned and looked at the house.

It was a mass of burning roof.

"Jenna!"

He was running and it wasn't fast enough. Dare was aware of his teammates joining him, converging on the garage. Dare kicked the door in as Vitus dragged him down so a wave of smoke and heat didn't hit him in the face.

Kirkland snickered. Mack was fitting the handcuff key he'd had in his shoe into the cuffs behind his back. The roof of the house was a fireball. Flames were dripping down the walls, the heat making the skin on his face prickle.

He rolled free and unlocked Mack.

"What the fuck?" Ricky yelled as they jumped into his car and peeled away, leaving him lying in the dirt.

Jenna felt the waves of heat hit her.

So intense.

As strong as ocean water, she felt them moving her like a leaf floating on the surface.

Only she didn't feel serene, like she would have at the beach. No, she was in hell. Her skin blistering from the heat. The cage had fallen over, leaving her staring up at the roof as it became a living wall of fire. She could see the different colors of the flames.

Red, orange, scarlet, ruby, and yellow.

Rolling like boiling water.

She wanted to cough and hack but the tape kept her mouth sealed. Her nose just wasn't big enough to draw in enough air. She felt herself suffocating.

Well, it beat burning to death.

Her vision was narrowing, darkness closing in like she was being lowered into a hole.

Deeper . . .

Deeper . . .

At last all she saw was Dare's face. Right above her. He was yelling but there was a ringing in her ears keeping her from understanding. She struggled for just enough breath to see him for a moment longer before darkness took her completely.

"It's locked!" Greer yelled.

"Pick it up!" Dare ordered. Jenna's eyes fluttered, her nostrils flaring as she fought for breath. "Don't quit on me, Jenna!"

The shark cage was hot, burning his hands as he held tight in spite of the pain. His team members dug in, giving everything they had.

At first, it didn't move. Dare stained, demanding more of himself as he felt the fire burning the skin on his nape.

But the thing budged. The team strained, forcing the cage through the opening where the garage door had been.

The air was icy cold by comparison. It hit their skin, making them shake as they shoved and forced the cage farther from the garage.

"Jenna!" Dare yelled as he reached in to yank the tape off her mouth.

"Get some water over here!" Vitus ordered.

There was a crash behind them as the roof fell in, sending a shower of sparks up into the early-morning light.

"Anyone have a crow bar?" Greer asked.

Emergency sirens were starting to be heard in the

distance. Someone was on a radio. Dare was focused on Jenna, reaching through the bars to press on her chest.

So close.

And yet too far away to save her life.

It was the torment he'd decided he couldn't face.

The pain was far worse than he'd ever imagined it could be. Vitus pulled him back as a firefighter brought in a power tool. Dare dropped to the ground, reaching through the bars to cover Jenna's face with a fire fighting jacket as sparks rained down from the blade cutting through the steel.

She loved the way he tasted.

Dare's kiss that was.

Jenna let out a little sigh as she opened her eyes and looked into his.

But as she drew in breath, her lungs were on fire. She hacked and contorted as her body tried to clear out whatever was in her lungs in a violent motion of purging.

Dare rolled her to her side, holding her as she fought to control her body.

"Easy Jenna . . . breathe . . . in . . . out . . ."

"I'm . . . trying!"

And with God as her witness, she was. Caught between the impossible and the necessary, she struggled to make her body work. Moments lasted for hours as she struggled and then suddenly, her chest filled and the air didn't get rejected. She savored a few long, deep breaths before her brain began to function again, running the moments of the fire through her memory as she struggled to sit up.

And then nothing mattered because Dare was beside

her, his hand against her cheek. He was warm and whole and hers.

No, nothing fucking mattered beyond that.

Kirkland was snickering. "That was too fucking easy."

He pressed the accelerator down harder, speeding along the road as first light broke. They came around a bend and skidded to a stop as they ran into the flashing red lights of police cars. There were dozens of vehicles, spread out on the side of the road. An entire battalion from the fire department as well as what looked like an equal number of federal agents.

And at the center of it all was his truck.

The girls from the truck were being treated and loaded into ambulances. The drivers were escorted to squad cars.

"Fuck," Mack muttered.

Kirkland fumbled to put the car in reverse but patrol cars had already boxed him in.

"Federal agents!" someone yelled. "Put your hands up!"

He looked around but all he saw were the rifles being aimed at him and Mack.

Compliance was the only option.

At least until he got to a place where his lawyers could work their magic. Kirkland followed orders, frustration drawing him tight as he was shackled and picked up to be walked to a patrol car.

And then the cheering started. The women moved forward, shouting and celebrating his capture. The officer taking him to a car pausing and dragging his feet to make sure they got a good long chance to cheer over his arrest.

Carl Davis was going to pay for the humiliation.

Kirkland intended to make sure of it.

"You used Jenna as bait. Sending her to that concert so I'd think she was in with Kirkland."

Kagan didn't shirk. He returned Dare's stare without flinching.

"Shadow Ops is my family," his section leader said.

"And that doesn't extend to the woman I love?" Dare inquired softly.

Kagan's lips twitched. "You were determined to walk away from her. What should be coming out of your mouth is a thank you."

Dare raised an eyebrow. "For almost getting her killed?"

"For making you see what you were about to lose." Kagan slowly drew in a breath as he looked across the way to where Jenna was sitting on the edge of a lowered tailgate. "What you were going to walk away from because of your choices made when you didn't realize how empty life is when you're alone."

There was a note in Kagan's voice Dare had never heard. It hinted at a secret, hidden somewhere in the past of his section leader.

"Don't ask," Kagan advised him. "The only heart any man has the right to manage is his own. I suggest you focus on the opportunity you scuttled. Thank me for making sure she came back into your spree of operation. You wouldn't have acted on it if I didn't make it snare your attention. I did you a favor."

Dare found himself staring at Jenna. Someone had given her a bottle of electrolyte water.

"I love her," Dare said.

"You're welcome," Kagan replied. "You're not going to the nest. I have other plans for you."

Dare turned his attention to his section leader.

"We need more than one location to bug out to, because Carl Davis is looking like he's going to win this thing." Kagan sent him a hard look. "We need to be prepared to shelter the men who have placed their lives on the line for this country."

Kagan offered Dare a small bag. "Details of your assignment. Take your wife and keep your head down. The storm is just starting to hit."

It was and yet Dare found himself viewing Jenna as a safe harbor where everything was just about perfect.

Carl ducked out of sight, taking the opportunity to wipe his brow. As far as the voters knew, he never broke a sweat. His security detail fell into step around him, shepherding him up a ramp and toward the presidential suite private elevators. They piled inside with him as his assistant babbled on about notes.

"Yes, thank you," Carl mumbled as the doors slid open and he took off toward the privacy of his suite. With only a few short weeks left, he'd be up at dawn.

So he planned to enjoy his privacy.

He was used to his men following him. It had become a way of life. He offered them a half-wave as he went through the door of the suite and let it close behind him.

"Fuck," he mumbled on his way through the meeting room and on toward the wet bar. He was reaching for the top of the ice bucket when he froze. A man was watching him in the mirror.

"Don't reach for your panic button," Kagan advised

softly. "It won't help you anyway. My men replaced yours hours ago."

Carl turned and faced Kagan. "You said you wouldn't kill me."

Kagan was dressed in a suit complete with cufflinks. "Good men . . . are men of character."

"What the fuck is that supposed to mean?" Carl gestured with his hands but he was really using the motion to hide the fact that he was pushing the little lapel panic pin he wore.

"Men of character will adjust to fit the circumstances, Carl," Kegan advised him softly. "Are you sure you want me to reevaluate my choices?"

Kagan had his back to the hallway. Carl enjoyed the sweet rush of relief as he watched two security men come toward him.

But they stopped at the entrance to the dining area and stared at him.

"The men who protect you are men of character," Kegan stated firmly. "My men."

Carl was at a loss for words. He floundered as he tried to grab his composure. "What are you trying to prove with this . . . this . . . display?"

Kagan walked closer to him. "You need to consider changing the type of people you associate with." He held up a tablet, showing a live feed of Kirkland sitting in a holding cell.

Carl felt his temper spike but there was one thing he'd learned over the years and it was to hold his true feelings inside.

"To your type?" Carl offered. "I presume that's what this little lesson is intended to be."

"It's a demonstration," Kagan explained. "One made necessary by threats you've made to shut down my

Shadow Ops teams. Now . . . something like that would rearrange the order of my life."

"I wouldn't do anything like that," Carl said. "Whoever you've been listening to has twisted my words."

One of the men in the hallway pulled a tablet from his jacket. He tapped it and held it up.

"What the fuck is going on with this bitch?"
Kirkland's voice played back.

"She can cause a whole lot of trouble for me," Kirkland informed Carl. "I need her cleaned up before she fingers me for that night on the docks. Servant set me up or I'd have killed her then."

Carl shoved the phone down. "Don't be stupid. You know how powerful some of those camera lenses are."

"If I go down, you do, too," Kirkland's voice came again.

"Servant and his team are fishing with her," Carl exclaimed in a harsh whisper. "Showing her off and seeing who surfaces. I brought you here to keep your head down. If she had anything of any value to add to the investigation, you'd already be facing a judge. Stay here, smile and be seen unaffected by her little press event. Don't be stupid enough to make a move towards her."

"But she knows my voice. Knows I'm involved in shady dealings down on the dock. There was a fucking body laid out next to her. One she knows I knew about," Kirkland growled. "I give you a healthy share of the profits from my empire. When are you going to get these Feds off my ass?"

"When I'm president, I will shut them down," Carl answered.

"That's five months away." Kirkland scowled.

"That is a Shadow Ops team," Carl said under his breath. *"As it stands, shutting them down will have to be done carefully or they could darken my reputation."*

"I pay you to take the risk."

"And I make sure you stay in business," Carl cut back. *"I can find someone else who will pay for my partnership. How long do you think you'll be running those prostitution rings if I don't shelter you? I can make it so you never get another load of girls in to staff your places. That will leave you with nothing but crack heads and runaways,"* Carl sniffed.

"Don't threaten me Kirkland, we're too deep in bed with each other for one of us to pull out now. Do it my way."

"What . . . what do you want?" Carl asked. He was shaking, collapsing back against the edge of the wet bar.

Kagan came closer, so that he could loom over him. "To protect and serve."

Carl shook his head. "I don't understand."

"Sleep on it," Kagan advised. "Think about who you want guarding you. Men like me . . . who still measure their actions against their conscience or men such as Kirkland, who is currently selling you out to lessen the charges against him."

"But . . . I've done too much . . ."

"And yet"—Kagan started to move away—"I'm more interested in what you could do, with the right information on the table."

He moved across the room, stopping in the hallway with his men.

"Don't disappoint me, Carl," Kagan advised.

Eric Geyer found his boss white-faced and sitting on the floor in front of the wet bar.

"Sir?" Eric was there, on one knee, searching Carl's wrist for a pulse. "What's wrong?"

Carl turned a haunted look toward Eric. "Kagan was here."

Eric stiffened. "What do you want me to do?"

It was a good question. The only one of any true importance. Carl let Eric help him up and place a soda in his hand. He sipped at the sweet beverage, feeling his blood sugar rise and with it, his determination.

He'd never backed down before.

No matter the odds.

No matter the risk.

"I want to make sure Kagan understands he isn't the only one who can bite."

Eric was listening intently. Carl put the glass down and stood, pacing around the dining room for a moment.

"Get a hitman," he said. "A really good one. I want Miranda Delacroix silenced forever."

"Are you sure?" Eric questioned. "She's sweet and kind and if it comes back to you, the stink will cling."

"She's just really good at playing the part the voters like to see," Carl spat. "That bitch recorded me talking to Kirkland at her benefit and she gave it to Kagan."

Eric's face reflected his horror.

"And you're tied to me," Carl hissed. "I go down, you go down alongside me. Kagan isn't the only one who can make people sweat. We kill Miranda and Kagan will get the message. I'm not going to become his puppet."

No, he was going to president.

And Miranda would be dead. It would be a warning to anyone else who got any ideas about trying to catch him with dirt on his hands. Kagan wasn't the only one with old-school values. Washington had a long history of sweeping the dirt under the rug if you wanted to survive. No one was above it either. Carl was going to make certain no one misunderstood what he expected from them in return for his favor.

"Home, sweet, home."

Dare spread his arms out wide. Jenna offered him a smile as she took in the vintage-era command center. Deep in the side of a mountain, it was like a time capsule from a sixties-era movie.

"It continues on for two miles into the bedrock." Dare informed her as he opened a roll of blueprints that cracked with age. "Ours for the remodeling."

Her new husband was looking at the yellowed paper, anticipation glowing in his eyes.

"You sound like retirement isn't going to be too terrible after all."

Dare looked up, a gleam in his dark eyes. "There's a whole lot of rooms for us to break in. . . . wife."

He dropped the blue prints and rushed her. Catching her around the waist and clasping her against his body. She squealed before relaxing and purring when he stroked the side of her face.

"I love you, Dare Servant."

"You'd better," he muttered. "Because otherwise, I'm going to become your stalker and chain you up in my mountainside complex because I can't live without you."

"Hmmm," she purred. "I understand stalkers are very devoted to their subjects."

"We are," he assured her as he stroked her face. "We definitely are."

"Get a room," Greer informed them as he came in with a tool box in hand. "Some of us have work to do."

Jenna rose onto her toes to press a kiss against Dare's mouth. The connection was soft and yet it sent a charge through her system that curled her toes.

Live in the moment . . .

Yeah, and she planned to savor every last one of them.

Read on for an excerpt from Dawn Ryder's
next Unbroken Heroes romantic suspense novel

Don't Look Back

Coming soon from St. Martin's Paperbacks

Thais remembered the bubble bath.

She felt a blush staining her cheeks but at least she was alone.

At last.

Working a case meant skimming through data. Tons of it. Looking for that one odd fact, which might lead to another and one more to form an evidence chain. They had the bullet and a short list of people who would put a hit out on Amanda. Finding the money, well, Thais stretched her neck and heard it pop. She'd been looking for the money all day.

She rubbed her eyes on the way towards the bedroom Dunn had pointed out as hers for the night. Working data had never been as hard as it was with Dunn in the room. The guy was a distraction but he wasn't lazy, she'd give him that. He'd been working as hard as the rest of the team.

The bubble bath . . .

With the doors of the suite closed behind her, Thais looked at the large slipper tub. It had gold feet and sat in front of floor to ceiling windows that overlooked a section of red rock. The spa town of Sedona was just

over the ridge, the private residence nestled into a section of private estates that came with enough land to
ensure privacy.

The tub sat in a hexagon section of glass so it could
overlook the rocks.

You baited him . . .

She had. Thais couldn't stop the memory from rising
up to play across her mind. She might have called Dunn
a civilian justly but he'd been involved in cases from
time to time over the last two years. Shadow Ops teams
needed to operate off grid, an action which was becoming harder and harder to pull off in a world of cell phones
and social media junkies.

Dunn's reputation as a recluse was the perfect resource. He invested a small fortune in keeping his
planes flying so no one really knew his location.

There was a rap on the door a moment before it
opened to reveal Dunn. She felt his arrival as much as she
witnessed it. All of her senses rippling with awareness.
He was better than a double expresso when it came to
waking her up.

And she couldn't allow it to keep growing. She dug
deep, looking for the professional persona she'd per-
fected over the years of working with Shadow Ops.

"I agreed to work a case with you, Dunn." She sent
him a hard look. "You don't like me calling you a civilian but coming in here tells me you aren't getting what
it means to be team mates. This isn't play time. I'm
working and you should be too."

He came forward, stopping for a moment near the
tub. "We've finished the day's work."

"A case is finished when it's closed," she replied. "A
good agent doesn't take time off when lives hang in the
balance."

Her retort earned her a half grin. He was devastating enough without his lips in that cocky grin. "And yet," he trailed a finger along the edge of the tub. "You've made use of down time on cases in the past."

Her cheeks warmed. "I shouldn't have."

"Why not?" he asked in a husky tone. "There is only so much we can do on this end. It's a waiting game now."

"One which would have been better served if you'd left me where my Section leader did." Thais latched onto the topic to avoid the issue of the tub.

And the fact that you knew Dunn was watching when you took that bath . . . teased him . . .

She had. Switched in as bait while Saxon Hale took their real witness off grid, Thais had indulged in a bubble bath in Dunn's cabin. She'd only suspected he'd been watching.

Now, she knew for certain he had.

"I won't apologize for getting you out of Homeland." His tone had sharpened. "Ever."

She felt their gazes lock, felt a reaction inside herself that was uncontrollable. She'd gone to a great deal of effort to make certain she wasn't the weak link of her team. She protected others but Dunn was making it clear he'd decided to cover her when she needed it. She shouldn't like the feeling but denying it was impossible and he knew it.

He was closer than she realized, making it necessary to tip her head up to maintain eye contact. He reached out and brushed her lips.

Straight across them, the connection sending a ripple of awareness through her.

"You can't deny the attraction between us, Thais," he whispered.

She turned, facing him head on. "I'm not. Just doing

the logical thing and walking away. Neither of us are looking for more than release."

Professional and cold.

Her delivery lacked none of the sharp edges she was known for in the field. She should have felt a sense of mild satisfaction, instead, Thais realized she felt hollow.

Like she was denying herself something she needed.

She drew in a sharp breath, pushing back a step.

She couldn't need.

"It's for the best, Bateson," she added.

The gauntlet was down now. Dunn's eyes narrowed, confirming her assessment of the situation a moment before he was coming towards her. She retreated, reacting to his approach, moving back until she was against the wall, his hands flattened on either side of her head.

He was going to kiss her.

The certainty of it crashed down on her like a wave. Stunning her with the force of the connection and wiping out everything except the feeling of the force of the water.

Only, he didn't kiss her.

Thais opened her eyes, and found Dunn's emerald ones fixed on her.

"I want to," he rasped out, his fingers flexing on the wall beside her head. "I want to smother you in a kiss hard enough to drown out your ideas of what should be between us in favor of what we both want."

"You don't want anything different." Thais reached up and pressed her own hand over her lips. She was letting her feelings out.

She mustn't.

"You," he rasped out, "are something I'd tried very hard not to think about."

The common ground between them was strangely alluring. Like a haven she might enter if she was willing to take the risk.

Don't kid yourself . . . he's not the sort of man a girl domesticates . . . he will always roam . . .

"Ye're hiding behind your badge, Thais," he muttered, his voice dipping down into a timbre that touched off a shiver inside her. "Label me as ye will but I'm more honest than you are."

Dunn pushed back, moving several paces away from her. "I want more from this relationship than professional interaction." His eyes flashed with hunger. "Much, much more. But I'm not going to overwhelm you. It's partners with full knowledge of what we're getting into or nothing."

He meant it.

And loathed it as much as she did.

Thais watched his jaw clamp tight with frustration before he turned and gave her a view of his back while he left the suite. She stayed against the wall for a long moment, needing the support as she ordered herself to stay where she was.

It was the last thing she truly wanted.